SERAFINA
and the
BLACK CLOAK

SERAFINA and the BLACK CLOAK

ROBERT BEATTY

EGMONT

EGMONT

We bring stories to life

First published in the USA in 2015 by Disney•Hyperion,
an imprint of Disney Book Group
First published in Great Britain 2016
by Egmont UK Limited
The Yellow Building, 1 Nicholas Road, London W11 4AN

Copyright © 2015 Robert Beatty
Designed by Maria Elias

The moral rights of the author and illustrators have been asserted

ISBN 978 1 4052 8378 6

www.egmont.co.uk

64661/1

A CIP catalogue record for this title is available from the British Library

Typeset by Avon DataSet Ltd, Bidford on Avon, Warwickshire
Printed and bound in Great Britain by CPI Group

Stay safe online. Any website addresses listed in this book are correct
at the time of going to print. However, Egmont is not responsible
for content hosted by third parties.

Please be aware that online content can be subject to change and
websites can contain content that is unsuitable for children.
We advise that all children are supervised when using the internet.

To my wife, Jennifer, who helped shape
this story from the beginning,

and to our girls
– Camille, Genevieve, and Elizabeth –
who will always be our first and
most important audience

Biltmore Estate

Asheville, North Carolina

1899

1

Serafina opened her eyes and scanned the darkened work-shop, looking for any rats stupid enough to come into her territory while she slept. She knew they were out there, just beyond her nightly range, crawling in the cracks and shadows of the great house's sprawling basement, keen to steal whatever they could from the kitchens and storerooms. She had spent most of the day napping in her favourite out-of-the-way places, but it was here, curled up on the old mattress behind the rusty boiler in the protection of the workshop, that she felt most at home. Hammers, wrenches and gears hung down from the rough-hewn beams, and the familiar smell of machinery oil filled the air. Her first thought as she looked around her and listened out into the reaching darkness was that it felt like a good night for hunting.

Her pa, who had worked on the construction of Biltmore Estate years before and had lived in the basement without permission ever since, lay sleeping on the cot he'd secretly built behind the supply racks. Embers glowed in the old metal barrel over which he had cooked their dinner of chicken and grits a few hours before. They had huddled around the cook fire for warmth as they ate. As usual, she had eaten the chicken but left the grits.

'Eat your supper,' her pa had grumbled.

'Did,' she had answered, setting down her half-empty tin plate.

'Your whole supper,' he said, pushing the plate towards her, 'or you're never gonna get any bigger than a little shoat.'

Her pa likened her to a skinny baby pig when he wanted to get a rise out of her, figuring she'd get so furious with him that she'd wolf those nasty grits down her throat despite herself.

'I'm not gonna eat the grits, Pa,' she said, smiling a little, 'no matter how many times you put 'em in front of me.'

'They ain't nothin' but ground-up corn, girl,' he said, poking at the fire with a stick to arrange the other sticks the way he wanted them. 'Everybody and his uncle likes corn 'cept you.'

'You know I can't stomach anything green or yellow or disgusting like that, Pa, so quit hollering at me.'

'If I was a-hollerin', you'd know it,' he said, shoving his poker stick into the fire.

By and by, they soon forgot about the grits and went on to talk about something else.

It made Serafina smile to think about her dinner with her father. She couldn't imagine much else in the world – except maybe sleeping in the warmth of one of the basement's small sunlit windows – that was finer than a bit of banter with her pa.

Careful not to wake him, she slunk off her mattress, padded across the workshop's gritty stone floor and snuck out into the winding passageway. While still rubbing the sleep out of her eyes and stretching out her arms and legs, she couldn't help but feel a trace of excitement. The tantalising sensation of starting a brand-new night tingled through her body. She felt her muscles and her senses coming alive, as if she were an owl stirring its wings and flexing its talons before it flies off for its ghostly hunt.

She moved quietly through the darkness, past the laundry rooms, pantries and kitchens. The basement had been bustling with servants all day, but the rooms were empty now, and dark, just the way she liked them. She knew that the Vanderbilts and their many guests were sleeping on the second and third floors above her, but here it was quiet. She loved to prowl through the endless corridors and shadowed storage rooms. She knew the touch and feel, the glint and gloom, of every nook and cranny. This was *her* domain at night, and hers alone.

She heard a faint slithering just ahead. The night was beginning quickly.

She stopped. She listened.

Two doors down, the scrabbling of tiny feet on bare floor.

She crept forward along the wall.

When the sound stopped, she stopped as well. When the sound resumed, she crept forward once more. It was a technique she'd taught herself by the age of seven: move when they're moving; stay still when they're still.

Now she could hear the creatures breathing, the scratching of their toenails on the stone and the dragging of their tails. She felt the familiar trembling in her fingers and the tightness in her legs.

She slipped through the half-open door into the storeroom and saw them in the darkness: two huge rats covered in greasy brown fur had slithered one by one up through the drainpipe in the floor. The intruders were obviously newcomers, foolishly scrounging for cockroaches when they could've been slurping custard off the fresh-baked pastries just down the hall.

Without making a sound or even disturbing the air, she stalked slowly towards the rats. Her eyes focused on them. Her ears picked up every sound they made. She could even smell their foul sewer stench. All the while, they went about their rotten, ratty business and had no idea she was there.

She stopped just a few feet behind them, hidden in the blackness of a shadow, poised for the leap. This was the moment she loved, the moment just before she lunged. Her body swayed slightly back and forth, tuning her angle of attack. Then she pounced. In one quick, explosive movement, she grabbed the squealing, writhing rats with her bare hands.

'Gotcha, ya nasty varmints!' she hissed.

The smaller rat squirmed in terror, desperate to get away, but the larger one twisted round and bit her hand.

'There'll be none of that!' she snarled, clamping the rat's neck firmly between her finger and thumb.

The rats wriggled wildly, but she kept a good, hard hold on them and wouldn't let them go. It had taken her a while to learn that lesson when she was younger, that once you had them, you had to squeeze hard and hold on, no matter what, even if their little claws scratched you and their scaly tails curled round your hand like some sort of nasty grey snake.

Finally, after several seconds of vicious struggling, the exhausted rats realised they couldn't escape her. They went still and stared suspiciously at her with their beady black eyes. Their snivelling little noses and wickedly long whiskers vibrated with fear. The rat who'd bitten her slowly slithered his long, scaly tail round her wrist, wrapping it two times, searching for new advantage to prise himself free.

'Don't even try it,' she warned him. Still bleeding from his bite, she was in no mood for his ratty schemes. She'd been bitten before, but she never did like it much.

Carrying the grisly beasts in her clenched fists, she took them down the passageway. It felt good to get two rats before midnight, and they were particularly ugly characters, the kind that would chew straight through a burlap sack to get at the grain inside, or knock eggs off the shelf so they could lick the mess from the floor.

She climbed the old stone stairs that led outside, then

walked across the moonlit grounds of the estate all the way to the edge of the forest. There she hurled the rats into the leaves. 'Now get on outta here, and don't come back!' she shouted at them. 'I won't be so nice next time!'

The rats tumbled across the forest floor with the force of her fierce throw, then came to a trembling stop, expecting a killing blow. When it didn't come, they turned and looked up at her in astonishment.

'Get goin' before I change my mind,' she said.

Hesitating no longer, the rats scurried into the underbrush.

There had been a time when the rats she caught weren't so lucky, when she'd leave their bodies next to her pa's bed to show him her night's work, but she hadn't done that in a coon's age.

Ever since she was a young'un, she'd studied the men and women who worked in the basement, so she knew that each one had a particular job. It was her father's responsibility to fix the elevators, dumbwaiters, window gears, steam heating systems and all the other mechanical contraptions on which the two-hundred-and-fifty-room mansion depended. He even made sure the pipe organ in the Grand Banquet Hall worked properly for Mr and Mrs Vanderbilt's fancy balls. Besides her pa, there were cooks, kitchen maids, coal shovellers, chimney sweeps, laundry women, pastry makers, housemaids, footmen and countless others.

When she was ten years old, she had asked, 'Do I have a job like everyone else, Pa?'

'Of course ya do,' he said, but she suspected that it wasn't true. He just didn't want to hurt her feelings.

'What is it? What's my job?' she pressed him.

'It's actually an extremely important position around here, and there ain't no one who does it better than you, Sera.'

'Tell me, Pa. What is it?'

'I reckon you're Biltmore Estate's C.R.C.'

'What's that mean?' she asked in excitement.

'You're the Chief Rat Catcher,' he said.

However the words were intended, they emblazoned themselves in her mind. She remembered even now, two years later, how her little chest had swelled and how she had smiled with pride when he'd said those words: Chief Rat Catcher. She had liked the sound of that. Everyone knew that rodents were a big problem in a place like Biltmore, with all its sheds and shelves and barns and whatnot. And it was true that she had shown a natural-born talent for snatching the cunning, food-stealing, dropping-leaving, disease-infected four-legged vermin that so eluded the adult folk with their crude traps and poisons. Mice, which were timid and prone to panic-induced mistakes at key moments, were no trouble at all for her to catch. It was the rats that gave her the scamper each night, and it was on the rats that she had honed her skills. She was twelve years old now. And that was who she was: Serafina, C.R.C.

But as she watched the two rats run into the forest, a strange and powerful feeling took hold of her. She wanted to follow them. She wanted to see what they saw beneath leaf and twig, to explore the rocks and dells, the streams and wonders. But her pa had forbidden her.

'Never go into the forest,' he had told her many times. 'There are dark forces there that no one understands, things that ain't natural and can do ya wicked harm.'

She stood at the edge of the forest and looked as far as she could into the trees. For years, she'd heard stories of people who got lost in the forest and never returned. She wondered what dangers lurked there. Was it black magic, demons or some sort of heinous beasts? What was her pa so afraid of?

She might bandy back and forth with her pa about all sorts of things just for the jump of it – like refusing her grits, sleeping all day and hunting all night, and spying on the Vanderbilts and their guests – but she never argued about this. She knew when he said those words he was as serious as her dead momma. For all the spiny talk and all the sneak-about, sometimes you just stayed quiet and did what you were told because you sensed it was a good way to keep breathing.

Feeling strangely lonesome, she turned away from the forest and gazed back at the estate. The moon rose above the steeply pitched slate roofs of the house and reflected in the panes of glass that domed the Winter Garden. The stars sparkled above the mountains. The grass and trees and flowers of the beautiful manicured grounds glowed in the midnight light. She could see every detail, every toad and snail and all the other creatures of the night. A lone mockingbird sang its evening song from a magnolia tree, and the baby hummingbirds, tucked into their tiny nest among the climbing wisteria, rustled in their sleep.

It lifted her chin a bit to think that her pa had helped build all this. He'd been one of the hundreds of stonemasons, wood-carvers and other craftsmen who had come to Asheville from the surrounding mountains to construct Biltmore Estate years before. He had stayed on to maintain the machinery. But when all the other basement workers went home to their families each night, he and Serafina hid among the steaming pipes and metal tools in the workshop like stowaways in the engine room of a great ship. The truth was they had no place else to go, no kin to go home to. Whenever she asked about her momma, her father refused to talk about her. So, there wasn't anyone else besides her and her pa, and they'd made the basement their home for as long as she could remember.

'How come we don't live in the servants' quarters or in town like the other workers, Pa?' she had asked many times.

'Never ya mind about that,' he would grumble in reply.

Over the years, her pa had taught her how to read and write pretty well, and told her plenty of stories about the world, but he was never too keen on talking about what she wanted to talk about, which was what was going on deep down in his heart, and what had happened to her momma, and why she didn't have any brothers and sisters, and why she and her pa didn't have any friends who came round to call. Sometimes, she wanted to reach down inside him and shake him up to see what would happen, but most of the time her pa just slept all night and worked all day, and cooked their dinner in the evening, and told her stories, and they had a pretty good life, the two of them, and she didn't shake him because she knew he didn't want to be shook, so she just let him be.

At night, when everyone else in the house went to sleep, she crept upstairs and snatched books to read in the moonlight. She'd overheard the butler boast to a visiting writer that Mr Vanderbilt had collected twenty-two thousand books, only half of which fitted in the Library Room. The others were stored on tables and shelves throughout the house, and to Serafina these were like Juneberries ripe for the picking, too tempting to resist. No one seemed to notice when a book went missing and was back in its place a few days later.

She had read about the great battles between the states with tattered flags flying and she had read of the steaming iron beasts that hurtled people hither and yon. She wanted to sneak into the graveyard at night with Tom and Huck and be ship-wrecked with the Swiss Family Robinson. Some nights, she longed to be one of the four sisters with their loving mother in *Little Women*. Other nights, she imagined meeting the ghosts of Sleepy Hollow or tapping, tapping, tapping with Poe's black raven. She liked to tell her pa about the books she read, and she often made up stories of her own, filled with imaginary friends and strange families and ghosts in the night, but he was never interested in her tales of fancy and fright. He was far too sensible a man for all that and didn't like to believe in anything but bricks and bolts and solid things.

More and more she wondered what it would be like to have some sort of secret friend whom her pa didn't know about, someone she could talk to about things, but she didn't tend to meet too many children her age skulking through the basement in the dead of night.

A few of the low-level kitchen scullions and boiler tenders who worked in the basement and went home each night had seen her darting here or there and knew vaguely who she was, but the maids and manservants who worked on the main floors did not. And certainly the master and mistress of the house didn't know she existed.

'The Vanderbilts are a good kind of folk, Sera,' her pa had told her, 'but they ain't *our* kind of folk. You keep yourself scarce when they come about. Don't let anyone get a good look at you. And, whatever you do, don't tell anyone your name or who you are. You hear?'

Serafina *did* hear. She heard very well. She could hear a mouse change his mind. Yet she didn't know exactly why she and her pa lived the way they did. She didn't know why her father hid her away from the world, why he was ashamed of her, but she knew one thing for sure: that she loved him with all her heart, and the last thing she ever wanted to do was to cause him trouble.

So she had become an expert at moving undetected, not just to catch the rats, but to avoid the people too. When she was feeling particularly brave or lonely, she darted upstairs into the comings and goings of the sparkling folk. She snuck and crept and hid. She was small for her age and light of foot. The shadows were her friends. She spied on the fancy-dressed guests as they arrived in their splendid horse-drawn carriages. No one upstairs ever saw her hiding beneath the bed or behind the door. No one noticed her in the back of the closet when they put their coats inside. When the ladies and gentlemen went on their walks around the grounds, she slunk up right next to them without them knowing and listened to everything they were saying. She loved seeing the young girls in their blue and yellow dresses with ribbons fluttering in their hair, and she ran along with them when they frolicked through the garden. When the children played hide-and-seek, they never realised there was another player. Sometimes she'd even see Mr and Mrs Vanderbilt walking arm in arm, or she'd see their twelve-year-old nephew riding his horse across the grounds, with his sleek black dog running alongside.

She had watched them all, but none of them ever saw her – not even the dog. Lately she'd been wondering just what would happen if they did. What if the boy glimpsed her? What would she do? What if his dog chased her? Could she get up a tree in time? Sometimes she liked to imagine what she would say if she met Mrs Vanderbilt face to face. *Hello, Mrs V. I catch your rats for you. Would you like them killed or just chucked out?* Sometimes she dreamed of wearing fancy dresses and ribbons in her hair and shiny shoes on her feet. And sometimes, just sometimes, she longed not just to listen secretly to the people around her, but to talk to them. Not just to see them, but to be *seen*.

As she walked through the moonlight across the open grass and back to the main house, she wondered what would happen if one of the guests, or perhaps the young master in his bedroom on the second floor, happened to wake and look out the window and see a mysterious girl walking alone in the night.

Her pa never spoke of it, but she knew she wasn't exactly normal-looking. She had a skinny little body, nothing but muscle, bone and sinew.

She didn't own a dress, so she wore one of her pa's old work shirts, which she cinched round her narrow waist with a length of fibrous twine she'd scavenged from the workshop. He didn't buy her any clothes because he didn't want people in town to ask questions and start meddling; meddling was something he could never brook.

Her long hair wasn't a single color like normal people had, but varying shades of gold and light brown. Her face had a peculiar angularity in the cheeks. And she had large, steady amber eyes. She could see at night as well as she could during the day. Even her soundless hunting skills weren't exactly normal. Every person she'd ever encountered, especially her pa, made so much noise when they walked that it was like they were one of the big Belgian draft horses that pulled the farm equipment in Mr Vanderbilt's fields.

And it all made her wonder, looking up at the windows of the great house. What did the people sleeping in those rooms dream of, with their one-coloured hair, and their long, pointy noses and their big bodies lying in their soft beds all through the glorious darkness of the night? What did they long for? What made them laugh or jump? What did they feel inside? When they had dinner at night, did the children eat the grits or just the chicken?

As she glided down the stairs and back into the basement, she heard something in a distant corridor. She stopped and listened, but she couldn't quite make it out. It wasn't a rat. That much was certain. Something much larger. But what was it?

Curious, she moved towards the sound.

She went past her pa's workshop, the kitchens and the other rooms she knew well, and into the deeper areas where she hunted less often. She heard doors closing, then the fall of footsteps and muffled noises. Her heart began to thump lightly in her chest. Someone was walking through the corridors of the basement. *Her* basement.

She moved closer.

It wasn't the servant who collected the garbage each night, or one of the footmen fetching a late-night snack for a guest – she knew the sound of their footsteps well. Sometimes the butler's assistant, who was eleven, would stop in the corridor and gobble down a few of the cookies from the silver tray that the butler had sent him to retrieve. She'd stand just round the corner from him in the darkness and pretend that they were friends just talking and enjoying each other's company for a while. Then the boy would wipe the powdered sugar off his lips, and off he'd go, hurrying up the stairs to catch up on the time he'd lost. But this wasn't him.

Whoever it was, he wore what sounded like hard-soled shoes – *expensive* shoes. But a gentleman proper had no business coming down into this area of the house. Why was he wandering through the dark passages in the middle of the night?

Increasingly curious, she followed the stranger, careful to avoid being seen. Whenever she snuck up close enough to almost see him, all she could make out was the shadow of a tall black shape carrying a dimly lit lantern. And there was another shadow there too, someone or something with him, but she didn't dare creep close enough to see who or what it was.

It was a vast basement with many different rooms, corridors and levels, which had been built into the slope of the earth beneath the house. Some areas, like the kitchens and the laundry, had smooth plaster walls and windows. The rooms there were plainly finished, but clean and dry, and well-suited to the daily work of the servants. The more distant reaches of the understructure delved deep into the damp and earthen burrows of the house's massive foundation. Here the dark, hardened mortar oozed out from between the roughly hewn stone blocks that formed the walls and ceiling, and she seldom went there because it was cold, dirty and dank.

Suddenly, the footsteps changed direction. They came towards her. Five screeching rats came running down the corridor ahead of the footfalls, more terrified than any rodents she had ever seen. Spiders crawled out of the cracks in the walls. Cockroaches and centipedes erupted from the earthen floor. Astounded by what she was seeing, she caught her breath and pressed herself to the wall, frozen in fear like a little rabbit kit trembling beneath the shadow of a passing hawk.

As the man walked towards her, she heard another sound too. It was a shuffling agitation like a small person – slippered feet, perhaps a child – but there was something wrong. The child's feet were scraping on the stone, sometimes sliding . . . the child was crippled . . . no . . . the child was being *dragged*.

'No, sir! Please! No!' the girl whimpered, her voice trembling with despair. 'We're not supposed to be down here.' The girl spoke like someone who had been raised in a well-heeled family and attended a fancy school.

'Don't worry. We're going right in here . . .' the man said, stopping at the door just round the corner from Serafina. Now she could hear his breathing, the movement of his hands, and the rustle of his clothing. Flashes of heat scorched through her. She wanted to run, to flee, but she couldn't get her legs to move.

'There's nothing to be frightened of, child,' he said to the girl. 'I'm not going to hurt you . . .'

The way he said these words caused the hairs on the back of

Serafina's neck to rise. *Don't go with him,* she thought. *Don't go!*

The girl sounded like she was just a little younger than her, and Serafina wanted to help her, but she couldn't find the courage. She pressed herself against the wall, certain that she would be heard or seen. Her legs trembled, feeling as if they would crumble beneath her. She couldn't see what happened next, but suddenly the girl let out a bloodcurdling scream. The piercing sound caused Serafina to jump, and she had to stifle her own scream. Then she heard a struggle as the girl tore away from the man and fled down the corridor.

Run, girl! Run! Serafina thought.

The man's steps faded into the distance as he went after her. Serafina could tell that he wasn't running full-out but moving steadily, relentlessly, like he knew the girl couldn't escape him. Serafina's pa had told her that's how the red wolves chase down and kill deer in the mountains – with dogged stamina rather than bursts of speed.

Serafina didn't know what to do. Should she hide in a dark corner and hope he didn't find her? Should she flee with the terror-stricken rats and spiders while she had the chance? She wanted to run back to her father, but what about the child? The girl was so helpless, so slow and weak and frightened, and, more than anything, she needed a friend to help her fight. Serafina wanted to be that friend; she wanted to help her, but she couldn't bring herself to move in that direction.

Then she heard the girl scream again. *That dirty, rotten rat's gonna kill her*, Serafina thought. *He's gonna kill her.*

With a burst of anger and courage, she raced towards the sound. Her legs felt like explosions of speed. Her mind blazed with fear and exhilaration. She turned corner after corner. But when she came to the mossy stone stairway that led down into the deepest bowels of the sub-basement, she stopped, gasping for breath, and shook her head. It was a cold, wet, slimy, horrible place that she had always done her best to avoid – especially in the winter. She'd heard stories that they stored dead bodies in the sub-basement in the winter, when the ground was too frozen to dig a grave. Why in the world had the girl gone down *there*?

Serafina made her way haltingly down the wet, sticky stairs, lifting and shaking off her foot after each slimy step she took. When at last she reached the bottom, she followed a long, slanting corridor where the ceiling dripped with brown sludge. The whole dank, disgusting place gave her the jitters something fierce, but she kept going.

You've got to help her, she told herself again. *You can't turn back.*

She wound her way through a labyrinth of twisting tunnels. She turned right, then left, then left, then right until she lost track of how far she'd gone. Then she heard the sound of fighting and shouting just round the corner ahead of her. She was very close.

She hesitated, frightened, her heart pounding so hard it felt like it was going to burst. Her body shook all over. She didn't want to go another step, but friends had to help friends. She didn't know much about life, but she did know that, knew that for sure, and she wasn't going to run away like a scared-out-of-her-wits squirrel just when somebody needed her most. Trembling all over, she steadied herself the best she could, sucked in a deep breath and pushed herself round the corner.

A broken lantern lay tipped on the stone floor, its glass shattered but the flame still burning. In its halo of faltering light, a girl in a yellow dress struggled for her life. A tall man in a black cloak and hood, his hands stained with blood, grabbed the girl by the wrists.

The girl tried to pull away. 'No! Let me go!' she screamed.

'Quiet down,' the man told her, his voice seething in a dark, unworldly tone. 'I'm not going to hurt you, child . . .' he said for the second time.

The girl had curly blonde hair and pale white skin. She fought to escape, but the man in the black cloak pulled her towards him. He tangled her in his arms. She flailed and struck him in the face with her tiny fists.

'Just stay still, and it will all be over,' he said, pulling her towards him.

Serafina suddenly realised that she'd made a dreadful mistake. This was far more than she could handle. She knew that she should help the girl, but she was so scared that her feet stuck to the floor. She couldn't even breathe, let alone fight.

Help her! Serafina's mind screamed at her. *Help her! Attack the rat! Attack the rat!*

She finally plucked up her courage and charged forward, but just at that moment, the man's black satin cloak floated upward as if possessed by a smoky spirit. The girl screamed. The folds of the cloak slithered around her like the tentacles of a hungry serpent. The cloak seemed to move of its own accord, wrapping, twisting, accompanied by a disturbing rattling noise, like the hissing threats of a hundred rattlesnakes. Serafina saw the girl's horrified face looking at her from within the folds of the enveloping cloak, the girl's pleading blue eyes wide with fear. *Help me! Help me!* Then the folds closed over her, the scream went silent and the girl disappeared, leaving nothing but the blackness of the cloak.

Serafina gasped in shock. One moment the girl was struggling to get free, and the next she had vanished into thin air. The cloak had consumed her. Overwhelmed with confusion, grief and fear, Serafina just stood there in stunned bewilderment.

For several seconds, the man seemed to vibrate violently, and a ghoulish aura glowed around him in a dark, shimmering haze. A horribly foul smell of rotting guts invaded Serafina's nostrils, forcing her head to jerk back. She wrinkled her nose and squinched her mouth and tried not to breathe it in.

She must have made some sort of involuntary gagging noise, for the man in the black cloak suddenly turned and looked at her, seeing her for the first time. It felt like a giant claw gripped her around her chest. The folds of the man's hood shrouded his face, but she could see that his eyes blazed with an unnatural light.

She stood frozen, utterly terrified.

The man whispered in a raspy voice. 'I'm not going to hurt you, child . . .'

Hearing those eerie words jolted Serafina into action. She had just seen what those words led to.

Not this time, rat!

With a burst of new energy, she turned and ran.

She tore through the labyrinth of criss-crossing tunnels, running and running, certain that she was leaving him far in the distance. But, when she glanced over her shoulder, the hooded man was flying through the air right behind her, levitated by the power of the billowing black cloak, his bloody hands reaching towards her.

Serafina tried to run faster, but just as she came to the bottom of the stairs that led up to the main level of the basement, the man in the black cloak grabbed her. One hand clamped her shoulder. The other locked on to her neck. She turned and hissed like a snared animal. She whirled and clawed in a wild circle and broke herself free.

She bounded up the stairs three at a time, but he followed right behind her. He reached out and yanked her head back by her hair. She screamed in pain.

'Time to give up now, little child,' he said calmly, even as the tightening of his fist slowly tore strands of her hair from her head.

'I ain't never!' she snarled, and bit his arm. She fought as hard as she could, scratching and clawing with her fingernails, but it didn't matter. The man in the black cloak was far too strong. He pulled her into his chest, entangling her in his arms.

The folds of the black cloak rose up around her, pulsing with grey smoke. The awful rotting odour made her gag. All she could hear was that loathsome rattling noise as the cloak slithered and twisted its way around her body. She felt like she was being crushed in the coil of a boa constrictor.

'I'm not going to hurt you, child . . .' came the hideous rasping voice again, as if the man wasn't of his own mind but possessed by a demented, ravenous demon.

The folds of the cloak cast a wretched pall over her, drenching her in a dripping, suffocating sickness. She felt her soul slipping away from her – not just slipping, but being yanked, being extracted. Death was so near that she could see its blackness with her own eyes and she could hear the screams of the children who had gone before her.

'No! No! No!' she screamed in defiance. She didn't want to go. Hissing wildly, she reached up and clutched his face, clawing at his eyes. She kicked his chest with her feet. She bit him repeatedly, snapping like a snarling, rabid beast, and she tasted his blood in her mouth. The girl in the yellow dress had fought, but nothing like this. Finally, Serafina twisted out of his grip and spun to the ground. She landed on her feet and leapt away.

She wanted to get back to her pa, but she couldn't make it that far. She fled down the corridor and dashed into the main kitchen. There were a dozen places to hide. Should she slip behind the black cast-iron ovens? Or crawl up among the copper pots hanging from the ceiling rack? No. She knew she had to find a better place.

She was back in her territory now, and she knew it well. She knew the darkness and she knew the light. She knew the left and the right. She had killed rats in every corner of this place, and there was no way she was going to let herself become one of those rats. She was the C.R.C. No trap or weapon or evil man was going to catch her. Like a wild creature, she ran and jumped and crawled.

When she reached the linen storage room, with all its wooden shelves and stacks of folded white sheets and blankets, she scampered into a crumbling break in the wall, in the back corner beneath the lowest shelf. Even if the man did notice the hole, it would seem impossibly small for anyone to fit through. But she knew it provided a shortcut into the back of the laundry.

She came out in the room where they hung and dried the fancy folks' bedsheets. The moon had risen outside, and its light shone through the basement windows. Hundreds of flowing white sheets hung from the ceiling like ghosts, the silver moonlight casting them into an eerie glow. She slipped slowly between the hanging sheets, wondering if they would provide her the concealment she needed. But she thought better of it and kept going.

For good or ill, she had an idea. She knew that Mr Vanderbilt prided himself on installing the most advanced equipment at Biltmore. Her pa had constructed special drying racks that rolled on metal ceiling tracks that tucked into narrow chambers where the sheets and clothes were dried with the radiant heat of well-sealed steam pipes. Determined to find the best possible hiding place, she made herself small and pressed herself through the narrow slot of one of the machines.

When Serafina was born, there had been a number of things physically different about her. She had four toes on each foot rather than five, and although it was not noticeable just by looking at her, her collarbones were malformed such that they didn't connect properly to her other bones. This allowed her to fit into some pretty tight spots. The opening in the machine was no more than a few inches wide, but as long as she could fit her head into something, she could push her whole body through. She wedged herself inside, into a dark little spot where she hoped the man in the black cloak wouldn't find her.

She tried to be quiet, she tried to be still, but she panted like a little animal. She was exhausted, breathless and frightened beyond her wits. She'd seen the girl in the yellow dress consumed by the shadow-filled folds and knew the man in the black cloak was coming for her next. Her only hope was that he couldn't hear the deafening pound of her heartbeat.

She heard him walking slowly down the hallway outside the kitchen. He'd lost her in the darkness, but he moved methodically from room to room, looking for her.

She heard him in the main kitchen, opening the doors of the cast-iron ovens. *If I'd hidden there*, she thought, *I'd be dead now.*

Then she heard him clanging through the copper pots, looking for her in the ceiling rack. *If I'd hidden there*, she thought, *I'd be dead again.*

'There's nothing to be frightened of,' he whispered, trying to coax her out.

She listened and waited, trembling like a field mouse.

Finally, the man in the black cloak made his way into the laundry room.

Mice are timid and prone to panic-induced mistakes at key moments.

She heard the man moving from place to place, rummaging beneath the sinks, opening and closing the cabinets.

Just stay still, little mouse. Just stay still, she told herself. She wanted to break cover and flee so badly, but she knew that the dead mice were the dumb mice that panicked and ran. She told herself over and over again, *Don't be a dumb mouse. Don't be a dumb mouse.*

Then he came into the drying area where she was and moved slowly through the room, running his hands over the ghostly sheets.

If I'd hidden there . . .

He was just a few feet away from her now, looking around the room. Even though he couldn't see her, he seemed to sense that she was there.

Serafina held her breath and stayed perfectly, perfectly, perfectly still.

3

Serafina slowly opened her eyes.

She didn't know how long she'd been asleep or even where she was. She found herself crammed into a tight, dark space, her face pressed up against metal.

She heard the sound of footsteps approaching. She stayed quiet and listened.

It was a man in work boots, tools jangling. Feeling a burst of happiness, she wriggled her way out of the machine and into the morning sunlight pouring through the laundry windows.

'Here I am, Pa!' she cried, her voice parched and weak.

'I've been gnawin' on leather lookin' for you,' her pa scolded. 'You weren't in your bed this mornin'.'

She ran forward and hugged him, pressing herself into his chest. He was a large and hardened man with thick arms and rough, calloused hands. His tools hung from his leather apron, and he smelled faintly of metal, oil and the leather straps that drove the workshop's machines.

In the distance, she heard the sounds of the staff arriving for the morning, the clanking of pots in the kitchen and the conversations of the workers. It was a glorious sound to her ears. The danger of the night was gone. She had survived!

Wrapped in her father's arms, she felt safe and at home. He was more accustomed to mallets and rivets than a kind word, but he'd always taken care of her, always loved and protected her. She couldn't hold back the tears of relief stinging her eyes.

'Where've ya been, Sera?' her father asked.

'He tried to get me, Pa! He tried to kill me!'

'What are you goin' on about, girl?' her pa said suspiciously, holding her by the shoulders with his huge hands. He looked intently into her face. 'Is this another one of your wild stories?'

'No, Pa,' she said, shaking her head.

'I ain't in any kinda mood for stories.'

'A man in a black cloak took a little girl, and then he came after me. I fought him, Pa! I bit him a good one! I spun round and clawed him, and I ran and ran and I got away and I hid. I crawled into your machine, Pa. That's how I got away. It saved me!'

'Whatcha mean, he took a girl?' her pa said, narrowing his eyes. 'What girl?'

'He . . . he made her . . . She was right in front of me, and then she vanished before my eyes!'

'Come on now, Sera,' he said doubtfully. 'You sound like you don't know whether you're washin' the clothes or hangin' 'em out.'

'I swear, Pa,' she said. 'Just listen to me.' She took a good, hard swallow and started at the beginning. As the story poured out of her, she realised how brave she'd actually been.

But her pa just shook his head. 'You've had a bad dream is all. Been readin' too many of them ghost stories. I told ya to stay away from Mr Poe. Now look at ya. You're all scruffed up like a cornered possum.'

Her heart sank. She was telling him the God's honest truth, and he didn't believe a word of it. She tried to keep from crying, but it was hard. She was going on thirteen and he was still treating her like a child.

'I wasn't dreamin', Pa,' she said, wiping a sniffle from her nose.

'Just calm yourself down,' he grumbled. He hated it when she cried. She'd known since she was little that he'd rather wrangle with a good piece of sheet metal than deal with a weepy girl.

'I've gotta go to work,' he said gruffly as he separated from her. 'The dynamo busted somethin' bad last night. Now get on back to the workshop, and get some proper sleep in ya.'

Hot frustration flashed through her and she clenched her fists in anger, but she could hear the seriousness in his voice and knew there was no point in arguing with him. The Edison dynamo was an iron machine with copper coils and spinning wheels that generated a new thing called 'electricity'. She knew from the books she'd read that most homes in America didn't have running water, indoor toilets, refrigeration or even heating. But Biltmore had all these things. It was one of the few homes in America that had electric lighting in some of the rooms. But if her pa couldn't get the dynamo working by nightfall the Vanderbilts and their guests would be plunged into darkness. She knew he had a lot of things on his mind, and she wasn't one of them.

A wave of resentment swept through her. She'd tried to save a girl from an evil black-cloaked demon-thing and almost got herself killed in the process, but her pa didn't care. All he cared about was his stupid machines. He never believed her about anything. To him, she was just a little girl, nothing important, nothing worth listening to, nothing anyone could count on for anything.

As she walked glumly back to the workshop, she fully intended to follow her pa's instructions, but when she passed the stairway that led up to Biltmore Estate's main floor she stopped and looked up the stairs.

She knew she shouldn't do it.

She shouldn't even think about doing it.

But she couldn't help it.

Her pa had been telling her for years that she shouldn't go upstairs, and lately she'd been trying to follow his rules at least some of the time, but today she was furious that he hadn't believed her.

It'd serve him right if I didn't listen to him.

She thought about the girl in the yellow dress. She tried to make sense of what she'd seen: the horrible black cloak and the wide-eyed fear in the girl's face as she disappeared. Where had the girl gone? Was she dead or somehow still alive? Was there still a chance she could be saved?

Snippets of conversation drifted down the stairs. There was some sort of commotion. Had they found a body? Were they all crying in despair? Were they searching for a murderer?

She didn't know if she was brave or stupid, but she had to tell someone what she'd seen. She had to figure out what had happened. Most of all, she had to help the girl in the yellow dress.

She began to climb the stairs.

Staying as small and quiet as she could, she crept up the steps one by one. A cacophony of sounds floated down to her: the echo of people talking, the rustling of clothing, dozens of different footsteps – it was a crowd of many people. Something was definitely happening up there. *We've got to keep to ourselves, you and I.* Her pa's warning played in her mind as she climbed. *There ain't no sense in people seein' you and askin' questions.*

She slunk to the top of the stairway, then ducked into an alcove on the main floor that looked onto a huge room full of fancy-dressed people who seemed to be gathering for some type of grand social event.

Massive, ornately crafted wrought-iron-and-glass doors led into the Entrance Hall, with its polished marble floor and vaulted ceiling of hand-carved oak beams. Soaring limestone arches led from this central room to the various wings of the mansion. The ceiling was so high she had the urge to climb up there and peer down. She'd been here before, but she had always loved the room and couldn't help marvelling at it again, especially in the daylight. She'd never seen so many glistening, beautiful things, so many soft surfaces to sit on and so many interesting places to hide. Spotting an upholstered chair, she felt an overwhelming desire to run her fingernails over the plush fabric. All the room's colours were so bright, and the surfaces were so clean and shiny. She didn't see any mud or grease or dirt anywhere. There were brightly coloured vases filled with flowers – to think! Flowers, actually *inside* the house. Sunlight flooded in from the sparkling, leaded-glass windows of the spiralling, four-story-high Grand Staircase and the glass-domed Winter Garden, with its spraying fountain and tropical plants. She squinted her eyes against the brightness.

The Entrance Hall teemed with dozens of beautifully attired ladies and gentlemen along with manservants in black-and-white uniforms helping them to prepare for a morning of horseback riding. Serafina stared at a lady who wore a riding dress made of white-piped green velvet and cranberry-red damask. Another woman wore a lovely mauve habit with dark purple accents and a matching hat. There were even a few children there, clothed as finely as their parents. Her eyes darted around the room as she tried to take it all in.

Serafina looked at the face of the lady in the green dress, and then she looked at the face of the lady in the mauve hat. She knew her momma was long dead, or at the very least long gone, but all her life, whenever she saw a woman, she checked to see if the woman looked like her. She studied the faces of the children too, wondering if there was a chance that any of them could be her brothers and sisters. When she was little, she used to tell herself a story that maybe she had come home one day to the house, muddy from her hunting, and her mother had taken her downstairs and stuck her in the belt-driven washing machine, and then gone back upstairs and accidentally forgot about her, just spinning and spinning away down there. But when Serafina looked around at the women and the children in the Entrance Hall and saw their blond hair and their blue eyes, their black hair and their brown eyes, she knew that none of them were her kin. Her pa never talked about what her momma looked like, but Serafina searched for her in every face she saw.

Serafina had come upstairs with a purpose, but now that she was here, the thought of actually trying to talk to any of these fancy people put a rock in her stomach. She swallowed and inched forward a little, but the lump in her throat was so huge she wasn't even sure she could get a word out. She wanted to tell them what she'd seen, but it suddenly seemed so foolish. They were all happy and carefree, like so many larks on a sunny day. She didn't understand. The girl was obviously one of these people, so why weren't they looking for her? It was like it had never happened, like she had imagined the whole thing. What was she going to say to them? *Excuse me, everyone . . . I'm pretty sure I saw a horrible black-cloaked man make a little girl vanish into thin air. Has anyone seen her?* They'd lock her up like a cuckoo bird.

As a tall gentleman in a black suit coat walked by, she realised that one of these men might actually be the Man in the Black Cloak. With his shadowed face and glowing eyes, there was no doubt that the attacker had been some sort of spectre, but she had sunk her teeth into him and tasted real blood, and he needed a lantern to see just like all the other people she'd followed over the years, which meant he was of this world too. She scanned the men in the crowd, keeping her breathing as steady as she could. Was it possible that he was here at this very moment?

Mrs Edith Vanderbilt, the mistress of the house, walked into the room wearing a striking velvet dress and a wide-brimmed hat. Serafina couldn't take her eyes off the mesmerising movement of the hat's feathers. A refined and attractive woman, Mrs Vanderbilt had a pale complexion and a full head of dark hair, and she seemed at ease in her role as hostess as she moved through the room.

'While we wait for the servants to bring up our horses,' she said happily to her guests, 'I would like to invite everyone to join me in the Tapestry Gallery for a little bit of musical entertainment.'

A pleasant murmur passed through the crowd. Delighted by the idea of a diversion, the ladies and gentlemen streamed into the gallery, an elegantly decorated room with its exquisitely hand-painted ceiling, intricate musical instruments and delicate antique wall tapestries. Serafina loved to climb the tapestries at night and run her fingernails down through the soft fabric.

'I'm sure that most of you already know Mr Montgomery Thorne,' Mrs Vanderbilt said with a gentle sweep of her arm towards a gentleman. 'He has graciously offered to play for us today.'

'Thank you, Mrs Vanderbilt,' Mr Thorne said as he stepped forward with a smile. 'This whole outing is such a wonderful idea, and I must say you're a most radiant hostess on this lovely morning.'

'You're too kind, sir,' Mrs Vanderbilt said with a smile.

To Serafina, who'd been listening to Biltmore's visitors her entire life, he didn't sound like he came from the mountains of North Carolina, or from New York like the Vanderbilts. He spoke with the accent of a Southern gentleman, maybe from Georgia or South Carolina. She crept forward to get a better look at him. He wore a white satin cravat round his neck, a brocade waistcoat and pale grey gloves, all of which she thought went nicely with his silvery-black hair and perfectly trimmed sideburns.

He picked up a finely made violin and its bow from the table where it had been lying.

'Since when do you play the violin, Thorne?' called one of

the gentlemen from New York in a friendly tone.

'Oh, I've been practising here and there, Mr Bendel,' said Mr Thorne as he lifted the instrument to his chin.

'When? On the carriage ride here?' Mr Bendel retorted, and everyone laughed.

Serafina almost felt sorry for Mr Thorne. It was clear from their playful banter that Mr Bendel and Mr Thorne were companions, but it was equally clear that Mr Bendel had serious doubts as to whether his friend could actually play.

Serafina watched in nervous silence as Mr Thorne prepared himself. Perhaps it was a new instrument to him and this was his first performance. She couldn't even imagine playing such a thing herself. At long last, he set the bow gently across the strings, paused for a moment to collect himself, and then began to play.

Suddenly, the vaulted rooms of the great house filled with the loveliest music she had ever heard, elegant and flowing, like a river of sound. He was wonderful. Spellbound by the beauty of his playing, the ladies and gentlemen and even the servants stood quietly and listened with rapt attention, and they let their hearts soak in every measure of the music he made.

Serafina enjoyed the sound of his playing, but she also watched his dexterous fingers. They moved so fast over the strings that they reminded her of little running mice, and she wanted to pounce on them.

When Mr Thorne was done, everyone applauded and congratulated him, especially Mr Bendel, who laughed in disbelief.

'You never cease to amaze me, Thorne. You shoot like a marksman, you speak fluent Russian and now you play the violin like Vivaldi! Tell us, man, is there anything you're *not* good at?'

'Well, I'm certainly not as skilled a horseback rider as you are, Mr Bendel,' Mr Thorne said as he set his violin aside. 'And I must say it has always been most vexing to me.'

'Well, stop the presses!' Mr Bendel called. 'The man has a chink in his armour after all!' Then he looked at Mrs Vanderbilt with a smile. 'So, when exactly are we going horseback riding?'

The other guests laughed at the two gentlemen as they quipped back and forth, and Serafina smiled. She enjoyed watching the camaraderie of these people. She envied the way they spoke to one another and touched each other and shared their lives. It was so different from her own world of shadow and solitude. She watched a young woman tilt her head and smile as she reached out and put her hand on the arm of a young gentleman. Serafina tried imitating the gesture herself.

'Are you lost?' someone said behind her.

Startled, Serafina whirled round and started to hiss, but then she stopped herself short. A young boy stood in front of her. A large black Dobermann with sharply pointed ears sat at his side, staring intently at her.

The boy wore a fine tweed riding jacket, a buttoned vest, woollen jodhpurs and knee-high leather boots. He was a little sickly-looking, a little frail even, but he had watchful, sensitive brown eyes and a rather fetching tussle of wavy brown hair. He stood quietly, staring at her.

It took every ounce of her courage not to run. She didn't know what to do. Did he think she was a vagrant who had wandered in? Or perhaps she looked like a dazed servant – maybe a chimney sweep or window-washing girl. Either way, she knew she was stuck. He'd caught her dead to rights exactly where she wasn't supposed to be.

'Are you lost?' the boy asked again, but this time she heard what sounded strangely like kindness in his voice. 'May I help you find your way?' He wasn't timid or shy, but he wasn't over-confident or arrogant, either. And it surprised her that he didn't seem angry at her for being there. There was a trace of curiosity in his tone.

'I-I-I'm not lost,' she stammered. 'I was just –'

'It's all right,' he said as he stepped towards her. 'I still get lost sometimes, and I've lived here for two years.'

Serafina sucked in a breath. Suddenly, she realised that she was speaking face to face with the young master, Mr Vanderbilt's nephew. She'd seen him many times before, standing at his bedroom window looking out at the mountains, or galloping his horse across the grounds or walking alone on the footpaths with his dog – she'd watched him for years, but she'd never been this close to him.

Most of what she knew about him she'd overheard from the gossiping servants, and when it came to the young master, they sure did prattle on. When he was ten years old, his family had died in a fire and he became an orphan. His uncle took him in. He became like a son to the Vanderbilts.

He was known as a loner. Some of the less charitable folks whispered that the young master preferred the company of his dog and his horse to most people. She'd overheard the men in the stables saying that he'd won many blue ribbons at equestrian events and was considered one of the most talented horseback riders around. The cooks, who prided themselves on preparing the most exquisite gourmet meals, complained that he always shared the food on his plate with his dog.

'I've explored pretty much every room on the first, second and third floors,' the young master said to her, 'and the stables, of course, but the other parts of the house are like foreign lands to me.'

As the boy spoke, she could tell he was trying to be polite, but his eyes kept studying her. It was nerve-racking. After all those years she'd been hiding, it felt so strange to have someone actually looking at her. It made her stomach twist, but at the same time her skin tingled all over. She knew she must look completely ridiculous standing before him in the remnants of her pa's old work shirt, and he must have noticed her hands were dirty and there were smudges all over her face. Her hair was as wild as a banshee's, and there was no hiding its streaked colour. How could he help but stare?

She reckoned he knew most of the guests and servants, and she could see him trying to figure out who she was. How out of place she must seem to him! She had two arms and legs like everyone else, but with her sharp cheekbones and her golden eyes she knew she didn't look like a normal girl. No matter how much she ate, she couldn't put any weight on the feral leanness of her body. She wasn't sure if she looked more like a skinny little shoat to the Vanderbilt boy or like a savage little weasel, but neither of those animals belonged in the house.

There was a part of her – maybe the smart part – that wanted to turn tail and run, but she thought that maybe the young master might be the perfect person to tell about the girl in the yellow dress. The silky-laced adults with all their high-falutin airs wouldn't pay a smudge-faced girl any mind. But maybe *he* would.

'I'm Braeden,' he said.

'I'm Serafina,' she blurted out before she could help herself. *You fool! Why did you give him your name?* It was bad enough that she'd allowed herself to be seen, but now he had a name to go with her face. Her father was going to kill her!

'It's good to meet you, Serafina,' he said, bowing, as if she deserved the same respect as a proper lady. 'This is my friend Gidean,' he said, introducing her to his dog, who continued to sit and study her malevolently with steady black eyes.

'Hello,' she managed to say, but she didn't appreciate the way the dog stared at her like it was only his master's command that kept him from chomping on her with his gleaming white teeth.

Gathering her courage, she looked at Braeden Vanderbilt nervously. 'Master Braeden, I came up here to tell you something that I saw . . .'

'Really? What'd you see?' he asked, full of curiosity.

'There was a girl, a pretty blonde girl in a yellow dress, down in the basement last night, and I saw a man in a –'

As the coterie of ladies and gentlemen began to flow out of the Tapestry Gallery and move towards the main doors, the handsome Mr Thorne broke away and approached Braeden, interrupting her.

'Are you coming, young master Vanderbilt?' he asked encouragingly in his Southern accent. 'Our horses are ready, and I'm anxious to see your latest riding skills. Perhaps we can ride together.'

Braeden's face lit up with a smile. 'Yes, sir, Mr Thorne,' he called. 'I'd like that very much.'

As soon as Mr Thorne rejoined the others, the young master's eyes immediately returned to Serafina. 'Excuse me, you were telling me what you saw . . .'

At that moment, Mr Boseman, the estate superintendent and her pa's boss, came stomping up the stairs. He'd always been a scowling-faced curmudgeon, and today was no exception. 'You there, who are you?' he demanded, clutching Serafina's arm so hard that she winced. 'What's your name, girl?'

Just when she thought it couldn't get any worse, a sudden commotion rose up in the main hall. A dishevelled, overweight, middle-aged woman still wearing her nightclothes came rushing down the Grand Staircase from the third floor. She crashed into the crowd in a flurry of hysterical panic.

'It's Mrs Brahms,' Mr Boseman said, turning towards the disturbance.

'Has anyone seen my Clara?' Mrs Brahms cried frantically, reaching out and grabbing the people around her. 'Please help me – she's gone missing! I can't find her anywhere!'

Mrs Vanderbilt moved forward and took the woman's hands in an attempt to calm her. 'It's a very large house, Mrs Brahms. I'm sure Clara is just off exploring.'

Worried discussion spread through the crowd. All the ladies and gentlemen of the riding party began talking to one another in confusion, wondering what was happening.

Miss Clara Brahms, Serafina thought. *That's the girl in the yellow dress.*

The whole time, Mr Boseman kept his hand clamped on her arm.

She wanted to leap forward and tell everyone what she'd seen, but then what would happen? *Where did you come from?* they'd demand. *What were you doing in the basement in the middle of the night?* There'd be all sorts of questions she couldn't answer.

All of a sudden, Mr George Vanderbilt, the master of the house, walked into the centre of the crowd and raised his hands. 'Everyone, may I please have your attention,' he said. All the guests and servants immediately stopped talking and listened. 'I'm sure you all agree that we need to delay our ride and search for Miss Brahms. Once we find her, we'll resume the activities of the day.'

George Vanderbilt was a slender, dark-haired, intelligent-looking gentleman in his thirties with a thick black moustache and keen, dark, penetrating eyes. He was well known for his love of reading, but he was a fit and healthy-looking man too, who seemed far younger than his years. And Serafina wasn't the only one who thought so. She had heard the servants in the kitchen joke that their master must have secretly discovered the Fountain of Youth. Mr Vanderbilt was a meticulous dresser, and as she admired his commanding presence, she couldn't help but notice his clothes too. In particular, his shoes. Like the other gentlemen present, he wore a gentleman's riding jacket, but instead of riding boots he wore expensive black patent-leather shoes. As he strode across the hard surface of the marble floor, his shoes made a familiar clicking sound . . . the same sound that she'd heard in the corridors of the basement the night before.

She looked at the other men's shoes. Braeden, Mr Thorne, and Mr Bendel wore riding boots in preparation for their outing, but Mr Vanderbilt was wearing his dress shoes.

He approached the lost girl's mother and consoled her. 'We're going to search this place from top to bottom, Mrs Brahms, and we'll keep looking until we find her.' He turned to the ladies and gentlemen and waved over the footmen and maidservants as well. 'We'll break up into five separate search parties,' he explained. 'We'll search the entire house, all four floors and also the basement. If anyone finds anything suspicious, report it immediately.'

Mr Vanderbilt's words struck fear into Serafina's heart. They were going to search the basement! The basement! That meant the workshop! With a mighty twist of her body, she yanked herself out of Mr Boseman's grip and darted away before he could stop her. She bounded headlong down the stairs into the basement. She had to warn her pa. The leftovers from last night's dinner, the mattress she slept on . . . they had to hide it all.

Serafina rushed up to her father in the workshop and grabbed his arm. Trying to talk and catch her breath at the same time, she gasped, 'Pa, there's a girl missing just like I said, and Mr Vanderbilt's searching the whole house!' Her words tumbled out with a mixture of urgency and pride. As she hurriedly reminded him of what she'd seen the night before, she was sure that he'd see now that she wasn't dreaming or making up stories.

'They're searchin' the house?' he asked, ignoring everything else. He turned and quickly gathered his cooking supplies and razor from the bench, then dragged her mattress into the hidden area he'd constructed behind the tool rack. There could be no evidence of their living there when the search party came through.

'What about the girl I saw disappear?' she asked in confusion. She couldn't figure out why he wasn't more interested in what she was telling him.

'Children don't just disappear, Sera,' he said as he continued his efforts.

Her heart sank. He still didn't believe her.

Her pa looked around the room one last time to make sure he hadn't missed anything, and then he looked at her. For a moment, she thought he was finally going to listen to what she was saying, but then he pointed at her hairbrush and snapped, 'For God's sake, girl, pick up your things!'

'But what about the Man in the Black Cloak?' she argued.

'I don't want you thinking about anything like that,' he barked. 'It was nothing but a nightmare. Now hush up.'

She flinched from the words. She couldn't understand why he was being so mean. But she could hear the worry in his voice along with the anger, and in the distance she could hear the search party coming down the stairs. She knew it wasn't just the threat of discovery that scared him. He hated any talk of the supernatural or any sort of dark and fiendish forces out in the world that he couldn't fix with his wrenches, hammers and screwdrivers.

'But it's real!' she demanded. 'The girl's actually gone, Pa. I'm telling the truth!'

'A little girl's got herself lost, that's it, and they're lookin' for her, so they'll find her, wherever she is. Get your wits about you. People don't just vanish. She's gotta be someplace.'

She stood in the centre of the room. 'I think we should both go out there right now and tell them everything I saw,' she declared boldly.

'No, Sera,' he said. 'They'll spit nails if they find me livin' down here. They'll fire me. Do you understand that? And God knows what they'll make of you. They don't even know you're alive, and we're gonna keep it that way. I'm talkin' to you dead straight now, girl. You hear me?'

The sound of the search party could be heard down the corridor, and it was coming their way.

Clenching her teeth, she shook her head in frustration and stood before him. 'Why, Pa? Why? Why can't people see me?' She didn't have the courage to tell him that at least one Vanderbilt already had, and that he knew her name. 'Just tell me, Pa, whatever it is. I'm twelve years old. I'm grown up. I deserve to know.'

'Look, Sera,' he said, 'last night, somebody sabotaged the dynamo, did it some real damage that I'm not sure I can mend. If I don't get it fixed by nightfall, there's gonna be hell to pay from the boss, and rightly so. The lights, the elevators, the servant-call system – this whole place depends on the Edison machine.'

She tried to imagine someone sneaking into the electrical room and damaging the equipment. 'But why would someone do that, Pa?'

The search party was making its way through the kitchens and would arrive in the workshop at any moment.

'I ain't got time to think about it,' he said, moving towards her with his huge body. 'I just gotta get it workin', that's all. Now do what I tell ya!'

He charged around the room and hid things with such roughness and loudness and violence that it frightened her. She crept behind the boiler and watched him. She knew that when he was like this she couldn't get anywhere with him. He just wanted to be left alone to do his job and work on his machines. But it was gnawing at her, and the more she thought about it, the madder she got. She knew it wasn't the right time to talk to him about everything she'd been thinking and feeling, but she didn't care. She just blurted it out.

'I'm sorry, Pa,' she said. 'I know you're busy, but please just tell me why you don't want anyone to see me.' She stepped out from behind the boiler and faced him, her voice getting louder now. 'Why have you been hiding me all these years?' she demanded. 'Just tell me what's wrong with me. I want to know. Why are you ashamed of me?'

By the time she was done, she was practically screaming at him. Her voice was so loud and shrill that it actually echoed.

Her pa stopped dead in his tracks and looked at her. She knew she had finally reached down inside him and grabbed that armoured heart of his. She'd finally stirred him up. She felt a sudden impulse to take it all back and dart behind the boiler again to hide, but she didn't. She stood before him and looked at him as steadily as she could, her eyes watering.

He stood very still over by the bench, his huge hands balled into fists. A visible wave of pain and despair seemed to pass through him all at once, and for a moment he couldn't speak.

'I'm not ashamed of you,' he said gruffly, his voice strangely hoarse. The searchers were now only one room away.

'You are,' she shot back. She was trembling in fear, but she wasn't going to give up this time. She wanted to shake him. She wanted to shake him to the core. 'You're ashamed of me,' she said again.

He turned away from her so that she couldn't see his face, just the back of his head and huge, bulky body. Several seconds of silence went by. Then he shook his head like he was arguing with himself, or furious with her, or both – she wasn't sure.

'Just keep your mouth shut and follow me,' he said as he turned and walked out of the room.

Scurrying after him, she caught up with him in the corridor. Her body felt queasy all over. She didn't know where he was taking her or what was going to happen. She could barely suck in breaths as he led her down the narrow stone stairs to the sub-basement and into the electrical room with the iron dynamo and thick black wires that spidered up the walls. They had left the search party behind them, at least for a little while.

'We'll hole up in here,' he said as he pulled the door shut with a heavy thud and locked them in. As he lit a lantern against the darkness, she'd never seen him look so serious, so grave and pale, and it frightened her.

'What's happening, Pa?' she asked, her voice shaking.

'Sit down,' he said. 'Ya ain't gonna like what I got to tell ya, but it might help ya understand.'

Serafina swallowed, sat on an old wooden spool of copper wire and prepared herself to listen. Her pa sat on the floor facing her, with his back against the wall. Staring down at the floor and deep in thought, he began to talk.

'Years ago, I was workin' as a mechanic in the train yard in Asheville,' he said. 'The foreman and his wife had just had their third baby boy and their home was full of joy, but while everyone else celebrated, I sat alone in a kind of self-made misery. I ain't proud of it, the way I was soppin' around that night, but things just weren't workin' out for me the way they were supposed to in a man's life. I wanted to meet a good woman, build a house in town and have children of my own, but years had gone by and it hadn't happened. I was a big man and not much to look at. I sweated all day on the engines, and those few times I encountered any womenfolk I could never find my words. I could talk about nuts and bolts till the mornin' come, but not much else.'

She opened her mouth to ask a question, but she didn't want to disrupt the story that was finally pouring out of her pa.

'That night, while everyone was tipping the jug,' he continued, 'I was feelin' pretty poor, and I headed out. I went for a long walk, just walkin' like ya do when you got too much on your mind to do naught else. I went deep into the forest, up through River's Gap and into the mountains. When night came, I just kept walkin'.'

It was hard for her to picture her father travelling through the forest. All those times he had warned her had led her to believe that he would never set foot in the forest. He hated the forest. At least he did now.

'Were you scared, Pa?'

'Naw, I weren't,' he said, shaking his head and still looking at the floor. 'But I shoulda been.'

'Why? What happened?' She couldn't even imagine what it was. The flicker of the lantern cast an eerie shadow on his face. She had always loved his stories, but this one felt closer to his heart than any story he had ever told.

'As I was walkin' through the woods, I heard a queer howlin' noise, like an animal in terrible, writhing pain. The bushes were movin' somethin' fierce, but I couldn't quite make out what it was.'

'Was it somethin' dyin', Pa?' She leaned toward him.

'I don't think so,' he said, looking up at her. 'The ruckus in the bushes went on for a spell, then the noise stopped all sudden-like. I thought it was over, but then a pair of amber-yellow eyes peered at me from the darkness. Whatever sort of man or beast it was, it circled slowly round me, taking one position and then another, studying me real careful, like it was trying to make a decision about me, whether I was worth eatin' or just lettin' be. I sensed a real power behind those eyes. But then the eyes disappeared. The beast was gone. And I heard a strange mewling, crying sound.'

She straightened her back and looked at him. 'Crying?' she asked in confusion. That definitely wasn't what she was expecting.

'I searched through the bushes. Blood covered the ground, and in the blood lay a pile of small creatures. Three of 'em were dead, but one remained just barely alive.'

She got off the wooden spool and crouched down beside her pa. She stared at him, totally absorbed in his story. In her mind, she could see the bloody creatures on the ground.

'But what kind of creatures were they?' she asked in amazement.

He shook his head. 'Like everyone else who lives in these mountains, I'd heard the stories of black magic, but I never gave them much credit until that night. I studied the one that was still alive the best I could in the darkness, but I still couldn't figure what kind of thing it was. Or more like my mind just couldn't believe it. But when I finally took up the creature in my bare hands and held it I realised that it was actually a tiny human baby curled into a little ball.'

Serafina's eyes opened wide in surprise. 'What? Wait. I don't understand. What happened? How did a baby get there?'

'The same question was runnin' through my own mind, believe me, but one thing I knew for certain: regardless of how she came into the world, I had to get this baby some help. I bundled her up in my jacket, hiked back down the hill and carried her out of the woods. I took her to the midwives at the convent and begged them to help, but they gasped at the sight of her, muttering that she was the devil's work. They said she was malformed, near to death and that there was nothing they could do to help her.'

'But why?' Serafina cried in outrage. 'That's terrible! That's so mean!' Just because something looked different didn't mean you just threw it away. She couldn't help but wonder what kind of world it was out there. The attitude of the midwives almost bothered her more than the idea of a yellow-eyed beast lurking in the night. But she felt a renewed glimmer of admiration for her pa as she imagined his huge, warm hands wrapped around that tiny little baby's body, giving it heat, keeping it alive.

Her father took a long, deep, troubled breath as he remembered that night, and then he continued his story. 'You have to understand the poor little thing had been born with her eyes closed, Sera, and the nuns said that she would never see. She'd been born deaf, and they said she would never hear. And it was plain enough to see that she had four toes on each foot instead of five, but that was the least of it. Her collarbones were malformed, and she had an unnaturally long, curving spine – all twisted-like – and she did not look like she could survive.'

The shock hit her like a blow. She looked up at her father in astonishment. 'I'm the baby!' she shouted, leaping to her feet. This wasn't just a story, this was *her* story. She'd been born in the forest. That meant her pa had *found* her and taken her in.

She was like a baby fox who'd been raised by a coyote. She stood in front of her pa. 'I'm the baby!' she said again.

Her father looked at her, and she saw the truth of it flickering in his eyes, but he didn't acknowledge it. He didn't say yes and didn't say no. It was like he couldn't reconcile his memory of that dark night with the daughter he had now, and he had to tell the story the only way he could: as if it wasn't her at all.

'The bones of the baby's back weren't connected to each other the way they should have been,' he continued. 'The nuns were half scared out of their wits at the idea of caring for this child, like it was some sort of demon spawn, but to me she was a little baby, a little chitlan, and you didn't abandon such a thing. Who cares how many toes she had!'

Serafina kneeled on the floor in front of him, trying to understand it all. She was beginning to see the kind of man her father was and maybe where she got some of her own stick-to-it-iveness. But it was all so confusing. How could she get anything from him if she wasn't even his?

'I took that baby away, fearin' them nuns would drown her,' he said.

'I hate them nuns,' she spat. 'They're terrible!'

He shook his head, not in disagreement, but more like the nuns didn't mean anything at all because they were the least of his problems.

'I didn't have any proper food,' he said, 'so I crept into a farmer's barn and milked his goat – stole a bottle too. Felt ashamed doin' these things, but I needed to get some food into her, and I couldn't see a better road. That night, I fed the little chitlan her first meal, and as bad off as she was, and with her eyes still closed, she drank it down real good, and I remember praying that somehow it'd help. The more I held her and watched her suck down that milk, the more I wanted her to live.'

'Then what happened?' She slid closer to him. She knew that outside the locked door of the electrical room, somewhere above them, the lawful inhabitants of Biltmore Estate were searching from room to room, but she didn't care. 'Keep goin', Pa,' she nudged.

'I looked for a woman who could mother the baby proper, but none of them would do it. They was sure she was gonna die. But two weeks later, while I was fixin' an engine with one hand and bottle-feedin' the chitlan with the other, somethin' happened. She opened her eyes for the first time and stared straight at me. All I could do was stare right back at her. She had these big, beautiful yellow eyes that just didn't stop. I knew then and there that I was hers, and she was mine, that we were kin now, and there was no denyin' it.'

Serafina was so mesmerised by his story that she barely blinked. The yellow eyes that her father spoke of were still looking at him, and they had been for twelve years.

He rubbed his mouth slowly with his hand, looked over at the dynamo, and then continued the story. 'In the time that followed, I fed the little chitlan every morning and every night. I slept with her tucked under my arm. I nestled her in an open toolbox beside me when I worked. When she started growing up a little, I taught her how to crawl and run about. I was tryin' my best to take good care of her – she was mine now, you see – but people started askin' questions and government types started comin' around. Men with badges and guns. One night when I was out workin' in the train yard, three of 'em waited until she wandered off a bit, and then they cornered her, trapped her in real tight. They was gonna take her away and put her someplace, God knows where, or maybe worse. I hit the first officer so hard that he went down bleedin' and he didn't get up, then I struck the second one and grabbed for the third, but he skedaddled on outta there. The little chitlan was all right, thank God, but I knew we were in trouble. They'd be comin' back with more men next time, chains for me, and a cage for the chitlan. I knew then that we had to go. We had to escape the pryin' eyes and yammerin' mouths in the city, so I quit the train yard and found a new job way up in the mountains, workin' the construction of a great house.'

She gasped as she realised that he hadn't just been hiding *her*; he'd been hiding *them*. *That's why we're in the basement*, she thought as a wave of relief passed through her. He was protecting her.

'I took care of her through good times and bad,' her pa continued, 'just doin' everything I could, and over the years the strange little creature that I found in the forest grew up into a fine little girl, and I did my best to forget how she came into the world or how I got her.'

And here, finally, her father paused and looked at her in earnest. 'And that's you now, Sera,' he said. 'That's you. It's plain to see that you're not like other girls, but you're not misshapen or hideous like them nuns said you'd be. You're remarkably graceful in your movements – fast and agile like I've never seen. You're not deaf and blind like they said, but real sharp in your senses. I've been protecting you every day for the last twelve years, and the God's truth: they've been the best twelve years of my life. You mean the world to me, girl. There's no shame here, none at all, just a strong desire to keep us both alive.'

When he stopped and looked at her with his steady dark eyes, she realised that she'd been sobbing, and quickly wiped the tears off her face before he got mad at her for crying. In some ways, she had never felt closer to her pa than at that moment, for his story had snagged her heart, but there was something else roiling up inside her too: her father wasn't her father. He'd found her in the woods and taken her. He'd been lying to her and everyone else for her entire life. All these years he'd refused to talk about her mother, just let her wonder on and on, and now here it was. The truth. Tears kept streaming down her face. She felt so stupid imagining fancy ladies and her mother forgetting her in a washing machine and all that stuff she used to think about when she was little. She'd spent countless hours wondering where she came from and he had known all this the whole time.

'Why didn't you tell me?' she asked him.

He didn't answer her.

'Why didn't you tell me, Pa?' she asked again.

Staring at the ground, he shook his head slowly back and forth.

'Pa . . .'

Finally, he said, 'Because I didn't want it to be true.'

She stopped and looked at him in shock. 'But it *is* true, Pa. You can't just wish things aren't true when they are true!'

'I'm sorry, Sera,' he said. 'I just wanted you to be my little girl.'

She was angry, very angry, but she felt a lump in her throat. He had finally reached deep down into his heart and told her what he was thinking, what he was feeling, what he was frightened of, and what he dreamed of.

And what he dreamed of was *her*.

She clenched her teeth and breathed through her nose and looked at him.

She was angry and confused and amazed and excited and frightened all at the same time. She finally knew the truth. At least some of it.

Now she knew that she didn't just *feel* different, she *was* different.

The thought of it terrified her: she was a creature of the night.

She came from the very forest that her pa had taught her to fear all her life and had forbidden her to enter. The thought of coming from that place repulsed her, scared her, but at the same time there was a strange confirmation in it, almost a relief. It made a twisted kind of sense to her.

She looked at her father, sitting with his back against the wall. Now that he had finally told her the story, he seemed exhausted, like a man who had shared a great burden.

He picked himself up off the floor, brushed off his hands and walked slowly to the other side of the room, deep in thought.

'I'm sorry, Sera,' he said. 'I reckon it ain't gonna do ya no good on the inside knowin' all that, but you're right, you're growin' up now, and ya deserved to know.' He came over to her and squatted down and held her so that he could look into her face. 'But whatever you do with it, I want you to remember this one thing: there's nothin' wrong with you, Sera, nothin' at all, you hear?'

'Yeah, I hear, Pa,' she said, nodding and wiping the tears from her eyes. There was turmoil in her heart, but one thing she knew for sure: her father believed in her. But, even as she stood there looking at him, thoughts and questions started weaving through her mind.

Would she have to stay hidden forever? Could she ever fit in with the people of Biltmore? Could she ever make any friends? She was a creature of the night, but what did that mean she could do? She looked down at her hand. If she grew out her fingernails, would they become claws?

In the distance she could hear the sound of the search party moving through the basement, and she tried to block it out. She looked over at her father again. After a long pause, she quietly asked the question that had been forming in her mind.

'What about my mother?'

Her pa shut his eyes for a second as he took a good, long breath, and then he opened his eyes, looked at her and spoke to her with unusual softness. 'I'm sorry, Sera. The truth is I don't rightly know. But when I see her in my mind I think she must have been beautiful, both lovely and strong. She fought hard to bring you into the world, Sera, and she wanted to stay with you, but she knew she couldn't. I don't know why she couldn't. But she gave you to me to love and take care of, and for that I'm much obliged.'

'So maybe she's still out there someplace . . .' Her voice trembled, uncertain. Her pa's story had made it feel like there was a tornado twisting inside her, but the thought of her momma felt like the bursting of the sun.

'Maybe she is,' he relented, gently.

She looked at him. 'Pa, do you . . . do you think that . . . do you know if she was human or –'

'I don't want to hear any talk 'bout that,' he interrupted her, shaking his head. She could see in the tightness of his mouth how upset her question made him. 'You're my little girl,' he said. 'That's what I believe.'

'But in the forest –' she began.

'No,' he cut her off, 'I don't want you to think about that. You live here. With me. This is your home. I've told ya before, and I'll tell ya again, Sera: our world is filled with many mysteries, things we don't understand. Never go into the deep parts of the forest, for there are many dangers there, both dark and bright, and they will ensnare your soul.'

She stared at her pa for a long time, trying to comprehend his words. She could see the seriousness in his eyes, and she felt it too, deep down in her heart. Her pa was the only person she'd ever had in the world.

She heard men coming down the corridor outside the door. They were searching the rooms of the sub-basement. The hair on her arms tingled, telling her to run.

She looked at her pa. After all he'd done for her by telling her this story, she didn't want to bring it up again, didn't want to make him angry, but she had to ask one last question.

'What about the man who took the girl in the yellow dress? What kind of demon is he, Pa? Does he come out of the forest, or do you think he's one of the fancy-dressed swells from upstairs?'

'I don't know,' he said. 'I've been prayin' to God in heaven that it was a figment of your imagination.'

'It wasn't, Pa,' she said softly.

He didn't want to argue with her any more, but he looked straight at her. 'Don't get it in your head you're gonna go out there, Sera,' he said. 'It's just too dangerous for us. You see why now. I know you're hankering to help her, and that does ya credit, but don't worry about the girl. She's their kin, not ours. They don't need our help. They'll find her. You stay out of it.'

At that moment, someone pounded on the heavy wooden door to the electrical room.

'We're searching the house!' a man shouted.

Serafina glanced around even though she already knew there was no way out of the room.

'Open this door!' shouted another man. 'Open up!'

5

The moment her pa opened the door, Mr Boseman and two other men stormed into the electrical room. Serafina clung to the metal racks on the ceiling, hidden among the hundreds of thick copper wires that ran to the floors above.

While her pa launched into an elaborate explanation of exactly how a dynamo generated electricity to the bewildered men, Serafina crawled along the ceiling, dropped silently to the floor behind them, and darted out through the open door.

She dashed down the corridor and crawled into a small coal chute, then curled up in the darkness and hunkered down.

She'd always had a hankering for sitting quietly in dark, confined spaces. As she peered out of the blackness through a small hole in the chute's iron door and watched the searchers go by one way and then the other, her mind kept going back to the story that her pa had told her about her birth. It infuriated her that he'd waited this long to tell her. Could it really be true? Had she actually been born on the ground one night out in the darkness of the forest? Her momma, whoever she was, must have been very brave.

But the more she thought about it, the more she reckoned that maybe her momma didn't just go sauntering into the forest that night to give birth. Maybe she already lived there. And if that was true then what kind of creature had her mother been? And what kind of creature did that make her? What if her pa had been wrong to take her?

It was all so confusing. She felt more unsettled and disjointed than ever. Suddenly, her pa wasn't her pa and Biltmore wasn't her home. And she still didn't have a momma.

She knew now that her pa had been hiding her because he was scared of what people would do to her. But it still confused her because her pa loved her, so couldn't other people love her too? What difference did it make when you slept and when you hunted? It seemed like everyone must love the feeling of lying in the warm sunlight of a window, or seeing a bird fly across the sky, or taking a walk on a cool, moonlit night when all the stars were overhead. She wasn't sure if most boys and girls her age could catch one rat or two with their bare hands, but she didn't think that it was too strange a thing either way.

As another search party moved past her, Serafina watched

them and shook her head. If Clara Brahms were alive and wanted to hide, there were plenty of places for her to do so. Adults, even a hundred of them running around in a panic, didn't seem to grasp all that was possible in a place like Biltmore. There were *thousands* of places to hide. She hoped they would somehow find Clara, despite what she had seen happen the night before, but she didn't think they would. Clara Brahms was *gone*.

You're too loud and moving too fast, she thought as the searchers went by. *You're never going to find her that way. You've got to catch the rat.*

Her pa had told her to leave them to it, that it wasn't any of her business, that they weren't her kin, but who was he to say who was kin and who wasn't? He stole babies out of the woods! What if Clara were still alive and needed her help? How could she just sit there and watch? What if the Man in the Black Cloak came again and took someone else? She resolved that she needed to find Braeden Vanderbilt again and tell him what she'd seen. It wouldn't be right not to. She'd always dreamed of having a friend, but what kind of friend was she going to be to Clara Brahms if she didn't try to help her?

When the corridor was clear, she crawled out of the chute and snuck away. Her plan was to creep upstairs, but when she passed the mossy stairway that led down to the lower levels of the basement she wondered if there'd be any sign of what had happened the night before. The young master would be far more likely to believe her story if she could bring him some sort of evidence of what she'd seen.

She slunk down the stairs, down and down again, into the damp darkness of the sub-basement until she came to the slanted, brown-dripping corridor.

She couldn't stop her breathing from getting heavier, but she kept going, telling herself that she'd be safe.

She crept through the darkness until she came to the spot where she'd seen the Man in the Black Cloak. There was no sign of Clara Brahms, but there were red drips on the wall. On the floor she found a tiny shard of glass.

From the broken lantern, she thought.

She searched the area but found nothing else.

On her way back, she followed the same series of corridors she had used to escape the demon or whatever it was. She studied the areas where she had battled for her life. She spotted something lying at the base of the wall that, at first glance, looked like a dead, rotting rat. It was the size and colour of one of the nasty vermin, but as she took a step closer her nose wrinkled. It gave off a putrid, foul smell, but it wasn't a rat. She clenched her teeth and got down onto her hands and knees and examined it. It was a glove lying crumpled on the floor. Images of the Black Cloak swirling around her rose up in her mind, the cloak cutting her off from all she knew and loved.

It's just a glove, you silly fool, she thought, smiling at her scaredy-cat thoughts, but when she picked it up, her mouth curled in disgust. Inside the glove there were bloody patches of skin.

It was so disgusting, far worse than any rat carcass she'd

ever found, but she forced herself to examine it more closely. The glove was made out of a fine, thin, black satin material. The flakes and patches of skin inside appeared as if they had sloughed off the hand that had last worn the glove. The skin had black spots and grey hairs. It was as if the owner of the glove hadn't just been old, but ageing rapidly, almost disintegrating. Her muscles twitched as she remembered fighting for her life. She had bitten and clawed in a wild frenzy. The glove must have fallen from his belt or pocket, for she remembered that his hands had been bare and bloody when she'd fought him.

Men's gloves were as common as top hats and canes, so it wasn't a very good clue. It didn't provide her evidence to show to the young master. But it did stiffen the idea that whoever or whatever the Man in the Black Cloak was, there was something wrong with him.

Anxious to get out of the damp and more determined than ever to find the young master, she scampered her way up to the main level of the basement.

Many of the rooms on this level had windows at the tops of the walls. Outside, she could see servants and guests searching the gardens, the Rambles maze and the many footpaths. She couldn't help but hope to see Braeden Vanderbilt among them.

She wondered if she could think of Braeden as her friend now, or if she were fooling herself. The God's honest truth was that she didn't even know what a friend was, other than what she'd read in books. If you meet someone face to face and they don't hiss at you and bite you, does that mean you're friends?

But, when she thought about it a little more, she remembered that she did in fact nearly hiss at the young master when they first met, so that wasn't ideal. Maybe they weren't friends at all. Maybe he thought she was nothing but a lowly dirt-scraper from the basement and she didn't warrant a second thought. She probably should have told him right off that she was the C.R.C. That would have been a lot more impressive. As it was, she just wasn't sure what sort of impression she'd made, except that she was dirty, rude, unkempt and had bad hair.

She darted up the stairs to the first floor. She took advantage of the chaos of the search to scurry unseen from one hiding spot to another. She moved silently, padding swiftly on soft feet. The adults spoke so loudly and made such a galumphing noise when they stomped all over the place that they were easy to avoid.

She dashed over to the Winter Garden, where she hid beneath the fronds of the tropical plants.

As Mrs Vanderbilt and two servants hurried down the corridor, Serafina scooted into the Billiard Room and made a narrow escape. She thought that even her rodent enemies would have been impressed by her quickness of foot on that particular manoeuvre.

Walled in rich oak panelling and appointed with soft leather chairs, the Billiard Room smelled of cigar smoke. Deep-hued Oriental carpets covered the floor. Black wrought-iron lamp fixtures hung down from the ceiling over the game tables. Animal heads and hunting trophies lined the walls. She liked those. The trophies on the walls reminded her of the rats she'd killed and laid at her pa's feet. So she and the Vanderbilts had that much in common. On the other hand, she had stopped doing that when she'd realised that it was the catching she liked more than the killing.

Just as she was about to leave the room, a footman came in with one of the maids. Serafina quickly dived beneath the billiard table.

'Maybe she's been giving us the slip at every turn, Miss Whitney,' the footman said, leaning down to look under the billiard table just as Serafina darted behind the sofa.

'She could be just about anywhere, Mr Pratt,' Miss Whitney agreed, looking behind the sofa just as Serafina hid in the green velvet curtains that adorned the windows.

'Do you know if anyone has checked the pipe organ?' Mr Pratt asked. 'There's a secret room back there.'

'The girl is a pianist, so she might be curious about the organ,' Miss Whitney agreed.

Taking a quick breath and using the curtain for cover, Serafina climbed up the window stile lickety-split, then wedged herself into the uppermost corner of the window. She had just enough time to see that Mr Pratt was wearing white gloves, a black tie and a black-and-white footman's livery, but she took special notice of his black patent-leather dress shoes.

'What do you mean, she's a pianist?' Mr Pratt asked.

'Tilly, on the third floor, told me the girl's some sort of musical prodigy, gives piano concerts all over the country,' Miss

Whitney said as she ran her hands through the curtains where Serafina had just been hiding.

Serafina held her breath and stayed very still. Miss Whitney was so close to her now that she could smell her sweet lavender-and-rose perfume. All Miss Whitney had to do was pull back the curtain and look up, and she'd see Serafina clinging there with a Cheshire smile. Despite her fear of being seen, Serafina couldn't resist noticing the details of the maid's outfit. She loved the pretty pink uniform with its white collar and cuffs, which the maids wore in the morning before changing into their more formal black-and-white uniforms in the afternoon.

'Come on. There's no one in here,' Mr Pratt said. 'We'll check the pipe organ.'

Serafina breathed a sigh of relief as Miss Whitney walked to the other side of the room.

Mr Pratt pushed the oak-panelled wall just to the right of the fireplace.

'Oh my!' Miss Whitney said in surprise, laughing nervously as a concealed door opened up. 'I've cleaned this room countless times, and I never knew that was there. You're always so clever, Mr Pratt.'

Serafina rolled her eyes at Miss Whitney's silliness. The maid was obviously besotted with this know-it-all footman. Serafina liked Miss Whitney, but the maid could sure use some help learning how to sniff out a rat. And that was exactly what Serafina thought about shiny-shoes Mr Pratt.

Mr Pratt laughed, clearly pleased with Miss Whitney's reaction to his little trick.

'How do you know about all these secret things?' Miss Whitney asked him. 'Do you skulk through the rooms at night when everyone else is sleeping?'

'Oh, I'm full of surprises, Miss Whitney, and not just about a little girl in a yellow dress – you wait and see,' he said. 'Come on . . .'

Yellow dress? How did he know what Clara was wearing when she disappeared? There was something about this footman that Serafina didn't like. He was too slick, too flirty, too tricky in his hoity-toity black livery, and she didn't trust him any more than she trusted a rat in the pastry kitchen.

I wouldn't go in there if I were you! She wanted to shout to Miss Whitney as they passed through the concealed door, but instead she listened to the rat's footsteps. They were similar to the footsteps she'd heard in the basement the night before, but he and Miss Whitney disappeared into the wall too quickly for her to be sure one way or the other.

As soon as they were gone, she climbed down and checked the area to the right of the fireplace to make sure she'd be able to find the concealed door if she ever needed it. A concealed door could be a very useful thing to a girl of her particular occupation. Measuring three oak panels tall and two oak panels wide, the door was disguised to look exactly like the wall. There was even a framed picture hanging there, a weirdly realistic tintype of a white-haired old man that she guessed was probably Mr Vanderbilt's long-dead grandfather, Cornelius Vanderbilt.

It pained her to think that not only did she not have a grandpa to tell her stories about the old times, she barely even had a pa any more. He was just someone who found her in a bloody heap and decided to steal goat's milk to keep her alive in his toolbox. He could be anybody. And she was still mightily perturbed at him for not coming straight with her sooner.

Below the hunting trophies that loomed above, the wall was covered with portraits of Vanderbilts. Mother, father, grandmother, grandfather, brothers and sisters and cousins. She found herself instinctively searching the faces to see if any of them resembled her. Was Clara Brahms alive someplace, wondering if her mother had forgotten her, just as Serafina often wondered about her own? But the difference was that Mrs Brahms hadn't forgotten her daughter, would never leave her behind. Clara Brahms's mother was still looking for her.

Serafina stepped closer to the wall of portraits. The last picture was another depiction of old Cornelius, the patriarch of the grand Vanderbilt family, walking proudly beside one of his iron steam trains, the blur of his motion giving him a ghostlike quality. It put shivers down her spine just looking at it. But the picture had gone a bit catawampus when Mr Pratt and Miss Whitney went through, so she straightened it out. When she touched the door, it glided open on smooth, well-oiled hinges. She took a deep breath, then slipped through.

. . .

To her surprise, the secret door led to the Smoking Room. From there, she found a similar passage into the Gun Room, with its racks of rifles and shotguns protected by panes of glass. Seeing her reflection in the glass, she spat on the back of her hand and wiped her face until she got a few of the larger smudges off her cheeks and chin. Then she smoothed her long brown-streaked hair back behind her ears in a few quick movements. She stood there and just stared at herself, wondering.

If her momma saw her, would she recognise her? Would she hug her and kiss her or would she look the other way and just keep walking? When strangers saw her, what did they think? What did they see, a girl or a creature?

As a group of estate guests walked past the room, she heard them talking in hushed voices that perked up her ears.

'I'm telling you it's true!' a young man whispered.

'I heard about it too,' whispered another. 'My grandmama told me that there's an old cemetery out there with hundreds of gravestones, but the bodies are missing!'

'I heard there's an old village,' said a third voice. 'It's all overgrown and taken back by the forest, like everyone who lived there abandoned their houses.'

Serafina had heard the tall tales passed around among the kitchen folk at night, but she'd never been too sure whether she was supposed to believe them or not.

Every place she went in the house that day, she overheard conversations – gentlemen discussing whether detectives should be called in to investigate the missing child; servants trading stories about suspicious guests; and parents arguing about the best way to protect their sons and daughters from getting lost in the giant house without being rude to the Vanderbilts. And now they were talking about the old cemetery in the woods.

She kept thinking about the Man in the Black Cloak. If he were one of these people, he could be lurking in any corridor or room. How do you tell a friend from an enemy just by looking at him?

It seemed like the further she went, the more questions she had. The only thing certain so far was that the search continued and they still hadn't found Clara Brahms. Either alive or dead.

Then she had an idea. If the Man in the Black Cloak was some sort of wraith that drifted out of the forest at night, or if he conjured himself out of the ether in the basement, then she probably wouldn't find very much evidence of him in the upper floors of the house. But if the Man in the Black Cloak was at least partially mortal and resided at Biltmore, then he'd have to stash his cloak someplace when he wasn't wearing it. If she could find the cloak, then maybe she could find the man.

The closets and storerooms throughout the house were some of her favourite hiding spots, so she knew them well. When ladies and gentlemen came to Biltmore, they usually exited from their carriages at the front door. But in bad weather they used the covered porte cochere at the north end of the house, near the stables. Always just out of sight, darting and dodging, creeping and crawling, she made her way there.

The coatroom was dark and cramped, which suited her just fine. She loved closets. As she pushed her way through the thick forest of coats, cloaks, stoles and capes, she searched the hangers one by one, looking for a long black satin cloak. When she reached the back wall of the coatroom without finding it, she couldn't help but feel a pang of disappointment.

As she crept out of the coatroom, she realised that she'd have to go to Braeden without any proof, but the truth was that she hadn't been able to find *him*, either.

You've got to think, girl, she heard her pa telling her in the tone he used when she couldn't reckon one of her lessons. *Use what you know, and think it through.*

An idea came to her. Knowing what she did about Braeden Vanderbilt, he'd either be with his dog or his horse or both. He loved horses. It would be the first thing he thought of. He'd go to the stables to help the stablemen look for Clara Brahms there. Or maybe he'd search the grounds on horseback. Either way, the stables seemed like the place to go.

The most direct path was through the porte cochere. There were quite a few people coming and going through this busy area, but she hoped that if anyone spotted her, they'd assume she was a scullery maid or a kindling girl going about her chores.

She took a deep breath and ran down the steps towards the archway that led to the stables. She moved fast. She thought she was going to make it. But just as she looked behind her to make sure no one was following her, she collided with a great smash into a large man in front of her. It knocked the wind out of her and nearly knocked her off her feet, but the man grabbed her by the shoulders and held her up with a brutal grip.

Her captor wore a full-length black rain cloak even though it wasn't raining. He had a peculiar pointed beard, crooked teeth, and an ugly, pockmarked face. She hadn't seen the face of the Man in the Black Cloak, but this is what she'd imagined he'd look like.

'What you lookin' at?' he demanded. 'Who is you, anyway?'

'I ain't nobody!' she spat defiantly, trying desperately to tear herself free and run, but the man's hands clamped her so tight that she couldn't escape. Now it was her turn to be the biting rat with its neck squeezed between finger and thumb. She noticed that he was standing in front of the open door of an awaiting carriage.

'You the new pig girl?' the man demanded. 'What you doin' up 'ere?' He tightened his grip so viciously on her arms that she let out a squeal of pain. 'I said, what's your name, ya little scamp?'

'None of your business!' she said as she kicked and fought any way she could.

The man had a terrible smell, like he needed a bath really, really bad, and his breath stank with the huge wad of putrefied chewing tobacco that bulged in his cheek.

'Tell me your name, or I'm gonna shake ya,' the man said even as he shook her. He shook her so violently that she couldn't catch her breath or get her feet on the ground. He just kept shaking her.

'Mr Crankshod,' a firm, authoritative voice said from behind her. It wasn't just a name. It was a command.

Startled, the ugly man stopped shaking her. He set her on her feet and began to smooth her hair, pretending that he had actually been taking care of her all along.

Gasping for breath, she turned to look at who had spoken.

There stood Braeden Vanderbilt at the top of the steps.

Serafina's heart sprang. Despite the terrible situation he'd caught her in and the angry expression on his face, she was glad to see Braeden.

The crab-crankedy Mr Crankshod, however, was far less pleased. 'Young Master Vanderbilt,' he grumbled in surprise as he bowed, wiped the tobacco spittle from his lip and stood at attention. 'I beg your pardon, sir. I didn't see you there. Your coach is ready, sir.'

Braeden looked at them both without speaking. Clearly, he wasn't pleased by what he'd just seen. The boy's Dobermann appeared ready to attack whichever of them his master told him to, and Serafina hoped that it was going to be the sputum-faced Mr Crankshod rather than her.

Braeden stared at Mr Crankshod, then slowly moved his eyes to her. Her mind whirled with potential cover stories. He had stopped the mountainous brute from shaking the living daylights out of her, but what could she say to explain her presence here?

'I'm the new shoeshine girl,' she said, stepping forward. 'Your aunt asked me to make sure your boots were well shone for your trip, sir, spit and polished good, sir. That's what she said, all right, spit and polished good.'

'No, no, no!' Mr Crankshod shouted, knowing it was a ruse. 'What's this, now, ya little beggar? You ain't no shoeshine girl! Who is ya? Where'd ya come from?'

But a smile of delicious conspiracy formed at the corner of Braeden's mouth. 'Ah, yes, Aunt Edith did mention something about getting my boots shone. I had quite forgotten,' he said, exaggerating the aristocratic air in his voice. Then he looked at her sharply and his eyebrows furrowed into a frown. 'I'm on my way to the Vances', and I'm running late. I don't have time to wait on you, so you'll just have to come with me and do it in the carriage on the way.'

Serafina felt the blood rush to her face. Was he serious? She couldn't go in a carriage with him! Her pa would kill her. And what was she gonna do all cooped up in there anyway, getting dragged around in a box by a bunch of four-legged black hoof-stompers?

'Well, come along, let's be quick about it,' Braeden said, his voice filled with the impatience of a lordly gentleman as he gestured towards the carriage door.

She had never been in a carriage in her life. She didn't even know how to get in one or what to do once she did.

The ill-tempered, rat-faced Mr Crankshod had no choice but to obey the young master's commands. He shoved Serafina towards the door, and she suddenly found herself in the dimly lit interior of the Vanderbilt carriage. As she crouched uncertainly on the floor, she could not help but marvel at the carriage's luxuriously appointed finery with its hand-carved woodwork, brass fixtures, bevelled-glass windows and plush paisley tufted seats.

Braeden followed her in with the grace of familiarity, and took a seat. Gidean sat on the floor, eyeing her with fanged intent.

Mind your own business, dog, she thought as she stared back at him.

Mr Crankshod shut the carriage door and climbed up onto the driver's bench with the other coachman.

Oh, great, rat face is driving us, Serafina thought. She had no idea how long a trip this would be or how she could send word back to her pa. He'd ordered her to hide in the basement, not get kidnapped by the young master and his stink-breathed henchman. But at least she'd finally be able to talk to Braeden alone about what she'd seen the night before.

The carriage seat looked too clean for her to sit on with her basement clothing, and she was supposed to be cleaning the young master's boots, so she knelt on the floor of the carriage and wondered how she was going to pretend to clean his boots when she didn't have any brushes or polish. Spit and polish was one thing, but just spit was another.

'You don't really have to clean my boots,' Braeden said softly. 'I was just going along with your story.'

Just as Serafina looked up at him and their eyes were about to meet, the horses pulled and the carriage jounced forward. In a moment as unusual as it was mortifying, she actually lost her balance.

'I'm sorry,' she mumbled as she fell against Braeden's legs and then quickly straightened herself up.

She glanced at the seat that she suspected she was supposed to be sitting on, but the dog stared at her with his steely eyes. When she moved towards the seat, the dog growled, low and menacing, baring his teeth as if to say, *If I can't sit on the seat, then neither can you.*

'No, Gidean,' Braeden chastised him. She couldn't decide if the young master had spoken the command because he wanted to protect her or if he just didn't want to get the inside of his carriage bloody. In any case, Gidean's ears crumpled and his head lowered under the force of his master's reprimand.

Seeing her chance, she slipped onto the seat opposite Braeden and as far away from the dog as possible.

As Gidean continued staring at her, she felt an overwhelming desire to hiss at him and make him back off, but she didn't think that would go over too well with the young master, so she held back the urge.

She had never liked dogs, and dogs had never liked her. Whenever they saw her, they barked. One time, she had to scurry up a tree to get away from a crazed foxhound, and her pa had to use a ladder to retrieve her.

When the carriage rumbled into a turn, Serafina looked out the window and saw the grand facade of the house. Biltmore Estate rose four stories high with its ornately carved grey stone walls. Gargoyles and ancient warriors adorned its dark copper edges. Chimneys, turrets and towers formed the spires of its almost Gothic presence. Two giant statues of lions guarded the massive oak doors at the entrance, as if warding off evil spirits. She had marvelled at those statues many times on her midnight prowls. She had always loved them. She imagined that those great cats were Biltmore's protectors, its guardians, and she could think of no more important job.

In the golden light of the setting sun, the mansion really could be quite startlingly lovely. But as the sun withdrew its brightness behind the surrounding mountains it cast ominous shadows across the estate, which reminded her of griffins, chimeras, and other twisted creatures of the night that were half one thing and half another. The thought of it gave her a shudder. In one moment, the estate was the most beautiful home you had ever seen, but, in the next, it was a dark and foreboding haunted castle.

'Lie down and be good,' Braeden said.

She looked at him in surprise and then realised that he was talking to the dog, not to her.

Gidean complied with his master's request and lay down at his feet. The dog seemed a little more relaxed now, but when he looked at Serafina his expression seemed to say, *Just because I'm lying down, don't think for a second that if you do something to my master I can't still kill you . . .*

She smiled to herself. She couldn't help it – she was beginning to like this dog. She could understand him, his fierceness and his loyalty. She admired that.

As she tried to get used to the rumbling motion of the moving carriage, she noticed that Braeden was studying her.

'I've been looking for you . . .' he said.

She stole a quick glance at him and then looked away. When she looked into his eyes, it felt as if he could tell what she were thinking. It was unnerving.

She tried to say something, but when she opened her mouth, she could barely breathe. Of course, she'd snuck around enough over the years to overhear people of all walks of life speaking to one another, so theoretically she knew how it was done. So many guests and servants had passed through Biltmore over the years that she could take on a rich lady's air or a mountain woman's twang or even a New York accent, but for some reason, she struggled mightily to find the right words – any words – to say to the young master.

'I – I'm sorry about all this,' she said finally. The annoying constriction in her chest seemed to strangle her words as she spoke them. She wasn't sure if she sounded anything like a halfway normal person or not. 'I mean, I'm sorry about being dumped into your carriage like luggage that wouldn't fit on the roof, and I don't know why your dog doesn't like me.'

Braeden looked at Gidean and then back at her. 'He normally likes people, especially girls. It's strange.'

'There are plenty of strange things happening today,' she said, her chest loosening up a bit as she began to realise that Braeden was going to actually talk to her.

'You think so too?' he said, leaning towards her.

He wasn't anything like what she imagined the young master of the Vanderbilt mansion would be, especially as good-looking and well educated as he was. She had expected him to be snobbish, bossy and aloof, but he was none of these things.

'I don't think Clara Brahms is hiding,' he said in a conspiratorial tone. 'Do you?'

'No,' she said, raising her eyes and looking at him. 'I definitely don't.' She wanted to pour it all out and tell him everything she knew. That had been her plan all along. But her pa's words kept going through her mind: *They ain't our kind of folk, Sera.*

Whatever he was, Braeden seemed to be a good person. As he was talking to her, he didn't judge her or discount her. If anything, he actually seemed to like her. Or maybe he was just fascinated by her in the same way he would be by a weird species of insect he'd never seen before, but, either way, he kept talking.

'She's not the first one, you know,' he whispered.

'What do you mean?' she said, drawing closer to him.

'Two weeks ago, a fifteen-year-old girl named Anastasia Rostonova went out for a walk in the evening in the Rambles, and she didn't come back.'

'Really?' she asked, hanging on his every word. She had thought she had something to tell him, but it turned out that he had just as much to tell her. A boy who whispered about kidnappings and skulduggery was the kind of boy she could learn to like. She knew the Rambles well, but she also knew that the shrubbery maze of crisscrossing paths caused many people great confusion.

'Everyone said Anastasia must have wandered into the forest and got lost,' he continued, 'or that she ran away from home. But I know they're wrong.'

'How do you know?' she asked, keen to hear the details.

'The next morning, I found her little white dog wandering around the paths of the Rambles. The poor dog was frantic, desperately searching for her.' Braeden looked at Gidean. 'I didn't know Anastasia well – she'd only been visiting with her father for a couple of days when she disappeared – but I don't think she would have run away and left her dog behind.'

Serafina thought that sounded about right. Braeden seemed as loyal to Gidean as Gidean was to him. They were friends, and she liked that. Then she thought about that poor girl and what might have happened to her.

'Anastasia Rostonova . . .' She repeated the funny-sounding name.

'She's the daughter of Mr Rostonov, the Russian ambassador,' Braeden explained. 'She told me that Russian girls always put an *a* on the end of their last name.'

'What did she look like?' she asked, wanting to make sure she hadn't got her kidnapped rich girls mixed up.

'She's tall and pretty, and she has long, curly black hair, and she wears elaborate red dresses that look really hard to walk in.'

'Do you think she vanished like Clara Brahms?' Serafina asked.

Before he could answer, something caught her eye through the carriage windows. There were trees on either side of the carriage. They were travelling down a narrow dirt road that wound through a thick and darkened forest, the very forest that her pa had warned her to never enter. And the very forest where she had been born. She couldn't help but feel a pang of trepidation. 'Where are we going, exactly?'

'My aunt and uncle are worried about me, so they're sending me to the Vances' in Asheville for the night to keep me out of harm's way. They ordered Crankshod to guard me.'

'That wasn't very smart,' she said before she could help herself. It wasn't a very polite thing to say, but for some reason, she was having a dickens of a time not telling Braeden the truth.

'I've always detested that man,' Braeden agreed, 'but my uncle depends on him.'

As she looked out of the window at the forest, she could

no longer see the horizon or the sun. All she could see was the thick density of the forest's huge old trees, black and decrepit, which grew so closely together that she could barely tell one from the other. It seemed a dark and foreboding place for anyone to even visit, let alone live, yet there was something that excited her about it too.

But then she felt a sinking sensation in her stomach. Somewhere, miles behind them, was Biltmore. Her pa would be wondering why she wasn't showing up for dinner.

No chicken or grits tonight, Pa. I'm sorry she thought. *Try not to worry about me.* A day ago, she had been leading a perfectly normal life catching rats in the basement, and now everything had turned so bizarre.

Pulling her gaze away from the forest, she finally turned to Braeden, swallowed hard, and began to say what she'd come for. 'There is something I need to tell –'

'How come I've never seen you before?' he interrupted.

'What?' she asked, taken aback.

'Where do you come from?'

'Yeah, good question,' she said before she could stop herself, imagining the bloody pile of dead creatures her pa had plucked her from.

'I'm serious,' he said, staring at her. 'Why haven't I seen you before?'

'Maybe you haven't been looking in the right places,' she shot back at him, feeling cornered.

But when she saw his eyes she realised that he wasn't going

to give up. Her temples began to pound, and she couldn't think straight. Why was he asking all these infernal questions?

'Well, where do *you* come from?' she asked, trying to throw him off the trail.

'You know I live at Biltmore,' he said gently. 'I'm asking about you.'

'I-I . . .' she stammered, staring at her lap. 'Maybe you met me before and just forgot,' she said.

'I would have remembered you,' he said quietly.

'Well, maybe I'm just visiting for the weekend,' she said weakly, looking at the floor.

He wasn't buying any of it. 'Please tell me where you live, Serafina,' he said firmly.

It surprised her when he said her name like that. It had tremendous power over her, like she had no choice but to look up at him and meet his gaze, which turned out to be a serious mistake. He was looking at her so intently that it felt as if he were casting a spell of truth on her.

'I live in your basement,' she said, and was immediately shocked that she'd actually uttered it out loud. He had powers over her that she did not understand.

He stared at her as her words hung in the air. She could see the confusion in his face and sense the questions forming in his mind.

She had no idea why she said it. It had just come flying out of her mouth.

But she'd done it. She'd said it out loud, straight to his face.

Please forgive me, Pa. She'd wrecked everything. She'd ruined their lives. Now her pa would be fired. They'd be kicked out of Biltmore. They'd be forced to wander the streets of Asheville, begging for scraps of food. No one would hire a man who'd lied to his employer, holed up in his basement and stolen food from him for his eight-toed daughter. No one.

She looked at Braeden. 'Please don't tell anyone . . .' she said quietly, but she knew there were no claws in that paw, nothing at all to protect her. If he wanted to, he could tell anyone – Mr Crankshod, Mr Boseman, even Mr and Mrs Vanderbilt – and then the life she and her pa had made together at Biltmore would be over. They might even go to prison for stealing food all those years.

Just as Braeden was about to speak, the horses screamed and the carriage slammed to a halt. She was hurled across the open space and crashed into him. Gidean leapt to his feet and began to bark wildly.

'Something has happened,' Braeden said fiercely as he quickly untangled himself from her and opened the carriage door.

It was pitch-dark outside.

She tried to hear what was out there, but her heart pounded so loudly that she couldn't hear a thing. She tried to calm herself down and really listen, but the forest was too quiet. There were no owls, no frogs, no insects, no birds – none of the normal night sounds she was used to hearing. Just silence. It was like every living creature in the forest was hiding for its dear life. Or already dead.

'Mr Crankshod?' Braeden asked uncertainly into the darkness.

No answer came.

The hairs on the back of Serafina's neck stood on end.

Braeden stepped partway out of the carriage and looked up at the driver's bench at the front. 'There's no one there!' he said in astonishment. 'They're both gone!'

The four horses were still in the harnesses, but the carriage had stopped dead in the road. Right in the middle of the forest.

7

Serafina climbed slowly out of the carriage and stood at Braeden's side. The forest surrounded them, black and impenetrable, the craggy-barked trees packed densely together. Her legs jittered beneath her, filled with nervous impulse. She tried to steady her breathing. Her whole body wanted to move, but she forced herself to stay with Braeden and Gidean.

She watched and listened to the unnaturally quiet forest, extending her senses out into the void. She couldn't hear a single toad or whip-poor-will. But it felt like there was something out there, something big but extremely quiet. She didn't even know how that was possible.

Gidean stood beside her on full alert, staring into the trees. Whatever it was, he sensed it too.

Braeden looked warily into the darkness that surrounded them and walked forward a few feet in the direction the carriage was facing.

'I wish I had a lantern,' he said. 'I can't see anything at all.'

The horses fidgeted in their harnesses, their hooves shifting uneasily in the gravel.

'When they're scared, they move their feet,' Braeden said sympathetically. 'They have no claws, no sharp teeth, no weapons. Their speed is their main defence.'

She marvelled at how Braeden didn't just see the horses but also understood how they thought.

When a breeze passed through the woods and rattled the branches of the trees, the horses spooked. All four of them pulled and tugged against their harnesses. It was like they were being attacked by some invisible predator. Squealing, the front two horses reared up on their hind legs and struck the air with their hooves.

As Serafina shrank back from the danger in frightened dismay, Braeden rushed forward and put himself between her and the horses. Standing in front of them, he raised his open hands to calm them. They towered above him, their eyes white with fear, their heads thrashing and their hooves flying. She was sure they were going to kick him in the head, or slam him with a shoulder, or trample him to death, but he stood with his hands raised, speaking to them in soft, gentle tones.

'It's all right. We're all here,' he said to them. 'We're all together.'

To her astonishment, the horses were calmed by his presence and his words. He touched their shoulders with his outstretched hands and seemed to bring the rearing horses back to the ground. Then he held the head of the lead horse in his hands and pressed his forehead to the horse's forehead so that they were looking at each other eye to eye, and he spoke to the horse in quiet, reassuring tones. 'We're in this together, my friend. We're going to be all right . . . There's no need to run, no need to fight . . .'

The lead horse breathed heavily through its nose as it listened to Braeden's words, then settled and became still. The other horses quieted as well, reassured by the young master.

'H-how did you . . . ?' she stammered.

'These horses and I have been friends for a long time,' he replied, but said nothing more.

Still astounded by what he'd done, she looked around at their surroundings. 'What do you think frightened them?'

'I don't know,' Braeden said. 'I've never seen them so scared.' He turned and looked down the road ahead of them. He squinted into the darkness and then he pointed. 'What is that up there?' he asked. 'I can't make it out. Does the road turn?'

She looked in the direction he pointed. It wasn't a turn in the road. A huge tree with thick, gnarly branches and a scattering of blood-red leaves lay across the road, completely blocking their path.

Suddenly, Mr Crankshod emerged from the darkness, trudging his way back to the carriage. 'We're gonna need the axe,' he grumbled angrily.

Serafina and Braeden looked at each other in surprise, then looked back at Mr Crankshod.

'Where have you been?' Braeden asked.

'We're gonna need the axe,' Mr Crankshod said again, ignoring the question.

'I'll get it, sir,' the assistant coachman said as he came running up from behind Mr Crankshod.

She hadn't noticed him before, but the assistant coachman was just a skinny boy with a mop of curly hair. He stood no taller than the shoulder of the lead horse and had thin arms and legs, bony knees and elbows, and a coltish skittishness about him. He wore a coachman's jacket, but it was several sizes too big in the shoulders and the sleeves were too long. His black coachman's top hat seemed ridiculously tall on his little head. The boy couldn't have been older than ten. He ran to the rear of the carriage, opened the wooden storage box and grabbed the axe, which looked huge in his hands.

'That's Nolan,' Braeden said, leaning towards her. 'He's actually one of the best carriage drivers we have, and he takes very good care of the horses.'

'Give it to me,' Mr Crankshod barked as he grabbed the axe out of Nolan's hands and stomped over to the fallen tree.

'I can help too, sir, I can,' Nolan said, tagging along behind him with a small hatchet.

'Naw, ya can't. Just stay out of the way, boy,' Mr Crankshod shouted. He seemed irritated that Nolan was even there.

Mr Crankshod heaved the axe behind him in a great, sweeping swing and slammed the blade into the centre of the trunk. The leaves of the tree shuddered with the force of the blow, but it hardly made any dent at all in the thick bark.

He swung the axe again and again, and finally cut through the bark. The wood chips began to fly. Serafina couldn't help but notice the brute strength of the man, but it was hard for her to tell if this was the same type of strength the Man in the Black Cloak had possessed.

'At this rate, we're gonna be 'ere all night,' Mr Crankshod complained, and just kept chopping.

'I'm sure I can help, sir, I'm sure I can,' Nolan said enthusiastically, standing by with his hatchet ready.

'I'm sure you can't! Now just get back and stay out of the way!' Mr Crankshod shouted. 'You're no use to anybody here, boy!'

As the grumpy Mr Crankshod made war on the tree, Serafina noticed Braeden looking around them, trying to figure out if there was a way to navigate the carriage round the obstacle. But the trees of this wicked forest grew so closely together that a man could barely get through them, let alone a carriage with a team of horses.

'Where are we?' Serafina asked.

'I think we're about eleven or twelve miles from the estate, a place called Dardin Forest,' Braeden said. 'There used to be an old town nearby.'

'Haven't been any people living in that village for years,' Mr Crankshod grumbled as he chopped at the tree. 'Nothin' but ghosts and demons left in these woods now.'

Serafina scanned the forest, filled with a sense of foreboding. It felt like they were being watched, but she couldn't figure out why she couldn't detect who or what was out there. Her ears twitched with nervousness. The trees slowly swayed back and forth in the wind. They were covered in strange grey lichen and strung with greyish-white moss, which hung down like the thin hair of an old dead woman. The branches buffeted and creaked, as if anxious in their plight. It appeared that many of the trees were dying.

She walked along the length of the fallen tree. She thought it was peculiar that the tree still held its red leaves this late in the year, but it was what she saw at the base of the trunk that truly disturbed her.

'Come look at this, Braeden,' she said.

'What have you found?' he asked as he came up behind her.

'I thought the tree must be an old snag that had rotted and fallen over in the last storm, but take a look . . .'

The stump of the tree didn't appear rotted, and it didn't have the fibrous appearance of a trunk that had been snapped by high winds. It was difficult to tell, but it almost appeared as if it had been gnawed by giant teeth or cut down with an axe.

'Look at the angle here,' Braeden said, gesturing at the side of the stump in anger and confusion. 'Someone purposely felled this tree so that it would block the road.'

Gidean barked and made Serafina jump a mile. As the dog kept barking, Braeden knelt at his side and put his hands on the dog's back. 'What's wrong, boy? What do you smell?'

'If it's all right with you,' Mr Crankshod said gruffly, 'we're not gonna wait around to find out.'

Spooked by the dog and apparently convinced that he'd cut through enough of the trunk, Mr Crankshod dropped the axe, braced his heavy boots against the earth and grabbed hold of the branches. He tried to drag the tree off the road, but it was far too large for him to budge.

Braeden and Nolan ran forward and tried to help. The whole time, Gidean just kept barking.

'Somebody hit that dog and shut it up!' Mr Crankshod shouted, spittle flying from his mouth.

'Mr Crankshod, I think we should turn the carriage round and go back the other way,' Braeden said sharply, obviously perturbed by his comment about the dog.

Mr Crankshod agreed, but at that moment a loud cracking sound filled the forest air. Serafina crouched, prepared to spring. A great shattering of wood erupted into an explosive crash as a large tree fell across the road behind them.

The horses squealed in panic and went up rearing and striking, pulling on their leather harnesses and dragging the carriage across the ground even though the brake was engaged and the wheels wouldn't turn. Their instinct was to run, whether they were free of the harnesses or not.

Braeden ran forward to help them.

'No, Braeden!' Serafina cried as she reached to stop him. The boy seemed determined to get himself killed by a horse kick.

Braeden leapt in front of the horses. He was able to calm them with a few soft words and quickly got them under control. Seeing that he was safe, Serafina scanned the forest in the direction of the fallen tree. That's when she realised that the worst had happened: the carriage, its four horses, the four humans and the dog were now trapped on a section of road between two trees.

Mr Crankshod, gripping the axe, stomped to the back of the carriage and shouted furiously into the darkness, 'Who's out there? Show yourselves, you rotten, filthy swine!'

Serafina looked into the darkness, waiting for an answer to come, but Mr Crankshod's words drifted out into the black nothingness without reply.

'Mr Crankshod,' Braeden said firmly, 'we need to go back to cutting the tree in front of us. The safest course now is to press on to Asheville.'

'I just hope we can get there,' Mr Crankshod carped beneath his breath, stomping back.

As Mr Crankshod, Braeden and Nolan worked on the tree, Serafina couldn't help but look behind the carriage where the most recent tree had fallen. Gidean was looking in that direction as well, his eyes black in the starlight.

'What do you think, boy?' she whispered as she crouched beside him and peered into the darkness. 'Is there something out there?' She and the dog were on the same side now.

She wondered about the second fallen tree. It couldn't be a coincidence. Someone was deliberately blocking them in so that they could not escape.

She scanned the forest. She had good senses, but she knew she couldn't smell nearly as well as Gidean, and he seemed to smell something right now. He wasn't barking any more, but was staring intently into the forest, waiting for something to appear. For all his faults as a dog, he was a brave defender.

But she hated this: the looking, the waiting, feeling like a trap was slowly surrounding them. She couldn't stand it. She didn't know how to defend; she knew how to *hunt*. And, right now, it felt like they were the ones being hunted, and she didn't like the feeling one bit.

She took a few steps forward into the trees to see how it felt. Her skin crawled with equal parts fear and excitement. She was drawn into the forest. Her instinct was telling her to go deeper.

She took a few more steps.

Gidean looked at her and tilted his head as if to say, *Are you crazy? You can't go in there!*

But then she padded quietly into the trees and ducked into the underbrush. She wanted to move, to prowl, to see what was out there, whatever it was. She wanted to be the hunter, not the hunted.

Leaving Gidean to guard the carriage, she crept deeper and deeper into the darkness of the forest, the very same black forest that her father had told her never to enter, the very same dark forest that Crankshod had said was filled with ghosts and demons.

But she was calm. She was in the right place. She figured if her mother could move through the forest at night, then so could she.

Suddenly, she heard the sounds of footfalls in the brush in front of her, as clear as a rat's footsteps in the basement, but much louder, much *larger*, moving through the leaves and the dirt. She wasn't sure whether it was an animal or a human.

As she crept closer to the sound, she crouched down but kept moving slowly forward. Sound and sight and feeling and smell – her whole body felt alive with sensation. With all her senses working, all her muscles in play, she stalked so slowly, so quietly, that she didn't make a single sound.

She heard the footsteps ahead of her more closely now. Feet crunching through autumn leaves. Walking at first and then breaking into a run. A man running through the underbrush. Some fifty yards out into the woods. She ran towards the sound, knowing that when a rat was moving, it couldn't hear nearly as well as when it wasn't.

When the man suddenly stopped, she stopped as well and remained perfectly still, holding her breath.

She knew the man must be listening for her, but she made no sound.

As soon as he started moving again, she moved as well, shadowing him.

But then something happened. The footsteps stopped. She felt a swooshing sensation of air on her face and head, like the beat of a vulture's wing. And then suddenly she heard a second set of footsteps behind her, between her and the carriage. How was that possible? Were there multiple attackers?

The forest erupted in a cacophony of sound. Leaves crashing. Sticks breaking. The rush of rapid movement. Her muscles exploded to life. It was an attack coming in from all directions.

In the distance, Gidean started barking and snarling and gnashing his teeth as if he were facing down Satan himself.

The carriage she thought. *They're attacking the carriage.* She turned and sprinted towards it, heedless of the sound she made. She glimpsed a flash of movement surge past her in the darkness but could not tell what it was. As she ran towards the carriage, she could see Braeden and Nolan. But where was Crankshod? He was the strongest person in their group, the man who was supposed to be protecting them.

'Look out, Braeden!' she shouted in warning. 'They're coming. Look out!'

Hearing her call, Braeden turned just in time to dodge the flashing shape of the incoming attacker. But then, in a startling movement of whirling black shadow, the attacker turned and was upon him again. Gidean charged in, snarling and biting. Nolan punched and kicked. Fighting, shouting, striking – all was confusion in a swirl of motion and battle.

Just as Serafina came within striking distance, a large black shape floated past her. She flinched so hard that her back hit a tree. Giant centipedes poured out of logs. Worms oozed up out of the earth. The Man in the Black Cloak had come. He was here in these woods. There weren't multiple attackers. There was only one. He seemed to float on the violence of the battle, his decaying, blood-dripping hands reaching outward as he came upon Braeden. It was clear he wanted the boy in particular. Serafina leapt forward to defend her friend. Gideon charged as well, but it was little Nolan, in a desperate act of shouting courage, who threw himself in front of the young master and blocked the attack.

The Man in the Black Cloak opened his arms and pulled Nolan to his chest. The slithering folds of the cloak wrapped around the boy. Nolan's shouts turned to screams. The grey smoke filled the forest. The rattling shook the trees. And then Nolan disappeared.

It took her breath away to see it again. 'No!' she cried out in anguish, anger and frustration.

Then the shaking came, and the glowing, and the terrible stench that followed. Every leaf on every tree around them suddenly fell to the ground, drenched with blood, and the ground itself became a stinking, horrific mud.

Expanded in size and now seemingly more powerful than ever, the Man in the Black Cloak advanced, heading straight for Braeden once more.

Braeden needed to fight or flee, but he stood frozen in shock by what he'd just seen happen to Nolan. He stared at the Man in the Black Cloak, unable to move.

Without thinking, Serafina charged forward and pounced on the man's back. She caterwauled a wild and crazed screech of anger. Her hands and feet clawed at the man with snarling ferocity.

The Man in the Black Cloak had no choice but to turn and fight her. He tried to pull her off his back and wrap her in his voluminous black cloak like he had the others, but Braeden pulled back a mighty swing and slammed the man's head with a large branch. Gideon lunged forward and bit the attacker repeatedly. Serafina tore herself free, rolled to the ground, spun and leapt back into the battle. All three of them pressed the attack.

The Man in the Black Cloak, his eyes still glowing with power, levitated upward. Three against one now, he had lost the element of surprise. He snapped the billowing folds of the Black Cloak with his arm, and a great explosion of air knocked Serafina off her feet. She went tumbling backwards as the Man in the Black Cloak withdrew into the forest and then was gone.

Gasping to catch her breath, Serafina scrambled to her feet and readied herself for the next attack, but it never came.

The battle was over.

She looked at her hands. Her fingers were slippery with blood and her fingernails had torn at the Man in the Black Cloak's rotting skin, but it was more than just the remnants of the battle. It was like the skin in the glove. He was disintegrating.

Through the darkness, she saw Braeden lying on the ground. Frightened that he'd been wounded, she ran over to him.

'Are you hurt?' she sputtered.

'I'm all right.' He gasped as she helped him onto his feet. 'What about you? Did he hurt you?'

'I'm all right,' she said.

'I . . . I . . . I don't understand, Serafina. What was that thing? What happened to Nolan?'

'I don't know,' she said, shaking her head in frustration.

'I mean, where did he go? Is he . . . is he . . . is he *dead*?'

She didn't know the answer to Braeden's questions. Thinking about poor little Nolan made her sick to her stomach, angry, frightened. He was just gone. How could she help him? It was the second time she'd battled the Man in the Black Cloak, and the second time she'd lost a friend.

'Come on. We gotta go before it comes back,' she said, touching his shoulder.

'What happened to Crankshod?' Braeden asked as he and Gidean followed her back towards the carriage and horses.

'I never saw him,' she answered.

'Do you think it got him too?' She could hear the fear and confusion in his voice.

'No, there's a rattling noise when it does it, and there was only one rattle.'

'You know what it is,' he said, grabbing her arm and bringing her to a stop. 'Tell me, Serafina.'

'I saw it last night,' she said. 'It took Clara Brahms the same way.'

'What? What do you mean? Where? Does this mean that Clara's dead? I don't understand what's going on.'

'Neither do I,' she said. 'But we've gotta go.'

Braeden picked up a stick from the ground and looked out into the forest. 'Whatever it is, it's still out there . . .'

She knew he was right. They had fought it off, but it was definitely still out there. She couldn't forget the image of Nolan leaping forward to save his master. She could still see the terror-stricken look on the boy's face right before he disappeared. As she looked at Braeden, she couldn't help the terrible sinking feeling that crept into her mind.

'Whatever it is,' she said, 'it didn't come for Nolan. It came for you . . .'

8

'The axe is gone,' Serafina said as she and Braeden searched the area around the carriage. Without the axe or anyone to help them move the trees, they couldn't clear the road in front of them or behind them. They were trapped.

'We can ride the horses,' Braeden suggested. But the trees grew so closely together in this part of the forest that the horses couldn't pass between them, which was almost a relief to Serafina, because she couldn't imagine clawing her way up onto the back of one of those stompers and expecting it not to kill her.

'We can walk,' she said.

'Eleven miles is a long way to walk in these woods,' he said. 'Especially at night . . .'

He kept looking around, obviously frustrated, and she was too, but there was something she liked about the fact that they were in this together. He was thinking of her as an ally. She'd never spent much time with other people, but she was beginning to see why people liked it. Although she was pretty sure that not everyone was as clever and kind as Braeden Vanderbilt.

'If we stay here, we can use the carriage for shelter,' he said. 'My uncle sent a rider ahead to tell the Vances that I was on my way. When I don't arrive, they'll come looking for me. I'm sure of it. I think we should wait for help.'

She didn't want to agree – she wanted to keep moving – but she knew he was probably right. She kept hearing the words he'd said to the horses: *We're in this together. We're going to be all right.* The words felt strangely reassuring to her as well.

She watched as Braeden unharnessed the horses for the night. The horses couldn't go far because of the fallen trees blocking the road, but at least they could move around. He gave them hay and water from the supply that Nolan had stowed in the back of the carriage. Prior to this, she had only seen horses from a distance, and they had always seemed like terribly wild and unpredictable beasts, but as she watched Braeden working with them, talking to them, and caring for them, they seemed to be such good-hearted creatures, far more intelligent than she'd realised.

'Horses usually sleep standing up,' Braeden said. 'And they always take shifts so that at least one of them is awake and alert for danger. If they sense something, they'll raise the alarm. You just have to know the signals.'

'Excellent. We have watch-horses,' she said with a smile, trying to cheer him up.

Braeden smiled in return, but she could see he was still very frightened by what had happened, and she was too. When a gust of wind passed through the trees, she reflexively spun round, fearful that the flying spectre had returned.

'What do you see?' Braeden asked.

'Nothing,' she said. 'It's just the wind.'

The night's cold had settled onto the forest, and with the moonlight that filtered down through the trees they could see their breath. When a screech owl gave an eerie trill in the distance, it startled Braeden, but the sound of the bird calmed Serafina. She had lived all her life hearing those sorts of sounds on her nightly prowls of Biltmore's grounds.

'Just an owl,' Braeden said as he exhaled.

'Just an owl,' she agreed.

As they climbed into the carriage, Braeden held the door open for her and helped her up the little steps, touching her back with his hand. It was as if they were entering the Grand Ballroom for the holiday dance. As a young gentleman, it was a natural gesture for him, probably just a habit, but it was a sensation she had never felt before. For a moment, that gentle touch of Braeden's hand against her back was all she could feel or think about. It was the first time in her life that anyone other than her pa had touched her in a kind and gentle way. She tried hard to tell herself that Braeden's touch probably meant a lot more to her than it did to him. He probably wasn't even aware that he'd touched her. She knew that he had danced and dined with many fancy-dressed girls. It was probably silly for her to think that he wanted to be friends with a girl who wore a shirt for a dress and couldn't ride a horse.

'Come on,' Braeden said quietly to Gidean, and the dog hopped up into the carriage with them. Braeden shut and locked the wooden door and shook it a few times to make sure that it was secure. Gidean circled twice, then took his position on the floor guarding the door.

'I'm sorry there aren't any blankets,' Braeden said, looking through the carriage's storage cabinets and trying to figure out how they were going to stay warm. 'Not even a good cloak to sleep under.'

'I'll pass on the cloak, thank you,' Serafina said with a smile, and Braeden laughed a little, but he seemed almost as nervous as she was to be crammed inside the carriage together, with nothing to do but look at each other in the darkness.

Braeden sat down and patted the seat beside him. 'Perhaps you should sit here, Serafina, on this side. We've got to stay warm somehow.'

Despite the uncomfortable tightness forming in her chest, she slowly moved towards him.

She hoped she didn't smell like the basement. If he was

accustomed to ladies like Anastasia Rostonova, with her lavish dresses, or even Miss Whitney, with her rose-scented perfume, she couldn't imagine that her own scent would be too pleasant for him. *Excuse me, Miss Serafina*, he would say, gagging and coughing, *on second thought, perhaps you should indeed sleep on the floor with the dog . . .*

But he didn't say that. She sat beside him, and the world didn't come to an end. As they snuggled together a little to stay warm, she fretted that he'd discover some bizarre characteristic about her that she didn't even realise was bizarre. She just hoped there wouldn't be a reason for her to take off her shoes in Braeden's presence and have him notice her missing toes. She didn't want him to get too close. Would he be able to feel her missing bones? She wasn't even sure which ones they were. How many bones did a person usually have, anyway?

She had always been content to snuggle into small places on her own, but she was surprised to find herself so comfortable cuddled up beside him. She was able to relax a little and breathe again.

Earlier that morning, when she'd woken up wedged in a metal drying rack in Biltmore's basement, the last place in the world she would have thought she'd spend her next evening was nestled in the velvet warmth between the Vanderbilt boy and his valiant guard dog. Gidean, for his part, seemed to have got over his initial reaction to her. They'd fought together on the same side, she and this dog, and maybe they were a little bit friends now, at least temporarily.

'Serafina, I need to ask you a question,' Braeden said in the darkness.

'All right,' she agreed, but she knew it wasn't going to be good.

'Why do you live in the basement?'

She didn't know if he considered her to be his friend or if they were just shoved together by happenstance and he was making the best out of a bad situation, but, after all they'd been through together, it didn't seem right to lie to him. And she didn't want to.

'I'm the machine mechanic's daughter,' she said finally. She just said it. Just like that. Out loud. Even as she said the words, she felt both pride and a sickening feeling of impending doom that she had betrayed her father.

'I've always liked him,' Braeden said casually. 'He fixed the buckle on my saddle and made it much more comfortable for my horse.'

'He likes you too,' she said, although she remembered that her pa had spoken more about the buckle than the boy that day.

'So, have you been down there in the basement all this time?' Braeden asked in amazement.

'I'm good at staying out of the way,' she said simply. She wanted to tell him that she was the Chief Rat Catcher, but she held her tongue, not sure how he would react to the thought of her grabbing rats. He might want to know when she had last washed her hands. She suddenly doubted if he even cared what she did. All sorts of rich and famous people and their children came to Biltmore, so why would Braeden care what she did all night?

'So you were down there in the basement when you saw the Man in the Black Cloak the first time . . .' he said. 'Who do you think it is?'

'I don't know,' she said. 'I don't even know if he's a human or a haint.'

'What's a haint?' Braeden asked, his eyebrows raised.

'A shade, a haint. You know, a ghost. The Man in the Black Cloak may be some sort of wraith that comes out of the woods at night. But I think he's a mortal man. I think he's one of the gentlemen at Biltmore.'

'What makes you think that?' Braeden said in surprise.

'His satin cloak, his shoes, the way he walks, the way he talks. There's something about him . . . like he thinks he's better than everyone else . . .'

'Well, he's certainly scarier than anyone I've met,' Braeden said, but then said no more.

She could tell that her theory that the Man in the Black Cloak was a gentleman at Biltmore had disturbed him.

They sat in silence for a long time. She could feel Braeden's warmth beside her, his breathing and the beating of his heart. She could smell the faint scent of wool, leather and horses on him. Regardless of what the two of them being in the carriage together might or might not really mean, for the moment, it brought her a wonderful sense of peace, a sense that she belonged, and that, despite everything that was going on, she was exactly where she was meant to be. It didn't make any sense to her, or even seem possible, but there was no denying that that was how she felt.

'I need to ask you to do me a favour,' she said quietly.

'All right,' he said.

'Please don't tell anyone about me and my father. He really needs his job. He loves Biltmore.'

Braeden nodded his head. 'I understand. I won't tell anyone, I swear.'

'Thank you,' she said, relieved.

It felt like she could trust Braeden. And his reputation among the kitchen staff for being a loner who preferred to spend time with his animal friends rather than human beings seemed totally unfair to her now.

As Braeden fell asleep, his breathing became slow and steady.

Remaining very still, Serafina turned to gaze upon him. She passed her eyes over his smooth, pale complexion. He was so clean. And his clothing fitted so well. His woollen jacket must've been made just for him. Even the buttons had been wrought with his very own initials, *BV*, etched upon every one. Mr and Mrs Vanderbilt must have commissioned those buttons, she thought. Did that mean they loved and cherished Braeden? Or was it just so that he would fit into their elegant society?

Her pa had told her the story of Mr Vanderbilt while they were washing up after supper one night in the workshop. Like many well-off gentlemen in society, George Vanderbilt used his inheritance to build a home. But he didn't build it in New York City like all the others. He built it in the remote wilds of western North Carolina, set deep in the densely forested mountains, miles and miles from the nearest town. The ladies and gentlemen of elite New York society thought this was extremely eccentric behaviour. Why would such a highly educated man born and raised in the civilised luxury of New York City want to live in the wilderness of such a dark and forested place?

Biltmore Estate took years to build, but when it was finally finished and everyone saw what George Vanderbilt had done, they understood his dream. He had constructed the largest, most magnificent home in America, surrounded by a working, self-sustaining estate and the gentle beauty of the Blue Ridge Mountains. He married a few years later. And everyone who was fortunate enough to earn an invitation came to the city of Asheville to visit George and Edith Vanderbilt. They were the rich, the famous and the powerful: senators, governors, great industrialists, leaders of foreign countries, favoured musicians, talented writers, artists and intellectuals of all kinds. And it was beneath this glittering world that her pa had raised her.

She looked at Braeden, and she remembered when he came to Biltmore two years before. The servants spoke of the tragedy in hushed tones. Mr Vanderbilt's ten-year-old nephew was coming to live at Biltmore because his family had died in a house fire in New York. No one knew how it started, perhaps an oil lamp or a spark from the cook fire in the kitchen, but the house caught on fire in the middle of the night. Gidean woke Braeden in a smoke-filled bedroom, pulled at his arm with his teeth and dragged him from his bed. With the walls and ceiling ablaze around them, they stumbled out of the burning house, choking and exhausted. They barely escaped with their lives. Gidean had saved him. It was only then that Braeden discovered that his mother, father, brothers and sisters were all dead. His entire family had been consumed by the fire. It made Serafina shudder to think about it. She couldn't stand the thought of losing her pa. How sad and lost Braeden must have felt to lose his whole family.

She had heard the servants talk about how hundreds of ladies and gentlemen, servants and folk of every ilk came out for the funeral. Four black horses pulled the black carriage stacked with eight coffins, as a little boy walked alongside, holding his uncle's hand.

She remembered watching the boy the day he arrived at Biltmore and wondering about him. The servants said he came with no luggage, no belongings whatsoever other than the four black horses, which his uncle agreed to ship by train from New York.

Moving closer to Braeden, she remembered what he'd said to her earlier that night: *These horses and I have been friends for a long time.*

From that day forward, she had kept a lookout for the boy. She often saw him walking the grounds in the morning. He spent long periods of time watching birds in the trees. He fished for trout in the streams, but, much to the consternation of the cook, he always released whatever he caught. When she watched him in the house, he didn't seem comfortable around boys and girls his own age, or most of the adults, either. He loved his dog and his horses, but that was all. Those seemed to be his only friends.

She remembered overhearing his aunt speaking to a guest once. 'He's just going through a phase,' Mrs Vanderbilt had said, trying to explain why he was so quiet at the dining table and so shy at parties. 'He'll snap out of it.'

But Serafina had a feeling that he never had.

His aunt and uncle lived in a world of extravagant parties, but, from a distance, Braeden seemed to find more accomplishment in riding a horse or repairing the wing of a wounded hawk than dancing with the girls at the resplendent proms. She remembered prowling around outside the windows of the Winter Garden when it was all lit up for a ball one summer's eve. She watched the girls in their lovely gowns sashaying this way and that, dancing with the boys, and drinking sparkling punch from a giant fountain in the centre of the room. She'd always wanted to be one of those girls in a fancy dress and shiny shoes. She remembered listening to the orchestra play and the people talking and laughing. Crouched down in the shadow beneath the windows, she could look over and see the silent gaze of the stone lions guarding the front doors of the house.

She didn't know how Braeden felt about her, but there was one thing for sure: she was *different*. Different from any girl he had seen before. She had no idea whether that fixed her as friend or enemy, but it was *something*.

It was the middle of the night now, and she knew that she should sleep, but she wasn't tired. The day hadn't left her exhausted. It had exhilarated her. Suddenly, the entire world was different from how it had been the day before. She'd never felt so alive in her life. There were so many questions, so many mysteries to solve. She kept praying that somehow, some way, despite everything she had seen, Clara, Nolan and Anastasia were still alive, and she could save them. She wanted to go outside and hunt through the woods in search of clues about the Man in the Black Cloak.

But she decided to stay where she was, content to remain curled up beside Braeden.

After a while, it began to rain a heavy rain, and she listened to the sound of it on the leaves of the trees and the roof of the carriage, and she thought it was a perfect sound.

Her eyes and ears open, she vowed that if the Man in the Black Cloak came again that night, she'd be ready.

When Serafina awoke the next morning, the gentle rays of the rising sun filtered through the carriage window, bathing her and Braeden in a soft golden light. Braeden slept soundly beside her. Gidean lay at their feet, quiet and restful.

Suddenly, the dog raised his head and perked his ears. Then she heard the sound as well: trotting horses, turning wheels, the rattle of approaching carriages . . .

She sprang up. She didn't know whether the carriages were bringing friends or enemies, but, either way, she didn't want to be seen. If she stayed in the carriage, she was trapped; she needed space to watch, to move, to fight.

She hated to leave him, but she touched Braeden on the shoulder. 'Wake up. Someone's here.'

Then she slipped out of the carriage and darted into the forest before he had even awoken.

Hiding in the bushes and trees some distance into the undergrowth, she watched Braeden and Gidean exit the carriage. Braeden rubbed his eyes in the sunlight and looked around for her, obviously wondering where she'd disappeared to.

'Over here! I found the carriage!' a man shouted as he climbed through the branches of the tree that had fallen across the road. Several carriages and a dozen men on horseback had come from Biltmore in search of Braeden. As the gang of men went to work with great two-man saws and lumber axes to hack away the tree, Mr Vanderbilt climbed his way through the branches, crossed over the fallen trunk and hurried towards Braeden.

'Thank God you're safe,' he said, his voice filled with emotion as they embraced.

Braeden was obviously glad and relieved to see his uncle. 'Thank you for coming for me.'

As they separated, Braeden pressed back his sleep-ruffled hair with his hands and scanned the trees. Then he looked towards the carriages and rescuers.

She knew he was looking for her, but she had hidden herself like a creature in the woods. She felt like a wild animal there, beneath the leaves of the rhododendrons and the mountain laurel. The forest wasn't something she feared, like she had the night before. It was her concealment, her protector.

'Tell me what happened, Braeden,' Mr Vanderbilt said, seeming to sense Braeden's anxiety.

'We were attacked in the night,' Braeden said, his voice ragged and his face splotchy with emotion. 'Nolan was taken. He's gone. Mr Crankshod disappeared right when the battle started, and hasn't shown up since.'

Mr Vanderbilt frowned in confusion. He put his hand on Braeden's shoulder and turned him towards the gang of workers cutting through the tree and clearing the road. In addition to the servants, Serafina recognised a dozen other men from the house, including Mr Bendel, Mr Thorne and Mr Brahms. She let out a small gasp. There was Mr Crankshod, working among them.

'Mr Crankshod said a group of bandits attacked,' Mr Vanderbilt said. 'He fended them off, but when he attempted to pursue them he became separated from the carriage and decided it was best to head back to Biltmore as fast as possible to fetch help. I was furious he'd left you, but in the end he was the one who led us here to you, so maybe he was right to do what he did.'

Serafina saw Braeden look at Mr Crankshod in surprise. The ugly man looked right back at him, his eyes betraying nothing.

'I'm not sure it was bandits, Uncle,' Braeden said uncertainly. 'I only saw one attacker. A man in a black cloak. He took Nolan. I've never seen anything like it. Nolan just vanished.'

'We'll send a mounted search party up and down this road

until we find the boy,' Mr Vanderbilt said, 'but in the meantime, I want to get you back to the house.'

As Braeden and Mr Vanderbilt spoke, Serafina watched Mr Crankshod. She wondered what the old rat was up to. Something wasn't right with him. He hadn't fought any bandits. He had simply disappeared. And now here he was again with a crooked tale of his own heroism.

The only good news was that it seemed like he hadn't spilled the grits about her existence to Mr Vanderbilt. Was Crankshod a hero? A villain? Or was he nothing more than a common rat-faced coward? She looked around at Mr Vanderbilt, Mr Crankshod and the other men. She was beginning to see how difficult it was to determine who was good and who was bad, who she could trust and who she had to watch out for. Every person was a hero in his own mind, fighting for what he thought was right, or just fighting to survive another day, but no one thought they were evil.

Gidean wasn't so forgiving. He charged towards Mr Crankshod right away and started barking and snarling at him.

Maybe dogs really can smell fear, Serafina thought. *Or at least cowardliness . . .*

It didn't look like Gidean was actually going to bite Mr Crankshod, but he wasn't going to let him off without a good barking-to. The other men watched in amusement, but Mr Crankshod was none too pleased by the dog's attention.

'Oh, shut up, you stupid mutt!' he shouted, and raised his arms to strike the dog with his axe.

Braeden and Serafina were too far away to help, but Mr Thorne clamped his hand onto Mr Crankshod's arm and stopped him mid-blow. 'Don't be a fool, Crankshod.'

'Aw, what the . . . Just keep that mangy cur away from me,' Mr Crankshod grumbled and stomped away.

Braeden ran over to Gidean and Mr Thorne. 'Oh, thank you, sir, thank you so much.'

'It's good to see you're all right, young master Vanderbilt,' Mr Thorne said cheerfully, patting Braeden's shoulder with his leather-gloved hand. 'Sounds like you'll have some big stories to tell everyone at dinner tonight about your adventure through the forest.'

'Did you see anyone else when you arrived?' Braeden asked him, still holding Gidean but looking around again for Serafina.

'Not to worry,' Mr Thorne said. 'Those yellow-bellied sorts aren't the type of men to stick around after an attack. I'm sure they're long gone by now.'

Despite his reassuring words, Serafina noticed that he was wearing an elegant dagger on his belt and wondered if he had half expected to encounter the bandits himself.

'I'm sure you're right, Mr Thorne,' Mr Vanderbilt said, shaking his head angrily as he walked up to them. 'But it's hard to believe that bandits would venture such a brazen attack so close to Biltmore. I'm going to ask the police to increase their patrols of the road.'

Braeden didn't seem to be listening to much of any of this. He just kept looking out into the trees. Serafina wanted to let him know she was all right, but she couldn't let all those men see her, and she definitely didn't want to have to explain who she was or why she had been in the carriage with Braeden, so she stayed quiet and out of sight.

Braeden squatted down and put his hands on Gidean, who was looking out into the trees in her direction. 'Can you smell her, boy?' he whispered.

'What are you doing?' Mr Vanderbilt asked gruffly.

Braeden stood, knowing that he'd been caught out.

'Who are you looking for, Braeden?' Mr Vanderbilt asked him.

Serafina sucked in her breath. That was the question she had been dreading. Who was Braeden looking for? This is where her and her pa's secret would come out. Braeden's answer to his uncle's question had the power to destroy her life.

When Braeden hesitated, Mr Vanderbilt frowned. 'What do you have to say, Braeden? Spit it out.'

Braeden didn't want to lie to his uncle, but he shook his head and looked at the ground. 'Nothing,' he said.

Serafina breathed a sigh of relief. He'd kept his promise. He wasn't going to tell.

Thank you, Braeden. Thank you, she thought, but then his uncle lit into him.

'You've got to buck up, son,' Mr Vanderbilt said. 'You're twelve years old now, and that's plenty old enough to handle yourself properly. Don't be scared of what's going on here. You've got to take charge of yourself. Be a man. We're only dealing with bandits here, thieves.'

'I don't think it was bandits,' Braeden said again.

'Of course it was. This is nothing a Vanderbilt can't handle. Do you agree?'

'Yes, sir,' Braeden said glumly, looking at the ground. 'Just hungry, I guess.'

Mr Thorne stepped in to rescue him. 'Well then, by all means, let's get some food in you,' he said enthusiastically, putting his arm round Braeden. 'Come on, I raided the kitchen on my way out. I brought a sack full of pulled-pork sandwiches and, if that doesn't suit, we'll dig right into the raspberry spoon bread.'

Braeden glanced one more time into the forest, then turned and followed Mr Thorne.

Serafina desperately wanted to give poor Braeden some clue that she was out there and that she was safe. If she had been any other kind of girl, she would have left some sort of token for him when she'd left, a signal of their connection – perhaps a silver locket, a lace handkerchief or a charm from her bracelet – but she was a wild girl and didn't have any of those possessions to give.

As the men gathered around Braeden, happy and relieved that they'd found him, Serafina noticed Mr Rostonov, the bearded and portly Russian ambassador, step away from the others and stand alone at the edge of the road. Braeden had told her that Mr Rostonov didn't know English too well. The poor man gazed tearfully into the forest, as if wondering whether his dear Anastasia had been murdered by what lurked in its shadows. He took out a handkerchief, wiped his eyes and blew his nose. Braeden had said that Mr Rostonov and his daughter were only scheduled to stay at Biltmore Estate for a few days before they returned home to their family in Russia in time for Christmas. But when Anastasia disappeared, he had stayed on, continuing the search for her. Mr Rostonov couldn't bear the thought of returning home to his wife without his daughter. Back over by the carriages, some of the men went over to Mr Crankshod, who was still put out by the incident with the dog, and thanked him for leading the search party to Braeden. But there was something about Crankshod, all smiling and greasy, that raised Serafina's hackles. What was he *really* doing? Where was he when the Man in the Black Cloak attacked? Did he work for him? Or was he *him*?

She looked suspiciously at Mr Vanderbilt too. She didn't like the way he was so tough on Braeden, telling him what to do and not to do and how to feel. He had no idea what Braeden had been through. He didn't listen any better than her pa, and he seemed far too quick to accept Mr Crankshod's story that it had been bandits.

Braeden had said that his aunt and uncle had secretly sent him away for the night, so few people would have known he was going to be on the road at that time. And he had said that his uncle trusted Mr Crankshod. Were they working together?

She tried to think it through. Was it really possible that Mr Vanderbilt was the Man in the Black Cloak? Did he have some terrible need to swallow up *all* the children at Biltmore?

After the men cleared the second tree from the road, those who weren't continuing on to search for Nolan climbed back into the carriages. The coachmen began the intricate task of turning all the carriages round in the tight quarters of the narrow road so that they could head back to Biltmore Estate.

'I want you to ride with me in my carriage, Braeden,' Mr Vanderbilt said. 'Mr Crankshod will drive us.'

'Yes, sir,' Braeden said, 'I understand, but we need to bring my horses home.' His horses had been harnessed, but there wasn't a coachman to drive them.

'I'll take care of it,' Mr Thorne volunteered. He walked over to the horses, patted their heads gently as they nuzzled him, then climbed up into the empty driver's seat and gathered the reins.

Serafina saw Braeden smile, relieved that Mr Thorne was willing to help, but something struck her as a bit odd. Many gentlemen were accomplished riders, but few had any experience with driving a carriage, which was a servant's job.

Mr Bendel, who was riding his thoroughbred, came up alongside Mr Thorne. 'Well, there you go, Thorne. You've got a fallback position if you ever lose your fortune.'

'I have to get a fortune before I can lose it,' Mr Thorne said humbly.

The two gentlemen laughed with each other, but then Mr Bendel became more serious, tipped his hat to Mr Thorne and Mr Vanderbilt, and joined the search party of half a dozen riders that was heading out to look for Nolan.

'Don't wait on supper for me,' Mr Bendel called back to his friends as he rode off with the other horsemen.

Soon the carriages were all moving and heading down the road towards home.

Serafina wanted desperately to go with them, but she knew she couldn't. She remained hidden in the bushes. She had to suppress a sense of panic that she was being left behind, that she'd never be able to find her way through the forest back to Biltmore. And she missed Braeden's company already. As she watched the carriages recede into the distance, she thought, *Goodbye, my friend*, and she hoped he was thinking the same.

But even as the carriages disappeared, she felt a tingling sensation course through her limbs. She should have been frightened to be in the forest alone. All her life she'd been told to stay away from it, but now here she was. Far from Biltmore. Alone in the trees. And she had an idea. She was downright keen on it. She just hoped that it wasn't going to get her lost. Or killed.

As she stepped onto the empty road and looked down the length of it, Serafina had a weird and foreign feeling from being so far away from her pa and Biltmore and all the commotion there. She half expected to burst into tears, go running after the carriages and wail, *Wait! Wait! You forgot about me!*

But she didn't. And she felt rather grown-up about it.

The sun was well up now and casting a lovely warm light on the trees. Birds were singing. There was a gentle breeze. Things weren't so bad in the forest.

But then she looked down the long road winding through the trees and remembered that she was eleven miles from home.

'I'll try to be home for dinner, Pa,' she said with a pang of uncertainty in her stomach, and she started walking. But she wasn't exactly heading for home. Not directly.

The Man in the Black Cloak had seemed to know the forest very well, and she remembered the tales of folk going missing. She had a creeping suspicion that the Man in the Black Cloak might be in some way connected to the abandoned village that she'd heard tell about. She had decided she was going to find the old village and see if it gave her any clues. Why would all the people in a town abandon their homes and leave?

There was a part of her, too, that was anxious to delve into the shadows of the forest, to see this mysterious world. It drew her, not just because she'd been forbidden by her pa to come here, but by the thorny truth of her pa's own account: she'd been *born* here.

She decided to walk on down the road a spell and see what she could see. Perhaps there would be an old sign pointing to the abandoned village, or perhaps she'd meet someone along the road who might be able to tell her how to get there. One way or another, it seemed like it would be pretty easy to find an entire town.

As she walked, her mind kept drifting back to her pa. She wished she could get a message to him. He'd be worried sick about her, especially with the horrible tales of disappearing children. She wondered if he ever got the dynamo working.

It created the one thing that everyone other than her needed so desperately at night: light. Who in the world would purposely damage an electric generator? And who would even know how to do something like that? Her pa was the only man on the estate who knew how it worked. Him, and maybe George Vanderbilt if he referred to one of the books in his library.

She thought that it was interesting how just about everyone had a special talent or skill, something they were naturally drawn to and good at, and then they worked years to master it. Nobody knew how to do everything. It wasn't possible. There wasn't enough time in the night. But everyone knew something. And everyone was a little different. Some people did one thing. Others did another. It made her think that maybe God intended for them to all fit together, like a puzzle made whole.

It still stunned her when she tried to imagine her big train-mechanic pa carrying a newborn baby out of the forest and taking care of her all those years. It had never occurred to her until now that she belonged anywhere but in the basement with her father, but now her mind ran wild with questions and ideas. She was anxious to get home, but, walking down that road, she felt a little exhilarated that she was free and on her own. She could go in any direction she chose.

She walked for an hour without seeing a soul, nothing but blue jays and chickadees twitching about her, a few squirrels chattering away at her and a mink dashing across the road in front of her like his life depended on it. She wasn't even sure she was still heading in the right direction any more, but she figured she couldn't go wrong if she stayed on the road.

Then she came to a three-way split.

The left road was the widest and seemed to be the most travelled. She got down on her hands and knees and studied the rocky ground. It was hard to tell, but she thought that maybe she could see the indention of carriage wheels. But the middle road was wide and clear as well, with occasional dents in the ground that might be from the hooves of horses. Either one of these roads could be the road to Biltmore.

Only the third road was different. It wasn't even right to call it a road, but what *used to be* a road. Two old, rotting fir trees had collapsed, making an X across the path. Thick vines of poison ivy and smothering creeper grew all around and seemed to strangle the two fallen trees. This road obviously hadn't been travelled by carriage or horseback in years. She wasn't even sure a person on foot could get through.

She didn't see any sign or marker that identified the road, but it seemed possible that an old, unused pathway like this might lead to the abandoned village. Maybe the state of the road choked off the town. Or maybe the forest took back the road when the townsfolk disappeared. In any case, if she had any hope of solving the mystery of the Man in the Black Cloak, she needed clues and information. Where did he come from? What was his story? How could she stop him?

Poison ivy had never affected her the way it did other people, but she still climbed carefully through the thicket of vines and thorns. On the other side of the two crossed trees, she came into a boscage of rotting, dead snags, with rocks on the ground as sharp as axe blades. The narrow, overgrown track twisted and turned, and dived down into a rocky ravine, and she couldn't see what lay beyond.

As she gazed at the darkened passage, a shiver went through her spine. She had no idea where it would lead her, but she started down the path.

10

$\mathcal{S}$erafina followed the shadowed path for a while, crawling over fallen trees and through nasty thickets, until she came to yet another split.

As she was trying to figure out which direction to go, she heard faint sounds drifting through the branches. The sounds had an eerie, unearthly quality to them. She thought it might be nothing more than the wind blowing through the trees, but when she listened very carefully it almost seemed like there were people calling to one another in the distance and children playing.

With no other clues to guide her, she decided to go towards the sounds and see what she could find. If she passed a house, then perhaps the inhabitants could point her in the right direction.

The path led her round a sharp curve and plummeted into a steep, bracken-choked ravine, then it climbed back out again, making its way among large moss-covered rocks and old trees twisted by wind and age. Desperate for soil, the trees' roots clung to the rocks like giant hands, their massive fingers plunging into the earth beneath them.

This place is terribly creepy, she thought, but she kept going, determined to keep moving forward.

Unlike normal trees, which grew upward towards the sunlight, these had gnarled, contorted branches, as if they had been twisted by agonising pain. Many of the trees stood dead and bare, withered by disease or some other killing force. Still more of the trees lay dead on the ground, their trunks criss-crossing one another as if a giant had pushed them over.

As she made her way, a mist rose up from the leaf-covered forest floor, and a fog set in that obscured her view of the terrain around her.

Oh, great. If I can't see, I'm gonna get lost for sure . . .

She turned around to head back towards the last split in the path, but the fog became so thick that even this simple navigation was impossible. She tried to control her fear, but she felt the panic rise up in her. She gulped for air as the mist surrounded her and she lost her sense of place and direction. She began to realise that she'd made a terrible mistake in leaving the main road.

Stay calm, she thought. *Just think it through . . . Find your way home. . . .*

Her foot hit a lump, and she tripped and fell forward onto the ground. Her hands and face touched something wet and slimy buried in the leaves. She gasped when she saw that it was the bloody carcass of a deer or some other large animal. Its body had been eviscerated, its guts ripped out. Its head and hind legs were missing, but from what was left over it appeared that it had been purposely cached here.

She gagged as she got up onto her feet, wiped her hands on the bark of a slimy tree and moved on, desperate to find the road.

When she heard voices ahead, she felt a swell of hope. She moved quickly towards them.

Maybe they're travellers, she thought. *Perhaps there's a hunting shack ahead.*

But then she stopped in her tracks. They were the same eerie noises she had heard before, but this time they were much closer: hoarse, raucous calling sounds, but with a strange, almost human quality, like some kind of weird children running and playing in the forest. A surge of fear swept through her. Her legs and hands buzzed with agitation. The sounds were above her and all around her now, and still she couldn't see them.

'Show yourself!' she demanded.

Something brushed past her shoulder and she whirled, crouching to the ground to defend herself. A burst of rushing air made her skin crawl as a black shape flew over her and then landed in a tree.

She looked around her. And then she saw them. First one,

and then another. They were surrounding her. The hoarse croaking sounds came from a conspiracy of thirteen ravens moving through the branches of the trees, calling to one another, speaking in their ancient codes. But the ravens weren't just conversing with each other – they were looking at her, flying around her, trying to communicate with her. As if frustrated by her lack of understanding, several of the ravens began diving at her with their claws. Were they attacking her or were they warning her? She didn't know.

'Leave me alone!' she shouted. She covered her head with her arms and ran to escape them. She dived into a thicket of brush, where the large birds couldn't fly. Driven by fear, she just kept running.

When she finally stopped to catch her breath, she looked behind her to see if they were still following. She found herself standing on something hard – some sort of flat surface. She looked down and saw a long, straight edge of grey stone.

Now what? she thought.

It was half buried, but she knelt on the ground and wiped away the dirt and leaves to expose the smooth, flat granite underneath.

Serafina read the words that someone had etched in blocky letters into the stone:

HERE LIES BLOOD, AND LET IT LIE,
SPEECHLESS STILL, AND NEVER CRY.

She felt a cold sweat pass over her. She looked around. There was another flat grey stone just a few feet away. She pulled the brush aside and read:

COME HITHER, COME HITHER, AND LAY WITH ME.
WE'LL MURDER THE MAN WHO MURDERED ME.
CLOVEN SMITH 1797–1843

All right, I don't like this place at all. These are graves . . .

She wiped her clammy hands on her shirt, then she took a few more steps, finding more graves beneath the undergrowth of the forest. The graveyard seemed like it went on and on. There were graves as far as she could see, most of them over-grown with vines and trees.

Many of the headstones were so close together that they couldn't possibly have bodies beneath them, just like the stories she'd heard. It was as if people had gone missing, their bodies never found, and these were but markers of the lost.

But as she delved deeper into the oldest parts of the abandoned cemetery she saw mounds where bodies had definitely been buried, and other graves that were empty holes, as if the coffins had been plundered or the dead had crawled out of the ground on their own.

She swallowed hard and tried to keep moving despite the trembling in her limbs.

In some places, the layers of earth appeared as if they had shifted, exposing broken, rotting coffins to the air. Some of the coffins jutted up out of the earth or were tangled beneath gnarled tree roots. She kept walking and reading the stones. A hundred years of old people, young people, brothers and sisters, friends and enemies, husbands and wives.

She had heard stories about this old cemetery, filled with hundreds of gravestones and monuments, even though no one alive could remember burying the people. Many of the local mountain folk wondered where all the dead people in this cemetery had come from. Whole families seemed to have perished in short spans of time.

There were tall tales that the mountain folk no longer used this cemetery because burying your loved ones here didn't necessarily guarantee that they would stay. The coffins shifted in the unstable earth. The bodies went missing. Your dead loved ones were seen wandering their old homes and streets, as if searching for a place to rest.

There were tales, too, of human beings shifting into the shape of wild animals, of sorcerers and witches with surpassing power, and horrible, disfigured creatures crawling through the forest.

She came upon two small mounds so close together, side by side, that they were nearly a single grave. One tombstone identified the two young sisters within:

OUR BED IS LOVELY, DARK AND SWEET.

COME JOIN US NOW AND WE SHALL MEET.

MARY HEMLOCK AND MARGARET HEMLOCK

REST IN PEACE AND DON'T RETURN.

When she read the words *don't return*, the hairs on the back of her neck tingled. What kind of strange place was this?

She had come in search of an old village, but all she'd found was its cemetery. She had a feeling that this was all that was left.

As Serafina walked, the dry autumn leaves crunched beneath her feet. Tree branches lay like emaciated dead fingers on the ground among the gravestones and monuments. Many of the monuments had toppled to the earth and lay broken and strewn while others had sunk deep into the ground. A few of the gravestones remained standing, sticking up several feet with spires or crosses, but they were so thickly covered in black and green moss and overgrown with vines that they were nearly indistinguishable from the wretched forest around them.

She read another:

DEATH IS A DEBT TO NATURE DUE,
WHICH I HAVE PAID, AND SO WILL YOU.

In another area, she found row upon row of crosses. An old, weathered plaque explained that these sixty-six crosses were the graves of an entire company of Confederate soldiers who were found dead one night, even though they never fought in any battle.

Further on, Serafina came to a glade, a little clearing in

the trees strangely without bushes, vines or undergrowth of any kind. This one particular part of the cemetery had not become overgrown, but remained an area of perfect green grass. In the centre of the glade stood a stone monument carved into the likeness of a winged angel. Stranger still was the fact that although there was fog all around the glade, there was no fog in the glade itself. Sunlight filtered through the mist and illuminated the angel's face and hair and wings with a gentle light.

'Now, she's pretty,' Serafina said as she stepped closer and read the inscription on the pedestal of the statue:

OUR CHARACTER ISN'T DEFINED
BY THE BATTLES WE WIN OR LOSE,
BUT BY THE BATTLES WE DARE TO FIGHT.

Serafina looked up at the angel and studied her. Dappled layers of green and grey moss and lichen covered the angel, and the black streaks of a hundred years of ageing stained her long dress and her beautiful face. Dark tears seemed to be falling down her cheeks, as if she had known great sadness. But her wings stretched upward into a fury, her head raised into an apocalyptic cry, as if calling those around her into a great battle.

What kind of battle? Serafina wondered.

In her right hand, the angel held a sword. The statue itself was made of stone, but the sword appeared to be made of steel, and the metal gleamed as if it was untouched by time. Curious, Serafina slowly reached out her hand and touched the edge of the blade. She gasped and pulled back, blood oozing from her finger. The edge of the sword was razor-sharp.

Then something caught her eye. She felt a pulse of fear. Her muscles tightened, readying themselves to flee. At the edge of the glade, a gravestone had tumbled over where a gnarled old willow tree had fallen and its upturned roots had created a small cave. She wasn't sure, but she thought she saw one of the shadows slowly move.

Then she was sure of it.

There was something stirring by the old grave.

11

Serafina had to remind herself to keep breathing, to stay calm. She felt her chest tightening, her breaths getting shorter and shorter. She wanted to turn and run, but she stayed and watched, her curiosity too strong to overcome.

She crept quietly through the graveyard to get a closer look.

She feared it might be a corpse crawling out of the ground. She imagined its rotting white hands digging through the dirt as it broke the surface. But as she got closer she realised it wasn't a corpse at all, but a very living creature.

It was some sort of small wildcat with yellowish-brown fur, black spots and markings, and a long tail. It took her several seconds to figure out that it was a baby mountain lion.

Suddenly, a second lion cub appeared. They charged each other, grabbing each other with their paws and tumbling in play, meowing and howling and swatting each other. They had the most adorable little yellow faces marked with black streaks and spots, and long white kitty whiskers.

Smiling, Serafina watched the cubs play in the bright green grass of the stone angel's sunlit glade. The fear she had felt just moments before began to melt away. She had always loved kittens.

She crouched down and moved a little closer. One of the cubs spotted her. Its ears perked up, and it stared at her, studying her. She thought that it would run away in fear. But it didn't. It gave her a raspy meow and ambled towards her as if it didn't have a care in the world.

She extended her arm, holding her hand still. The brave little cub slowed down, but it kept coming towards her, watching her, inching closer and closer. When it reached her, it sniffed her fingers and rubbed the side of its mouth along the length of her hand. Serafina smiled, almost giggled, pleased that the cub didn't fear her.

She sat down in the grass, and the cub climbed right into her lap, pawing playfully at her fingers. She wrapped her arms around the cub and hugged its warm, fuzzy little body to her chest. It was good to have some company that didn't scare the living daylights out of her. The other cub came over, and soon she was lovin' on both of them as they tumbled and rolled around her, and they rubbed themselves against her and purred.

'What are you sweet little babies doing here?' she asked. After all she'd been through, it felt more than agreeable to be accepted by these wonderful little creatures. It felt like a homecoming.

Soon, they were all up and about. She chased the cubs around the glade, pretending to swat at them with her paw, then they chased her. She got down on her hands and knees. One of the cubs ran behind the pedestal of the stone angel, came round the other side and peeked at her, his dark little eyes blinking as he pretended to stalk her. He darted out playfully, running sideways with his back arched into a mock attack as he leapt upon her. Then the other cub joined in, grabbing her arms and legs, trying to tackle her, and soon they were all brawling and growling. The adorable, kittenish attack made Serafina laugh out loud.

And her laughter carried through the misty forest.

She kept playing and wrestling with the cubs, feeling a pure and oblivious childlike pleasure that she hadn't felt in a long time.

Then she sensed severe and immediate danger. She turned and saw something hurtling towards her out of the mist. At first, it seemed to be floating like a ghost, but then she realised it wasn't a ghost at all.

It was running. Fast. Straight towards her.

A wave of dread washed through her as she realised that by playing with these cubs she'd made a terrible, terrible error in judgement. The angry, full-grown mother mountain lion charged towards her. The lioness would kill her to defend her cubs.

Fear jolted Serafina into motion. The lioness leapt through the air, her claws and teeth bared. Serafina knew she was going to die, but she tried to duck. The impact of the lioness's attack slammed into her so hard that it knocked her off her feet. She and the vicious beast tumbled across the grass in a brawling, snarling mass of hissing, teeth and claws.

Serafina battled with all her strength. She had never in her life fought anything so physically powerful. She knew there was no way to defeat her; she was but a kitten compared to this wild beast. Her only hope was to get away as fast as she could. She kicked her feet and flailed her fists. She beat the lioness with a stick, screaming all the while.

When the lioness tried to bite her neck and deliver her deadly blow, Serafina slammed her hands into the lioness's face and tore at her eyes, then whirled herself into a wild, twisting frenzy. Her attacks distracted the big cat just long enough to break herself free. Serafina sprang up and darted away like a scalded dog.

The lioness chased her, but she sprinted with an incredible burst of fear-induced speed. She scrambled into the thick bushes like a squirrel and just kept running. She ran and she ran. She ran until her whole chest hurt with thumping pain.

She crossed a rocky stream, then went through a thick stand of pines, and then delved into a thicket of thistles and blackberry thorns. She climbed up hills and over rocks and just kept running as far as she could.

Finally, exhausted, she ducked beneath a bush like a rabbit and listened for the sounds of her pursuer. She did not hear her.

She imagined that the lioness, satisfied that she had chased off the intruder, had returned to her cubs. She could picture the mother lion scolding them for playing with a stranger and pushing them angrily back into their den beneath the roots of the tree.

Panting and wounded, Serafina pressed on through the forest, determined to put as much distance as possible between her, the cemetery and the mountain lion's den. She vowed to never return to that terrifying place.

When she finally stopped for a moment to catch her breath, she stared around her. Nothing looked familiar. It was then that she realised that she was completely and utterly lost.

12

Serafina kept moving and soon found herself travelling along the top edge of a rocky, tree-covered ridge. In her panic to escape the lioness, it seemed that she'd run halfway up a mountain.

Exhausted, she finally stopped to rest and check her wounds. Her clothing had been torn. The length of twine that once held her pa's shirt round her body had broken and was gone. Claw marks sliced her arms and legs. Her head hurt. Several tooth marks punctured her chest. She was pretty torn up, but it wasn't nearly as bad as she had expected.

It hurts, but I'm gonna live, she thought. *Assuming I can find my way home.* She had thought that the forest couldn't be nearly as bad as her pa described, but it had turned out to be a far darker, more dangerous place than she'd ever imagined. With everything she'd seen so far, she didn't think she could survive another night here. But she was still miles from the house, stuck on a ridge, and she didn't even know in which direction to go.

She looked up at the dark, cloudy sky, trying to find the position of the sun, then she scanned the surrounding landscape for clues and landmarks. With no compass, no map and no idea where she was in relation to Biltmore Estate, how could she make sure she was going in the right direction?

She was already cold when it started raining.

'Oh, great,' she said, shouting up at the clouds. 'Thank you! That's really nice, you stupid sky!'

She hated getting wet. This was a miserable place. She just wanted to get home. She missed her pa something awful. She longed for a glass of milk, a piece of fried catfish, a warm little cook fire in the workshop and her dry, cosy bed behind the boiler. Yesterday she'd been slinking gracefully across the plush carpets of Biltmore's elegant rooms, and today she was stuck out in the cold, wet, stupid, raining world.

As the rain poured down, she tried to hide under the boughs of a pine tree, but it didn't help. The big drips onto her sopping head and neck just made her more miserable. Rivulets of water flowed across the rocky ground beneath her. Wet and bedraggled, she clung to the trunk of the tree, terrified that she'd slip down the steep slope of the mountainside. She wanted her pa to get his ladder and rescue her like he had when she was little, but she knew he wouldn't even know where to look for her.

Then, as she watched the water trickle across the ground, a thought occurred to her.

Water runs downhill. Downhill, and into rivers.

She had been following the contour of the ridge because it had been easiest, but now she had a different idea. What if she climbed straight down the steepest slope of the mountain and used the trunks of the trees and the branches of the rhododendrons as a sort of ladder? She'd get down a lot quicker.

She stepped closer to the edge and peered tentatively over the cliff. It was a long way down, but she grabbed the first branch to see if it would hold her. Suddenly, her foot slipped in the wet leaves, her fingers broke free from the branch and she plummeted down the mountainside.

The swooping sensation of free fall instantly filled her entire body. She slid down feet first, screaming. She tried to stay upright and reached out for the bushes to break her fall, but then she hit a tree trunk, and it knocked the wind out of her. She pitched in one direction, then the next, hurtling down the mountain. She hit a branch. She spun. She hit a rock. She plunged. Suddenly, she was somersaulting end over end. All the while she fell, tumbling down the mountainside in a great wave of autumn leaves. The rush of speed and the wind against her face made her feel like she was flying, but then she hit another tree, the force slamming a painful grunt from her chest, and she flipped and rolled until she finally crashed, breathless and hurting, at the bottom of the ravine.

She lay there for several seconds, unable to move. Her whole body hurt. She'd been punched and battered and stabbed.

'Well, that was one way to get down,' she groaned.

When she was finally able to get on her feet, she brushed herself off and limped on her way.

She followed a small stream that trickled into a creek. Thirsty, she lay flat at the stream's edge and lapped up the clear mountain water like an animal.

The stream led her to a waterfall that crashed into a tumultuous pool thirty feet below.

Does this waterfall have a name? she wondered. If she knew that, then maybe it would help her understand where she was and give her a better chance of finding her way home. *What river is this?*

But then she realised that it didn't matter exactly where she was. A river wasn't a place. A river was movement. She remembered something her pa had taught her. All the rivers in these mountains wound through complicated, twisting routes, but eventually they all flowed in one direction, into the mighty French Broad River.

The Blue Ridge Mountains were some of the oldest mountains in the world. The river had been flowing here for millions of years and had helped shape the mountains into what they were today. And, most importantly, she knew that the French Broad River flowed through the grounds of Biltmore Estate, right past the mansion. The river was the way home.

She climbed down the wet, slippery rocks at the edge of the

waterfall, then made her way along the craggy shoreline. Confident in her direction now, she travelled as fast as she could. She had to reach her pa, who she knew must be worried sick about her, and she wanted to see Braeden. She wasn't sure if she had abandoned him by sneaking into the woods, or if he'd abandoned her by going home in his uncle's carriage; but they'd separated, and it made her stomach hurt. The more time that went by, the less certain she became of how she should feel. Was Braeden actually her friend, or was her mind just imagining it, like when she imagined herself as being friends with the butler's assistant who stopped and ate the cookies? All her life, she had pretended that she had friends, but was it true this time?

She and Braeden had only known each other for a short while, but she let the memories of their time together wash over her. To someone like her, it felt like a lifetime of friendship. She was like a starved animal wolfing down a scrap and thinking it had eaten a full meal. But she had no idea if he missed her the way she missed him.

She walked for hours, following the river until it flowed into a much wider, flatter river that she hoped was the French Broad, but she wasn't sure. She was tired, hungry and sore from her wounds. She just wanted to get home.

As the sun slowly withdrew behind the trees in the western sky, she tried to push herself faster. She didn't want to get caught in the forest another night, for that's when the mountain lion, the Man in the Black Cloak and whatever other demons might crawl out of the cemetery would be on the prowl. But it was no use. The sun abandoned her, the birds and the other daytime sounds went dead and the darkness settled into the trees like a black oil.

Exhausted, she stopped to catch her breath and rest a spell. She knew it was dangerous to linger in the open. Wet and shivering, she crawled into a hole beneath the hollowed roots of a tree at the river's edge, curled into a little ball and peered out into the darkness.

She was a failure. That's what she thought. She had hoped to find answers in the forest, but all she'd found was wretchedness.

From her little cave beneath the roots, she looked downstream along the gravelly shore of the river. The air around her was cold and still, but the river rippled with a steady rushing sound, and she could taste its moisture on her lips. The waxing moon rising above the mountains cast a silvery light across the deep-flowing black water. Mist oozed out of the forest and drifted across the river like a legion of ghosts.

A wolf called in the distance, a long, plaintive, lonely howl that put a shiver up her spine. The wolf was miles away, up on the mountains. But then she nearly jumped out of her skin when a much closer wolf answered the call with a returning howl.

Red wolves were elusive, almost mythological beasts, seldom seen by anyone, but they were well known for being fierce warriors that fought in packs, tearing their enemies with their gleaming white fangs.

The wolf close to her howled again, and a dozen wolves on

the other side of the river lit up the air with a bloodcurdling chorus of howls. Goose bumps rose on her arms.

She did not hear it approach for it moved like a ghost through the mist, but she saw the wolf come slowly out of the forest and look out across the river. She stayed very still among the roots and watched it. She could smell the musky scent of its coat and see its moonlit breath in the air.

It was a young wolf, long and lean, with a deep coat of reddish-brown fur, a slender nose and tall ears. The fur on its right shoulder was bloody from a wound.

She held her breath and stayed quiet. *The wolf doesn't know I'm here*, she thought. *I'm one with the forest. I'm camouflaged and silent.*

But then the wolf turned its head and looked straight at her, its eyes as keen and penetrating as any creature she had ever seen.

Her muscles bunched as she prepared herself for the attack.

But then the wolf's ear twitched. Serafina heard it too. There was something large moving through the forest, travelling along the river shore towards them.

The wolf looked in the direction of the sound, and then he looked back at her. He stared at her for several seconds, even as the sound moved towards them. Then, to her astonishment, the wolf walked into the river. He kept walking until he was up to his shoulders in the water, then the river swept him away and all she could see was his head as he tried to fight against the current. He was swimming towards the howls of his brothers and sisters on the other side of the river. And he was swimming away from the thing coming towards her.

Suddenly, she felt abandoned, vulnerable.

The river made too much noise for her to hear exactly what was coming towards her, but it was getting closer. Sticks breaking. Footsteps. Two feet. It wasn't the mountain lion or another wolf that had scared the red wolf across the river, but a man. Was it the Man in the Black Cloak?

As she huddled down into the dirt, a hideous giant centipede crawled across her hand. She flinched and stifled a scream.

Her lungs demanded more air. Her legs tensed, wanting her to run. But it was too late. The attacker was too close. A smart rabbit doesn't break cover when the predator is upon her. She *hides*. She pushed herself further back into the dark little hole beneath the roots.

A flickering light came through the trees. She heard the pushing of bushes and the scraping of bark and the muffled clanking of metal and wood.

It's a lantern, she thought. *The same kind of lantern the Man in the Black Cloak used the night he took Clara Brahms.*

Trembling, she crouched low and readied herself for battle.

13

Serafina watched the man raise his lantern and look around him as he broke through the underbrush. It was clear that he was searching for something, but, more than that, he was *frightened*. Even with his lantern and the nearly full moon, he could not see as well in the forest's darkness as she could. When the man took another step, she recognised the familiar creak of his leather work boot. That's when she realised that it wasn't the Man in the Black Cloak. It was her pa, in a long, dark brown weather cloak. Despite his warnings, and despite his fear, he had delved deep into the forest to rescue her.

She gasped, crawled out of her hole and ran towards him.

'I-I'm here, Pa! I'm here!' she stammered, crying as she threw her arms round him.

He squeezed her tight for a long time. It was like being hugged by a gentle bear. She clung to his huge, warm body.

As he exhaled in relief, she could feel the shattering worry pouring out of him. 'Sera, aw, Sera, I . . . I thought you'd disappeared like the other children.'

'I ain't disappeared, Pa,' she said, her voice quivering like she was a little girl again.

Seeing her torn clothing and the scratches on her arms even in the poor light of his lantern, he asked, 'What happened to you, Sera? You have another run-in with a raccoon?'

She didn't even know where to begin in telling him everything that had happened to her, and she knew he wouldn't believe her anyway. He would think it was just another one of her cockamamy stories.

'Got terribly lost,' she said, shaking her head in shame, and it was the truth. Tears streamed down her face.

'But you're all right?' he said, looking her over. 'Where's it hurt?'

'Just wanna get home,' she said, burying her head in the folds of his cloak. She remembered how angry she'd been at him for not telling her about her birth, and how she'd convinced herself that he wasn't on her side, but she realised now how foolish she'd been. Nobody in the world had ever done more for her than her pa, and nobody in the world had ever loved her like he did.

When the wolves across the river exploded into howls, it made her pa flinch.

He looked around. 'I hate wolves,' he said with a shudder as he put his arm round her shoulders and pulled her along. 'Come on. We've gotta get out of here.'

She happily went with him, but as the wolves continued their howling, it sounded different to her than it had before. The howls weren't the lonely searching calls spread across the vast distances of mountain ridges, but excited yip-howls, all from the same location. She couldn't help but feel that they weren't howls of menace, but of joy and reunion. *You made it, brother.* She thought of the wounded red wolf crossing the river. *You made it home.*

Her pa held the lantern out in front of them as they travelled, like a guide leading them through the night. She was glad to let him lead the way.

'You got to the river and followed it like I taught ya,' he said as they walked.

'I wouldn't have made it otherwise,' she said.

Soon, they left the trees of the forest behind them and then continued for another mile. Finally, they climbed up the bank of the great river and saw the Biltmore mansion shining in the moonlight on the high ground in the distance. They still had a ways to go, but at least she could see it now. The faint smell of wood smoke drifted on the cold winter air and filled her with a powerful longing for home.

The local folk called the magnificent house 'The Lady on the Hill', and tonight she could see why. Biltmore looked majestic with her light grey walls and slate-blue rooftops, her chimneys and towers stretching upward and the reflection of the moon glistening on her gold and copper trim, like something out of a fairy tale. Serafina had never been so glad to see her home in all her life.

Her pa took her gently by the shoulders and looked into her face. 'I know you're drawn to the woods, Sera,' he said. 'You've always been pulled by your curiosity, but you've got to stay outta there. You've got to keep yourself safe.'

'I understand,' she said. She sure couldn't argue with him that it wasn't dangerous.

'I know you're good in the dark,' he said, 'best I ever seen, but you gotta resist the urges, Sera. You're my little girl. I'd hate to lose you all the way.'

When he said *all the way*, it haunted her. She realised then that he felt like he was already losing her. She could hear the despair in the raggedness of his voice and see it glistening in his eyes as he looked at her. This was his greatest fear; not just that she would be hurt or killed in the forest, but that her wildness would draw her in, that she'd become more and more wild. More wild than human.

She looked up at him and met his small brown eyes, and saw the reflection of her amber eyes in his. 'I'm not gonna leave ya, Pa,' she promised.

He nodded and wiped his mouth. 'Come on, then,' he said, wrapping his arm round her. 'Let's get ya home and dry, and get some supper in ya.'

• • •

By the time they reached the mansion, the workers had come in from the farms and fields. Most of the mansion's doors had been closed up and locked. The shutters and shades had been drawn against the demons that lurked in the night.

As Serafina and her pa headed for the basement, she was surprised to see that the stables were filled with people and activity. Oil lamps glowed brightly in the night.

She and her pa couldn't help but pause to see what the commotion was about. A returning mounted search party, a dozen riders strong, stormed into the inner courtyard, filling the air with the clatter of horse hooves striking the brick paving. They'd been looking for Clara Brahms and the other victims. As the riders dismounted and the stablemen hurried out to tend to the horses, the parents of the missing children gathered around.

Nolan's pa, who was the stable blacksmith, begged for news of his son, but the riders shook their heads. They'd found nothing.

Poor Mr Rostonov was there as well, struggling to ask questions in his Russian-hindered English as he held on to his daughter's little white dog. The shaggy creature barked incessantly, growling at the horses as if chastising them for the failure of the search.

Watching Mr Rostonov, the Brahmses, and Nolan's pa in their desperate struggle to find their children, Serafina's heart filled with an aching sadness. It made her guts churn to think about it, to think about her part in it all. She had to find the Man in the Black Cloak.

'Come on,' her pa said as he pulled her away. 'This whole place is comin' apart at the bolts, equipment breakin' for no reason, folks losin' their children. It's a bad business all around.'

As they ate their dinner together huddled around their little cook fire in the workshop, her pa talked about his day. 'I've been working on the dynamo, but I can't figure out how to fix it. The floors upstairs are pitch-black. The servants had to pass out lanterns and candles to all the guests, but there weren't enough of them to go around. Everyone's frightened. With all the guests in the house and the disappearance of the children, this couldn't have come at a worse time . . .'

She could hear the pain in his voice. 'What are you going to do, Pa?'

'I've gotta get back to it,' he said. It was only then that she realised that he'd stopped his work in order to look for her. 'And you need to go to bed. No hunting tonight. I mean it. Just hunker down and keep yourself safe.'

She nodded her head. She knew he was right.

'No hunting,' he said again firmly; then he grabbed his tool bag and headed out.

As her father's footsteps receded down the corridor, heading for the stairs that led down to the electrical room in the sub-basement, she said, 'You'll figure it out, Pa. I know you will.' She knew he would never hear the words from so far away, but she wanted to say them anyway.

She found herself sitting alone in the workshop. The Man in the Black Cloak had taken a victim each night for the last two nights in a row. With the dynamo broken, she imagined him walking through the darkness of Biltmore's unlit corridors tonight with a crooked smile on his face. It was going to be easy pickings for him.

She sat on the mattress behind the boiler. When she was out on the mountain ridge in the rain, this was all she wanted – to be dry and well fed and comfortable in her bed. But now that she was here, it wasn't where she wanted to be. Her pa had told her to go to sleep, and she knew she should – her body was tired and sore – but her mind was a swirl of memories and sensations, hopes and fears.

There was only one person in the world who would believe what had happened to her in the forest that day. There was only one person who'd understand everything she'd been through, and he lived in a room on the second floor at the far end of the house. She missed him. She was worried about him. And she wanted to see him.

When she and Braeden were stranded in the carriage, they were together, they were on the same side, they were as close as close could be. But now that they were both back home again, he in his bedroom and she in the basement, he seemed further away than when she was lost in the mountains. There were too many forbidden stairs and doors and corridors between them.

They ain't our kind of folk, Sera, her pa had said, and she could only imagine what Mr and Mrs Vanderbilt would say about her if they knew she existed.

Using a wet rag she found in the workshop, she tended to

her wounds and cleaned herself up the best she could. Although she lived in a dirty place filled with grease and tools, she liked to keep herself clean, and her adventure in the mountains had left her as muddy as a mudpuppy on a rainy day. She took off her wet clothes, wiped her face and neck, her hands and arms, and all the way down her legs until she was spotless once more.

When she was done she changed into a dry shirt, but she'd lost her only belt. She found an old leather machine strap on one of the shelves and used a knife to slice it lengthwise so that it was about an inch wide. She poked holes in it and cut thinner strips of leather to fasten it. When she was done, she cinched the leather belt round her waist to see what it looked like on her. She was so thin that she could wrap it round her waist twice, but she thought it looked very nice. If her pa had been there, he would have said that it made her look halfway to half-grown. She had always wanted to wear a dress too, like all the other girls, but she'd never been able to find a discarded one, and she didn't think it was right to steal one. For now, she was happy with her new belt. She bowed and pretended she was a young woman meeting a friend at the market. She smiled and twittered and pretended to tell a story that made her friend laugh.

Somewhere between washing the blood and mud off her face and seeing herself in her new belt, she decided that if she could survive a haunted forest, find her way through a misty cemetery and narrowly escape a highly perturbed mountain lion, then maybe she could sneak into a Vanderbilt's bedroom while he was sleeping. One way or another, she needed to solve the mystery of the Man in the Black Cloak, and that wasn't going to get done with her taking a nap behind the boiler. The Man in the Black Cloak was going to walk again tonight. He was going to take another child. She was sure of it. And the one he wanted was Braeden Vanderbilt. She had to protect him.

The house was quiet and dark. There was a palpable fear in the air. With no electric lights, the Vanderbilts and their guests had gone to bed early, holing up in the safety of their rooms, next to their small brick fireplaces. A once bright and grand home had been robbed of light and had become a dark and haunted place.

She knew Mr Vanderbilt's room and Mrs Vanderbilt's room were both on the second floor, connected by the Oak Sitting Room, where they shared their breakfast each morning. She didn't want to go anywhere near there. She turned left down the corridor toward the southern end of the house, where she knew Braeden's bedroom overlooked the gardens.

She crept past door after door, but they all looked annoyingly similar. Finally, she came to one adorned with a running horse carved in relief in its centre panel, and she smiled. She'd found him.

Crouched outside Braeden's door, she realised that the real risk she faced wasn't just that someone would catch her, but that Braeden wouldn't want her there. He hadn't invited her to his room that night. He hadn't even said he wanted to see her ever again. What if her whole theory of their friendship had been pure and utter imagination on her part? What if he was glad to get rid of her in the forest that morning? Maybe he didn't want anything to do with her any more. He certainly wouldn't want her sneaking into his room late at night.

So she devised a plan. She would peek in, and if her presence there didn't feel right she'd turn tail quick as a wink.

She slowly turned the knob and pushed on the door. When she slipped inside the room, Braeden was fast asleep in his bed. He lay on his stomach beneath several layers of blankets, his cheek against the white pillow, his arms up around his head. He looked plum tuckered out, like there wasn't anything in the world that could wake him, and she was glad that he was able to sleep. Gidean slept on the floor beside him. She was relieved to see that they were both safe.

Sensing her entrance, Gidean opened his eyes and growled.

'Shh,' she whispered. 'You know me . . .'

Gidean's ears went down in relief when he recognised her voice, and he stopped growling.

Now, that's a good dog, she thought. And it was a pretty good sign that her hopes for friendship with Braeden weren't on the completely wrong mountaintop. She'd get a chuckle out of that – if she became friends with the dog but not the boy.

She gently closed the door behind her and locked it. At first, she thought it was the foolish adults who had forgotten to lock the door and protect Braeden from whoever or whatever was making their children disappear, but then she realised that it was the type of door that could only be locked from the inside. She couldn't decide whether to be angry with him or pleased. She couldn't help but smile a little when she realised that maybe he'd left it unlocked for her. Maybe he was hoping that she would come.

Standing quietly by the door, she gazed around the room. The warm embers of the fire glowed in the fireplace. The red oak-panelled walls were covered with paintings of horses, cats, dogs, hawks, foxes and otters. His shelves were filled with books about horseback riding and animals. Award plaques and blue ribbons from equestrian events were everywhere. Soon they would need to build the young master a new room for all his first-place finishes. Knowing the Vanderbilts, it wouldn't be just a room but a whole wing.

It felt good to be there with Braeden, to be in the warmth and darkness of his room. She could see that this was his refuge. But she had the feeling that maybe even here, in this seemingly protected place, they weren't completely safe. Something was telling her that she should stay on her guard, at least a little while longer.

Careful not to wake him, she moved quietly over to the window and scanned the grounds for signs of danger. The moon cast a ghostly silver light across the Rambles, a maze of giant azaleas, hollies and other bushes. The branches of the trees swayed in the wind. It was in the Rambles that Anastasia Rostonova had disappeared, leaving her little white dog behind to search the empty paths for her.

As she looked down from the second floor to the moonlit gardens below her, she could almost imagine seeing herself a few nights before, walking across the grounds towards the forest's edge, two rats clenched in her fists.

She looked behind her at Braeden, lying in the bed. Then she looked out across the forest once more. An owl glided on silent wings across the canopy of trees and then disappeared.

I am a creature of the night, she thought.

When she finally began to feel tired, Serafina pulled herself away from the window. She went over to the fireplace and felt the warmth of its glowing coals. Then she pulled a blanket off the leather chair and curled up on the fur rug on the floor in front of the fire. She fell asleep almost immediately. For the first time in what seemed like a long time, she slept soundly and dreamed deeply for hours. It felt good to be home.

In the middle of the night, she awoke slowly to the gentle sound of Braeden's voice. 'I was hoping you would come,' he said. It didn't seem to surprise him at all to wake and find her curled up by his fireplace. 'I was worrying about you all day.'

'I'm all right,' she said, her heart filling with warmth as much from the tone of his voice as the words he spoke.

'How did you make it home?' he asked.

She told him everything, and for the first time, it all began to feel real in her mind and in her heart. It didn't feel like just a dream or a child's fantasy, but actually true.

Braeden turned onto his back and listened to her account with rapt attention. 'That's amazing,' he said several times.

When she was done, he paused for a long time, as if he were envisioning it all in his mind, and then he said, 'You're so clever and brave, Serafina.'

She couldn't suppress a sigh as all the fear, uncertainty and helplessness that had built up inside her drifted away.

They sat quietly in the darkness for a long time, he in his bed and her by the fireplace, not moving or talking, and it felt good just to be there for a while.

She got up slowly, took a few steps over to the window, and then faced him. She could see his eyes looking at her as she stood in front of him in the moonlight. She imagined her skin must look very pale to him, almost ghostly, and her hair almost white in color.

'I'm going to ask you a question,' she said.

'All right,' he said softly, sitting up in his bed.

'When you look at me, what do you see?'

Braeden went quiet and did not answer. The question seemed to scare him. 'What do you mean?'

'When you look at me, do you see . . . do you see . . . a normal girl?'

'Clara Brahms is different from Anastasia Rostonova, and you are different from both of them,' he said. 'We're all different in our own way.'

'I understand what you're saying, but am I . . .' She faltered. She didn't know how to ask it. 'Am I strange-looking? Do I act strange? Am I some sort of weird creature or something?'

It stunned her when he did not reply right away, when he did not immediately deny it. He didn't say anything at all. He hesitated. For a long time. Every second that went by was like a dagger in her heart because she knew it was true. She felt like leaping out of his window and running into the trees. His reaction confirmed that she was strange and contorted beyond reckoning!

'Let me ask you a question in return,' he said. 'Have you had a lot of friends during the course of your life?'

'No,' she said soberly, thinking that now he was being particularly cruel if this was his way of explaining just how grotesque she was.

'Neither have I,' he said. 'The truth is, besides Gidean and my horses, I've never had a good friend my own age, someone I really trusted and wanted to be with through thick and thin. I've met a lot of girls and a lot of boys, and I've spent time with them, but . . .'

His voice faltered. He could not explain. And she could feel the hurt inside him, and her heart went out to him despite the fact that he'd practically called her a monster to her face just moments before.

'Keep going . . .' she said softly.

'I-I don't know why, but I haven't made any friends that are . . . like . . . that are . . .'

'Human,' she said.

He nodded. 'Isn't that strange? I mean, isn't that *very* strange? After my family died, I didn't want to talk to anyone any more or be with anybody. I didn't want to wonder when I was going to see them next. I just didn't want to. I wanted to be alone. My aunt and uncle have been very kind. They've brought all sorts of boys and girls here to see if I was interested in making friends. I sat with them at dinner because my aunt and uncle wanted me to sit with them. I danced with the girls because they wanted me to dance with them. I never said anything mean to any of the girls or the boys, and felt nothing but kindness toward them, and maybe they never even knew what I was feeling. There was nothing wrong with them, but, for some reason, I would just rather be with Gidean, or taking a walk watching the birds, or looking for new things in the forest. My uncle brought my cousins here to explore the forests with me, but they started playing a game with a ball, and soon I drifted away from them. I don't understand it. There's nothing wrong with any of them. I think there's something wrong with *me*, Serafina.'

Serafina looked at Braeden, and she spoke very softly, not sure she wanted to know the answer to the question she was about to ask. 'Was it like that when you met me?'

'I don't . . . I . . .'

'Would you just as soon I go?' she said quietly, trying to understand.

'No, it's . . . it's hard to explain . . .'

'Try,' she said, praying that he wasn't just about to tell her that he felt nothing for her and just wanted to be alone.

'When I met you, it was *different*,' he said. 'I wanted to know who you were. When you ran down the stairs and disappeared, I was frantic to find you again. I searched all over, every floor. I checked every closet and looked under every bed. Everyone else was looking for Clara Brahms, may God be with her, but I was looking for *you*, Serafina. When my aunt and uncle decided to send me away to the Vances, I pitched a fit of temper like they'd never seen before. You should've seen the look on their faces. They had no idea what had got into me.'

Serafina smiled. 'You really didn't want to leave Biltmore that bad?' Still smiling, she took a few steps forward and sat on the edge of the bed beside him.

'You have no idea how my heart leapt when I saw stupid old Crankshod shaking the daylights out of you in the porte cochere,' he said. 'I thought: There she is! There she is! I can save her!'

Serafina laughed. 'Well, you could have come a little earlier and saved me a good shaking!'

Braeden smiled, and it was good to see him smile, but then he remembered her question and turned more serious again as he looked at her. 'But then, later, during the battle in the forest, and in the carriage that night, and when you disappeared the next morning, that's when I realised how different you really were from anyone I had ever met. Yes, you are different, Serafina . . . very different . . . maybe even strange, like you say . . . I don't know . . . but . . .' His words faded, and he did not continue.

'But maybe that's all right with you,' she said tentatively, thinking she understood him.

'Yes. I think it's what I like about you,' he said, and there was a long pause between them.

'So, we're friends,' she said finally, her heart beating as she waited for his answer. It was a statement, but it was also a question, to be confirmed or denied, and it was the first time in her life she had ever asked someone that question.

'We're friends,' he agreed, nodding his head. 'Good friends.'

She smiled at him, and he smiled in return. Her chest filled with a sensation like she was drinking warm milk.

'I also want to tell you this, Serafina,' he said. 'I don't think there's anything wrong with you. And maybe there's nothing wrong with me, either. I don't know. We're just different from the others, you and I, each in our own way. You know what I mean?'

He climbed out of the bed. 'I have a present for you,' he said as he lit an oil lamp on his nightstand. 'I know you don't need the light, but I do. Otherwise, I'm going to stub my toe on the bed.'

'A present? For me?' she said, not really hearing anything else he said.

Presents were something she'd read about in *Little Women* and other books, something people exchanged when they liked each other. She had never been able to figure out why her pa never celebrated her birthday, but now that he'd told her the story of her birth, she realised that it probably dug up dark and painful memories that he preferred to forget. It didn't help that buying sentimental presents that weren't useful was akin to a sin in his book. And the one time he tried to make her a gift, she ended up with a doll that looked suspiciously like a crescent wrench. The truth was she had never received an actual wrapped present in her life, but the thought of it excited her.

'Why do I deserve a present?' she asked Braeden as she crawled farther onto the bed.

'Because we're friends, right?' he said as he handed her a medium-size lightweight box wrapped in decorative paper and tied with a crimson velvet bow. 'I hope you don't mind what it is.'

She looked at him and raised an eyebrow. 'Well, that's foreboding. What is it, a black satin cloak?'

'Just open it,' he said, smiling.

She untied the bow, thinking of how different the soft velvet felt in her fingers compared to the rough twine that she once cinched round her waist. But, having no practice at it, she didn't know how to unwrap the beautiful paper. Braeden had to show her how.

Finally, she lifted the lid off the box.

She gasped. What she saw in the box struck a deep chord in her heart. It was a gorgeous winter gown. It had long sleeves of dark maroon velvet and a corset of richly patterned charcoal-and-black velour, all trimmed in lynx-grey piping, its silver threads shimmering in the flickering light of the oil lamp.

'Oh, it's wonderful . . .' she said in amazement as she lifted the dress out of the box. The material felt so soft and warm that she kneaded it with her fingers and touched it to her face. She had never seen such a beautiful dress in her life.

She pulled her hair back behind her head and tied it with the red bow from her present. Then she went to the mirror and draped the dress in front of her to see what she looked like. When she saw her image, it almost seemed like a completely different person staring back at her. She wasn't a wild creature from the forest any more, but a beautiful little girl who belonged wherever she went. She stared at the girl for a long time.

As she marvelled at the exquisite details of her new gown, a dark thought crept into her mind. She didn't want to be rude, but her curiosity won that battle as fast as water running downhill. She turned to Braeden.

'I already know what you're going to ask,' he said.

'We've only known each other for a short time, so how did you get this dress so quickly?'

He looked at the pictures on his wall.

'Where did it come from, Braeden?'

He looked at the floor.

'Braeden . . .'

Finally, he looked at her and answered, 'My aunt had it made.'

'But not for me.'

'She wanted me to give it to Clara.'

'Ah,' Serafina said, trying to come to grips with it.

'I know, I know, I'm really sorry,' he said. 'She never wore it, though, I swear. She never even saw it. I just really wanted to give you something nice and I didn't have anything. I didn't mean any offence by it.'

Serafina gently touched his arm. 'It's a beautiful gown, Braeden. I love it. Thank you.' She leaned towards him and kissed him on the cheek.

Braeden smiled, happy.

She enjoyed seeing him pleased, but the dress made her think of Clara again. 'So, why were the Brahms invited to Biltmore?' she asked.

'I don't know,' Braeden said. 'I think my aunt and uncle heard that Clara was a prodigy and they thought it would be nice to meet her and have her play for the guests.'

'And your aunt saw how sweet and pretty she was, how educated and talented, and she wanted you to be friends with her.'

He nodded. 'Part of my aunt's grand plan to find a friend for me. She really liked Clara, in particular, but I only spoke to her a few times so I didn't know her very well.'

As Braeden spoke, Serafina's ears picked up the sound of

someone approaching. She heard footsteps coming slowly down the hall. She set aside the dress. 'Do you hear that?' she whispered. 'Someone's coming!'

'I hear it,' Braeden said in a low voice.

Gidean rose to his feet and went straight to the closed door.

'Douse the light!' she whispered.

Braeden quickly followed her suggestion, striking them into darkness.

Staying quiet, they stopped and listened.

From the sound of the shoes, she thought that it might be Mr Vanderbilt coming to check in on his nephew. She'd been caught, she thought. She'd been caught bad and there wasn't going to be any way to get out of it! The shoeshine-girl ruse wasn't going to work this time. She wondered if she could hide under the bed, or fling some sort of crazy excuse at him and then skedaddle down the corridor before he got a good look at her. But then she heard the slithering noise.

It was the Man in the Black Cloak.

He was coming down the corridor.

He was searching.

Every night he came.

He was relentless.

'I have a secret way out,' Braeden whispered.

'Let's just be real quiet,' she said. 'Stay very still.' Leaving Braeden near the bed, she moved forward through the darkness and joined Gidean at the door, worried that he'd start barking and give their presence away. She touched the dog's shoulder, letting him know that if a fight came they'd fight it together.

The sound came closer and closer until the Man in the Black Cloak was right outside the door.

He stopped there, listening, waiting, as if he could sense them inside the room. He knew they were in there.

She could hear him breathing. She picked up the foul scent of the cloak as the stench wafted through the crack under the door.

The Black Cloak began its slow, slithering, rattling motion.

Gidean growled.

The doorknob slowly turned.

15

Serafina watched the doorknob rotate a quarter turn and then come to a stop with a click of metal on metal. She had locked the door when she came in, and she remembered the weight of it, with its solid, inch-thick oak panels. It seemed nearly impossible for anyone to break the door. She just hoped that the Man in the Black Cloak couldn't pass through it using some sort of dark magic.

She could feel him breathing on the other side of the door, seething.

She waited, holding on to Gidean.

After several seconds, the doorknob returned to its normal position and the footsteps resumed, continuing slowly down the hallway. She let go of Gidean, and they all finally started breathing normally again. She looked at Braeden.

'That was a close one,' she whispered.

'I'm glad you got here before he did,' Braeden said.

She went over and climbed back onto the bed. They lay in the darkness, listening to the sounds of the house – expecting running footsteps or a cry of terror in the night – but all they heard was the crackle of the fire and their own steady breathing as they drifted in and out of sleep.

Serafina woke the next morning to the sound of Braeden's aunt knocking urgently on his locked bedroom door.

'Braeden, it's time to get up,' Mrs Vanderbilt said. 'Braeden?'

Serafina slipped off the bed and looked for a place to hide.

'Here . . .' Braeden whispered as he pulled back a decorative brass vent cover on the wall beneath his desk.

'Braeden, are you all right in there?' his aunt asked through the door. 'Please open up, darling. You're worrying me.'

Serafina crawled into the air passage, and Braeden replaced the cover behind her. She watched him through the grille as he shoved the dress under his bed then glanced around the room to make sure there wasn't any other evidence that she'd been there. Gidean studied his master with interest, the dog's pointed ears raised upward and his head tilted to the side in enquiry.

'You don't say a word,' Braeden warned him, and Gidean lowered his ears.

Finally, Braeden walked over to the door and opened it. 'I'm here. I'm all right.'

His aunt swept into the room, wrapped her arms round him and held him. That's when Serafina realised that Mrs Vanderbilt really did love Braeden. She could see it just in the way she clutched him.

'What's happened?' Braeden asked his aunt uncertainly.

'The pastor's son disappeared during the night.'

When she heard the news of another victim, Serafina felt a terrible knot in her stomach. That made three children in three nights now. It was like something was driving the attacker anew, pushing him harder and harder. She'd been so relieved that she and Braeden had been able to escape the Man in the Black Cloak by hiding in Braeden's locked room, but now she realised all that meant was that he got someone else. Another child was gone. She had eluded the demon, but she had not *stopped* him.

Knowing that she had to find some way out other than through Braeden's room, she crawled down the passage to see where it would lead. She came to an intersection of two other passages. She took the one on the right, where she came to another split. There appeared to be a whole network of secret passages running through the house. *So this is where the rats have been hiding all these years.*

She crawled past vents that led into the various private rooms of the house – sitting rooms, hallways, bedrooms, even bathrooms. She saw maids making beds, and guests getting dressed for the day. Everyone was whispering in worry and confusion. No one understood what was happening. They were talking about shades and murderers. Biltmore had become a haunted place where children disappeared.

She saw the footman, Mr Pratt, walking hurriedly down a corridor with Miss Whitney. 'No, no, Miss Whitney, this is no normal killer,' Mr Pratt was saying as they went by.

'That's an awful thing to say!' Miss Whitney protested. 'How do you know they're dead?'

'Oh, they're dead, believe me. This is a creature of the night, something straight from hell.'

The phrase shocked Serafina. *Creature of the night*, he'd said. But *she* was a creature of the night. She'd used the phrase herself. Were creatures of the night evil? Did that mean *she* was evil? It horrified her to think that she was in some way associated with or like the Man in the Black Cloak.

'Well, what are we going to do about it? That's what I want to know,' a man shouted.

She crawled a few feet through the passage in the direction of the man's voice and looked down through a metal grate into the Gun Room. From her vantage point, she could see a dozen gentlemen standing and talking about what was going on.

'There is nothing we can do,' Mr Vanderbilt said. 'We have to let the detectives do their job.'

Mr Vanderbilt knew all the ins and outs of Biltmore better than anybody. He designed the place. Why all the hidden staircases and secret doors? And he was rich, so he had the money and power to do whatever he wanted. And he was a Vanderbilt, so no one would ever suspect him. Was this why he'd built a mansion in the middle of a dark forest?

So now here Mr Vanderbilt was, telling everyone that there was nothing they could do but wait for the detectives to do their work. He was undoubtedly the person *paying* the private detectives, so they'd come up with whatever answer he wanted them to.

The other gentlemen shook their heads in frustration.

'Perhaps we should bring in one of the well-known detective agencies from New York,' Mr Bendel suggested. 'These local chaps are asking everybody a lot of prying questions, but they don't seem to be getting the job done.'

'Or perhaps we should organise another search party,' Mr Thorne suggested.

'I agree,' Mr Brahms said. 'The detectives seem to think that one of the servants is taking the children, but I don't think we should rule out that it could be anyone in the house. Even one of us.'

'Maybe it's you, Brahms,' Mr Bendel snarled, clearly not appreciating his implication.

'Don't be ridiculous,' Mr Vanderbilt said, getting between them. 'It's not one of us. Just calm down.'

'The womenfolk are terrified,' said a gentleman she didn't recognise. 'Every night, another child disappears. We've got to do something!'

'Do we even know if the attacker is an outsider or someone inside Biltmore?' someone else asked. 'Maybe it's a total stranger. Or one of our own men – Mr Boseman or Mr Crankshod.'

'We don't even know if there *is* an attacker,' Mr Bendel said. 'We haven't found any proof that these are kidnappings. For all we know, these children just ran away!'

'Of course there's an attacker,' Mr Brahms argued, becoming more and more upset. 'Someone's taking our children! My Clara would never run away! Mr Thorne is right. We need to organise another search.'

Mr Rostonov said something in a mix of Russian and English, but no one seemed to pay him any mind.

'Perhaps the children are falling into some kind of hole in the basement or something,' Mr Bendel suggested.

'There aren't any holes in the basement,' Mr Vanderbilt said firmly, offended by the suggestion that Biltmore itself might be a dangerous place.

'Or maybe there's an uncovered well somewhere on the grounds . . .' Mr Bendel pressed on.

'The main thing is that we need to protect the remaining children,' Mr Thorne said. 'I'm especially concerned for the young master. What can we do to make sure he stays safe?'

'Don't worry,' Mr Vanderbilt said. 'We'll keep Braeden safe.'

'That's all well and good, but we have to organise another search party,' Mr Brahms said again. 'I have to find my Clara!'

'I'm sorry, Mr Brahms, but I just don't think that's going to do any good,' Mr Vanderbilt said. 'We've searched the house and grounds several times already. There's got to be something else we can do, something more effective. There has to be answer to this terrible puzzle . . .'

Mr Rostonov turned to Mr Thorne and touched his arm for assistance. *'Nekotorye ubivayut detyey,'* he said to him.

'Otets, vse v poryadke. My organizuem novyi poisk, Batya,' Mr Thorne said in reply.

Serafina remembered that Mr Bendel had mentioned that Mr Thorne spoke Russian, but it still surprised her to hear it. Mr Thorne went on to translate what was going on for Mr Rostonov and tried to reassure him.

She thought it was kind of Mr Thorne to help Mr Rostonov, but suddenly Mr Rostonov became very upset and looked at Mr Thorne in extreme confusion. *'Otets?'* he asked him. *'Batya?'*

Mr Thorne blanched, as if he realised that he'd made a dreadful mistake in his Russian. He tried to apologise, but as he did so Mr Rostonov became even more upset. Everything Mr Thorne said to him made him more and more agitated.

Serafina watched all this in fascination. What had Mr Thorne said to Mr Rostonov that caused him such anguish?

'Gentlemen, please,' Mr Vanderbilt said, frustrated with the arguing. 'All right, all right, we'll do it. If that's what you think should be done, then we'll organise another search effort, but this time we'll search slowly and systematically from one room to the next, and we'll post guard positions in each room that we've completed.'

The other men heartily agreed with Mr Vanderbilt's plan.

They were clearly relieved that some sort of agreement had been reached and there was something they could do. The feeling of uselessness was unbearable. It was a feeling Serafina had in common with them.

The men streamed out of the room to organise the search – all but poor Mr Rostonov, who remained behind, red-faced and upset.

She frowned. Something wasn't right.

She had planned to use the air vents to find a way to get down to the first floor and then make her way to the basement to rejoin her pa, but now she had a different idea.

She turned round and crawled quickly back to Braeden's room. She stopped at the vent cover and listened. When she didn't hear Mrs Vanderbilt's voice, she slowly cracked open the vent and peeked inside. Gidean stuck his nose into the crack and growled. Surprised, she recoiled, her back arching like a witch's best friend as she hissed at him. 'It's me, you stupid dog! I'm on the good side, remember?' *At least I think I am*, she thought, remembering Mr Pratt's comment about the evil nature of creatures of the night.

Gidean stopped growling and stepped back, his face happy with relief and his little tail nub wagging.

'Serafina!' Braeden said excitedly as he pulled her out of the vent. 'Where did you go? You were supposed to wait for me in there, not crawl away! You'll get lost in all those passages! They're endless!'

'I wasn't going to get lost,' she said. 'I liked it in there.'

'You have to be careful. Didn't you hear my aunt say that another boy's gone missing?'

'Your uncle is organising a search party.'

'How do you know that?'

'Do you know what the Russian word *otets* means?' she asked abruptly, ignoring his question.

'What?'

'*Otets*. Or the word *batya*. What do those words mean?'

'I don't know. What are you talking about?'

'Do you know anyone who speaks Russian?'

'Mr Rostonov.'

'Besides him.'

'Mr Thorne.'

'Definitely besides him. Anyone else?'

'No, but we do have a library.'

'The library . . .' she said. That was a good idea. 'Can we go?'

'You want to go to the library *now*? What for?'

'We need to look something up. I think it's important.'

She and Braeden crawled rapidly, one behind the other, through the secret passages of the house. For all his talent in befriending animals and his other good qualities, Braeden sounded like a herd of wild boars trampling through the passage.

'Shh,' she whispered. 'Quietly . . .'

'All right, Little Miss Softpaws,' Braeden retorted, and urged her forward with a push of his head. 'Just keep moving.'

For the next few yards through the passage, Braeden made every effort to move more quietly, but he was still too loud.

'I'm going to get in big trouble if my uncle catches us doing this,' Braeden said as they passed another vent.

'He can't even fit in here,' she said happily.

They crawled past the second-floor living hall and then down the length of the Tapestry Gallery until they reached the south wing of the house.

'There it is,' Braeden said finally.

She peered down through the metal grate into the Biltmore Library Room, with its ornate brass lamps, oak-panelled walls and plush furniture. The shelves were lined with thousands of books.

'Come on,' she said, and pushed through the grate.

Thirty feet above the floor, Serafina balanced on the high ledge of the hand-carved crown moulding that supported the vaulted ceiling, with its famous Italian painting of sunlit clouds and winged angels. She climbed down the upper shelves like they were the rungs of an easy ladder. From there, she scampered like a tightrope artist along a decorative wrought-iron railing. Darting quickly over to the high mantel of the massive black marble fireplace, she leapt lightly onto the soft Persian rugs on the floor and landed on her feet.

'That was fun,' she said with satisfaction.

'Speak for yourself,' said Braeden, who was still thirty feet up in the air, clinging desperately to the highest bookshelf, looking scared out of his wits.

'What are you doing up there, Braeden?' she whispered up to him in confusion. 'Quit fooling around. Come on!'

'I'm not fooling around,' Braeden said.

She could see now that he was truly terrified. 'Put your left foot on the shelf right below you and go from there,' she said.

She watched as he slowly, clumsily climbed down. He did pretty well at first, but then lost his grip on the last bit, fell a short distance, and landed on his bottom with a relieved sigh.

'You made it,' she said cheerfully, touching his shoulder in congratulations.

He smiled. 'Let's just use the normal door next time, all right?'

She smiled and nodded. She liked how he was already thinking there was going to be a next time.

She gazed around at all the books lining the shelves. She'd never been here in the light of day. She thought back to all the books her pa had brought her, and how she would spend hours poring over the pages under his guidance, sounding out the letters until they became words and sentences and thoughts in her mind. Always wanting more, she would keep reading long after he'd gone to sleep. Over the years, she'd read hundreds of books, each one opening a whole new world to her. She marvelled at how this one room contained the thoughts and voices of thousands of writers, people who had lived in different countries and different times, people who had told stories of the heart and of the mind, people who had studied ancient civilisations, the species of plants and the flow of rivers. Her pa had told her that Mr Vanderbilt had many keen interests and studied the books in his library; he was considered one of the most well-read men in America. As she looked around the room at all the leather-bound tomes, the intricate knickknacks on the tables and the inviting soft furniture, it felt like she could spend hours here just exploring and reading and taking afternoon naps.

'That's Napoleon Bonaparte's personal chess set,' Braeden said when he noticed her looking at the ornately carved pieces arranged in perfect rows on a delicate rectangular table. She didn't know who Napoleon Bonaparte was, but she thought it would be great fun pushing the beautiful pieces off the edge of the table and watching them fall to the floor.

'What's that?' she asked, pointing to a small, dark oil painting in a wooden frame sitting on one of the tables among a collection of other items. The painting was so faded and worn that it was difficult to make out, but it appeared to depict a mountain lion stalking through the undergrowth of a forest.

'I think it's supposed to be a catamount,' Braeden said, looking over her shoulder.

'What's that?'

'My uncle said that years ago the local people used to use the phrase *cat of the mountains*, but over time it was shortened to *cat-a-the-mountains*, and eventually it became *catamount*.'

As Braeden spoke, she leaned close to the painting and tried to make out the details. It was difficult to tell, but the shadow of the cat looked weird and all ajumble in the bushes behind it. It almost seemed like the lion was casting the shadow of a human being. She vaguely remembered the remnants of an old folktale that she'd heard years before.

'Are catamounts changers of some sort?' she asked.

'I don't know. My uncle bought the painting in a local shop. My aunt thinks it's ugly and wants to get rid of it,' Braeden said, then pulled her away. 'Come on. You wanted to know the meaning of a Russian word. Let's look it up.' He led her to the corner behind the huge brass globe. 'The foreign languages are over here.' He scanned the titles of the books, saying each one as if he enjoyed the sound of the words. '*Arabic, Bulgarian, Cherokee, Deutsch, Español*.' It was clear that Braeden's uncle, who was fluent in eight languages, had taught him a few things. Now that they were in the world of words and books rather than scaling the precipitous heights, Braeden was back in his element. '*French, Greek, Hindi, Italiano, Japanese, Kurdish, Latin, Manx –*'

'I like the sound of that one,' Serafina interjected.

'Some sort of old Celtic language, I think,' Braeden said before continuing. '*Norman, Ojibwa, Polish, Quechua, Romanian*. Got it. Here it is. *Russian!*'

'Great. Look up the word *otets*.'

'How do you spell it?'

'I'm not sure.'

'We'll have to go by the sound of it . . .' he said as he flipped through the pages until he came to the spot he wanted. 'Nope, that's not it.' He tried another guess. 'Nope, that's not it, either. Oh, here it is. *Otets.*'

'That's it!' she said, grasping his arm. 'That's what Mr Thorne called Mr Rostonov that upset him so badly. Is it some kind of terrible insult or accusation? Is it a sharp-fanged demon or something?'

'Umm . . .' Braeden said, frowning as he read the entry. 'Not exactly.'

'Well, what's it mean?'

'Father.'

'What?'

'*Otets* means "father" in Russian,' Braeden said, shaking his head. 'I don't understand. Maybe you misunderstood what Mr Thorne said. Why would he call Mr Rostonov "Father"?'

She had no idea, but she pushed closer to get a better view of the entry in the book.

'I can't imagine Mr Thorne making a mistake like that,' Braeden said. 'He's very smart. You should see him play chess. He even beats my uncle, and *nobody* beats my uncle.'

'He seems to be amazing at nearly everything,' she scoffed.

'Well, you don't have to be mean about it. He's a good man.'

She took the book from Braeden and kept reading. It explained that *otets* was the formal way a child would address a parent in public. But the more intimate way, used only within the family, was the word *batya*, which translated roughly to 'daddy' or 'papa.'

She frowned in confusion.

They were the same age and completely unrelated. Why in the world would Mr Thorne repeatedly address Mr Rostonov as his papa?

16

As Serafina and Braeden crawled back into the ventilation system, she asked, 'Do you know all the gentlemen who are currently guests at Biltmore?'

'I've met most of them,' Braeden said as he closed up the vent cover behind them, 'but not all of them.'

'Do you know which rooms they're staying in?' she asked as they made their way on their hands and knees along the shaft back towards his bedroom.

'The guests are on the third floor. Servants live on the fourth.'

'But do you know the specific rooms?'

'I know some of them. My aunt put Mr Bendel in the Raphael Room. The Brahmses are in the Earlom Room and Mr Rostonov is in the Morland Room. It goes on and on. Why?'

'I have an idea. If the Man in the Black Cloak is one of the gentlemen at Biltmore, then he needs to store his cloak someplace when he's not using it. I've checked the closets and coat rooms on the first floor, but I want to check the bedrooms too.'

'You want to sneak into people's private bedrooms?' Braeden asked hesitantly.

'They won't know,' Serafina pointed out. 'As long as we're careful, they won't catch us.'

'But we'll be looking through their private belongings . . .'

'Yes, but we need to help Clara and the others. And we need to stop the Man in the Black Cloak from doing this again.'

Braeden pursed his lips. He didn't like this idea. 'Isn't there some other way?'

'We just need to look,' she said.

Finally, he nodded his head.

Serafina followed Braeden along the shaft. Mr Vanderbilt had called in private detectives, who now stood guard at various points in the corridors of the house. As long as they stayed in the ventilation system they were safe, but moving through the other parts of the house unseen was going to be far more difficult than before.

Serafina could tell that all the searches and the presence of the detectives weren't bringing solace to Biltmore's anxious inhabitants. She sensed that both the guests and the servants were losing hope. From what she overheard people saying to one another, there was an increasing sense that the children weren't just missing but dead. She had to defend her own heart from the same terrible conclusion. She'd seen them vanish, but her pa had told her that everyone had to be someplace. Even dead bodies had to be someplace.

We've got to keep looking, she kept telling herself. *We can't give up. We've got to help them.* But when the members of the various search parties began to return without any sign of the children, people were more disheartened than ever.

Serafina and Braeden snuck into the Raphael Room and looked through Mr Bendel's belongings.

'Mr Bendel is always so cheerful,' Braeden said. 'I don't see how he could have hurt anyone.'

'Just keep looking,' she whispered, determined to stay focused.

She found all sorts of expensive clothing in Mr Bendel's finely decorated travelling chests, including many stylish gloves and a long, dark grey cloak, but it wasn't the Black Cloak.

Next, they checked the Van Dyck Room, with its finely detailed terracotta-coloured wallpaper, its dark mahogany furniture and many paintings hanging by wires on the walls.

'Mr Thorne has always been very kind to me,' Braeden said. 'I don't see how it could possibly be him.'

Ignoring him, Serafina searched the room as thoroughly

as she could, digging through all the old chests that he'd left unlocked. She found no trace of the cloak.

'You like him too much,' she said as she searched under the mahogany bed.

'I do not,' Braeden protested.

'We'll see.'

'He saved Gidean's life when Mr Crankshod was going to kill him with an axe,' Braeden said.

Serafina frowned. In Braeden's mind, the man who saved his dog could do no wrong. When they heard someone coming, they darted back into the ventilation shaft as quickly as they could.

'I don't think it's any of the gentlemen at Biltmore,' Braeden said as they made their way to the next room. 'It must be some kind of demon from the forest like we were talking about before, or maybe it's a stranger from the city who isn't known to us.'

Serafina agreed that the lack of clues was discouraging, but there were still at least a dozen more rooms to check. They moved on to the Sheraton Room and the Old English Room.

When they searched the Morland Room, she looked into each of Mr Rostonov's beautiful, hand-painted travelling cases. Her heart filled with sadness when she found a chest filled with lovely Russian dresses. They were such amazing gowns, with deep frills and exotic patterns.

'It doesn't feel right to be here,' Braeden said uncomfortably.

As they were crawling through a shaft to the next room,

they heard several women talking in a hallway on the level below. They shinnied down a shaft to get a closer look.

'That's my aunt's room,' Braeden said nervously.

'Let's stay quiet . . .' Serafina whispered, then peered through a grate to look into the room.

When Serafina looked down into Mrs Vanderbilt's room, she beheld the glittering purple-and-gold French-style bedroom, with its elegant, curvy furniture and fancifully trimmed mirrors. She thought it was the most beautiful room she had ever seen. It wasn't rectangular in shape like a normal room, but oval. The gold silk walls, the bright windows and even the delicately painted doors were curved along the lines of the oval. The bed coverings, draperies and furniture upholstery were all finely cut purple velvet. The room positively glowed with sunlight, and she would have loved to curl up on Mrs Vanderbilt's bed. She was just about to suggest to Braeden that they risk climbing into the room when Braeden grabbed her arm.

'Wait. There's my aunt,' he said as Mrs Vanderbilt came slowly into the room, followed by her lady's maid and her household assistant.

'These are such lonely and frightening times,' Mrs Vanderbilt said with sadness. 'I would like to do something for the families, something to bring everyone together and strengthen our spirits. This evening, we'll gather in the Banquet Hall at seven o'clock. The electric lighting still isn't working, so stoke up the fires and bring in as many candles and oil lamps as you can. Arrange it with the kitchen so that we can provide everyone with something to eat. It won't be a formal sit-down dinner or any sort of party, mind you; it's just not the appropriate time for that, but we must do something.'

'I'll go down to the kitchens and talk to the cook,' her assistant said.

'I think it's important that we gain the comfort of spending some time together, whether we're frightened, grieving or still holding on to hope,' Mrs Vanderbilt said.

'Yes, ma'am,' her lady's maid said.

Serafina thought it was kind of Mrs Vanderbilt to arrange the gathering.

It was well known at Biltmore that Mrs Vanderbilt liked to learn the names and faces of all the children of both the guests and servants, and when Christmas came she and her lady's maid would go shopping in Asheville and the surrounding villages and buy each one of the children a special gift. Sometimes, if she heard that a child wanted a particular present that wasn't available in the area, Mrs Vanderbilt would send away to New York for it, and it would miraculously arrive a few days later on the train. On Christmas morning, she would invite all the families to gather around the Christmas tree, where she would hand each child his or her gift: a porcelain-faced doll, a soft toy bear, a pocket knife – it all depended on the child. Serafina remembered her own Christmas mornings, sitting in the basement, curled up on the stone floor at the bottom of the stairs, listening to the children laughing and playing with their toys above her.

Over the next few hours, the word spread, and the guests and servants began preparing for the upcoming gathering.

'My aunt and uncle are going to want me to be there, so I've got to go,' Braeden said glumly. 'I wish you could come with me. You must be as hungry as I am.'

'I'm starving. It's going to be in the Banquet Hall, right? I'll be there in spirit. Just don't let anyone play the pipe organ,' Serafina said.

'I'll sneak you some food,' he said as they parted.

While Braeden went to his bedroom to dress for the gathering, Serafina snuck into position. She moved through the secret passages behind the upper levels of the organ that she'd learned about from Mr Pratt and Miss Whitney. There she hid in the organ loft, among the seven hundred brass pipes, some reaching five, ten, twenty feet in height. From here she had a wonderful bird's-eye view of the room.

The Banquet Hall was the largest room she'd ever laid eyes on, with a barrel-vaulted ceiling high enough for a hawk to soar in. Rows of flags and pennants hung down from above, like the throne room of an ancient king. The stone walls were adorned with medieval armour, crossed spears and rich tapestries that looked extremely old but well worth climbing someday. In the centre of the room there was a massively long oak dining table ringed with hand-carved chairs intended for the Vanderbilts and sixty-four of their closest friends. But tonight no one was sitting at the table. The servants had laid it out with a cornucopian buffet of food. In addition to the selection of roast beef, brook trout, chicken à l'orange, endless trays of vegetables and rosemary potatoes au gratin, there were all sorts of chocolate desserts and fruit tarts. The pumpkin pie, like all pumpkin pie, looked like something a dog would eat, but the whipped Chantilly cream on top of it looked delicious.

She watched in silence as weary, saddened people streamed into the room, exchanged a few words with Mrs Vanderbilt, and then joined the gathering. In what appeared to be a valiant effort to stay upbeat, Mr and Mrs Brahms came in and tried to eat some food and find some solace in the company of the others. Mr Vanderbilt went over and spoke to them, and they seemed to find great comfort in his words and touch. He then went over to the pastor and his wife and consoled them about their lost son. He went next to Nolan's distraught mother and father. Nolan's father was the blacksmith, but he and his wife were welcome here. Mr Vanderbilt spoke with them for a long time. The more she watched him, the more her feelings towards him softened. There seemed to be true and genuine caring in him, not just for his guests, but for the people who worked for him as well.

Braeden, following his uncle's example and looking particularly neat in his black jacket and vest, did his best to talk with a young red-haired girl in a blue dress. The young lady appeared to be more than a little frightened by everything that had been going on. There were other children there as well, looking scared and sullen. Mr Boseman, the estate superintendent, was in attendance, along with Mr Pratt and Miss Whitney and many other familiar faces. It seemed to her that the only person missing was poor old Mr Rostonov. Serafina overheard one of the manservants come in and say that Mr Rostonov had sent word that he was too heartsick to attend.

She glanced over at Mr Thorne and Mr Bendel, who were standing together near the fire. Mr Thorne looked haggard and tired. When he started to cough a little, he covered his mouth and turned away from Mr Bendel. It appeared Mr Thorne might be feeling ill or coming down with a cold. Such a difference from the other times she'd seen him. Nobody was feeling good tonight.

When she saw that nearly everyone was present, Mrs Vanderbilt turned to Mr Thorne and put her hand on his shoulder. 'Perhaps you would be kind enough to play something for us . . .'

Mr Thorne looked reluctant.

'Indeed,' Mr Bendel said encouragingly. 'We could all use a bit of cheering up.'

'Of course. I would be honoured to oblige,' Mr Thorne said quietly, wiping his mouth with his handkerchief and gathering himself. It took several seconds, but he seemed to find a second wind. He glanced around the room as if looking for inspiration.

'Shall I send the footmen for your violin?' Mrs Vanderbilt asked, trying to be helpful.

'No, no, thank you. I was thinking I would give that magnificent pipe organ a try . . .' Mr Thorne said.

Serafina panicked. She had heard the pipe organ many times before from the basement. She couldn't even imagine how loud it would be when she was crouching among its pipes. It would break her eardrums for sure! She hurried to wiggle herself out of her hiding spot and escape.

At the same time, Braeden rushed forward and grabbed Mr Thorne's arm. 'Perhaps you could play the piano instead, Mr Thorne. I do love the piano.'

Surprised, Mr Thorne paused and looked at his young friend. 'Is that what you would prefer, Master Braeden?'

'Oh, yes, sir. I'd love to hear you play.'

'Very well,' Mr Thorne said.

Much relieved, Serafina smiled at her ally's quick thinking and crawled back into her hiding spot.

Braeden risked a quick glance up towards her, his face momentarily betraying a self-satisfied grin. She couldn't help but smile in return.

Mr Thorne walked over to the grand piano.

'I thought you played the violin,' Mr Bendel said.

'Lately, I've been tinkering a bit with the piano as well,' Mr Thorne said quietly.

He sat down in front of the piano slowly, almost shyly, as if he were uncertain. He sat there for several long seconds while everyone waited. And then, without taking off his satin gloves, he began to play. He played a soft and enchanting sonata with the grace of a virtuoso. The piece he had selected was not too sad, and not too happy, but was lovely in its own way, and it seemed to bring everyone together in mood and spirit. Serafina marvelled at how music seemed to have an almost magical ability to unite the emotions of the people in a room. Everyone seemed to truly love and appreciate Mr Thorne's playing except Mr and Mrs Brahms, who seemed to grow sadder with every note he played. Mrs Brahms began to sob and pulled out her handkerchief, and then her apologetic husband had to take her away. The other guests continued to listen to Mr Thorne's music as he finished the sonata.

'Thank you, Mr Thorne,' Mrs Vanderbilt said, trying to stay positive. She looked around at everyone. 'Why don't we all see if we can have a little bite to eat and something to drink?'

Braeden approached Mr Thorne shyly. 'You play wonderfully, sir.'

'Thank you, Braeden,' Mr Thorne said with a small smile. 'I appreciate it. I know you are a young man of discerning taste.'

'A few weeks ago, when you first arrived at Biltmore, you told us a delightful story about the boy with three wishes.'

'Yes?' Mr Thorne looked at him.

'Do you have any others?' Braeden asked, looking around at the red-haired girl in the blue dress and the other children. 'Could you tell us another story?'

Mr Thorne paused and looked at Mrs Vanderbilt, who nodded in agreement, looking proud of her nephew for his consideration of the others. 'I think that would be wonderful if you could, Mr Thorne. We'd all enjoy it.'

'Then I shall endeavour to try,' Mr Thorne agreed, nodding. He slowly waved his arm to the children. 'Let's all gather around the hearth.'

As Braeden and the other children sat in the glowing light of the fire, Mr Thorne lowered his voice into a dramatic tone and began to tell a story.

Watching and listening from the organ loft, Serafina could see that the children were leaning forward, following the story intently. Mr Thorne's voice was soft at times, and then booming with force at other times. She found herself longing to gather around and listen with the other children. Her heart ached to be a part of the world he depicted – a place where all the boys and girls had mommas and papas and brothers and sisters. A place where the children played together in bright fields, and when they got tired lay about in the shade of a giant tree on top of a hill. Serafina wanted to be in that world. She wanted to live that life. The story made her long to see her momma and hear her voice. And when the story was done she thought Mr Thorne must be one of the most magnificent storytellers she had ever heard.

Mrs Vanderbilt watched Braeden sitting among the other children and looking up at Mr Thorne. There was a contented look on her face. Braeden was finally making friends.

Serafina studied Mr Thorne. There was no denying that he had warmed her heart. She'd loved his music and his story. And he had brought a sense of community and togetherness to the sad gathering for a little while. Braeden and Mr Bendel were right – he was a man of many talents.

Afterwards, as the gathering was breaking up, Mrs Vanderbilt approached Mr Thorne and gently embraced him. 'Thank you, sir, for all you've been doing for us. I especially appreciate the way you've befriended Braeden. He thinks the world of you.'

'I just wish I could do more,' Mr Thorne said. 'These are such difficult times for everyone.'

'You're a good man, Montgomery,' said Mr Vanderbilt as he walked up and shook Mr Thorne's hand in gratitude. 'Later this evening, I would like to invite you and Mr Bendel to join me in the Billiard Room for cognac and cigars. Just us friends.'

'Thank you very much, George,' Mr Thorne said, bowing slightly. 'I'm honoured. I look forward to it.'

As Serafina watched the interaction, something didn't sit quite right with her. Mr Thorne looked sombre, as he should at a sorrowful gathering such as this, but she noticed something else too. As Mr Vanderbilt spoke with him, Mr Thorne had the same look on his face that a possum gets when he's gnawing on a sweet tater he's grubbed out of the garden. He seemed pleased with himself – too pleased, and not just for his flawless playing and his wonderful story. He seemed delighted by the personal invitation to join George Vanderbilt's inner circle. Braeden had told her that his uncle and Mr Thorne had only known each other for a few months, but now she could see there was a stronger connection developing between them, a growing personal bond. The Vanderbilts were one of the most famous, wealthy and powerful families in all of America, and Mr Thorne had just made himself a most valued friend.

She looked over at Braeden to see if he, too, sensed something was amiss, but he wasn't even looking at Mr Thorne. As everyone was leaving the room, he was walking along the buffet table, discreetly stuffing pieces of breaded chicken into his pocket. Then he snatched a little jar of clotted cream from the scone tray. She couldn't help but feel her mouth watering at the sight of the glorious food. She'd forgotten how hungry she was, and Braeden seemed to know exactly what she liked.

As he followed his aunt and uncle out of the room, Braeden looked up at her.

She signalled for him to meet her outside. There was much to talk about.

She knew Mr Thorne was well liked, but, to her, he was too talented, too kind, too *something*. And she still couldn't figure out why he had called Mr Rostonov 'Papa'.

She couldn't put it all together, but she smelled a rat.

17

Serafina met Braeden outside in the darkness at the base of the great house's rear foundation, where they hoped no one would see them. The forested valley of the French Broad River lay below them, and the black silhouette of the mountains layered into the distance. A mist was rising up from the canopy of the valley trees as if the entire forest were breathing.

'Did you see how well Mr Thorne played the piano?' Serafina asked in disbelief. 'Did you know he could do that?'

'No, but he can do a lot of things,' Braeden said, pulling the bits of chicken out of his pocket and handing them over to her.

'You're right. He can,' she said as she gobbled the chicken down. 'We keep saying that, but how is it possible?'

'That's just the way he is,' Braeden said as Serafina slurped up the clotted cream.

'But what do you know about Mr Thorne?' she asked as she wiped her mouth. 'I mean, what do you really *know* about him?'

'My uncle says that he should be an inspiration to us all.'

'Yes, but how do you know you can trust him?'

'I told you. He saved Gidean. And he's been very helpful to my aunt and uncle. I don't understand why you dislike him so much.'

'We've got to follow the clues,' she said.

'He's a good man!' Braeden said, becoming increasingly upset. 'You can't just go around accusing everyone. He's been nothing but nice to me!'

She nodded in understanding. Braeden was a loyal person. 'But stop for a second. Who is he, Braeden?'

'He's a friend of Mr Bendel and my uncle.'

'Yes, but where does he come from?'

'Mr Bendel told me that way back before the War Between the States, Mr Thorne owned a large estate in South Carolina. It was burned and destroyed by the union troops. He'd been born and raised a rich man, a landowner, but he lost every penny and had to flee for his life.'

'He doesn't seem poor now,' she said, confused by the story.

'Mr Bendel said that after the war Mr Thorne was so poor he could barely survive. He had no house, no property, no money and no food. He became a homeless drunk, wandering through the streets, swearing obscenities at any Northerner who happened to walk by.'

Serafina frowned. 'This is Montgomery Thorne you're talking about, the man who can do everything? Your description doesn't match with the Mr Thorne I've seen.'

'I know, I know,' Braeden said in exasperation. 'That's what I'm saying. He's had a hard life, a bad life, but he turned himself round. He's been nothing but kind to me. You have no cause to think ill of him.'

'Just finish the story you were telling me. What else? What happened to him? How'd he get here?'

'Mr Bendel told me that one night, after drinking too much in a pub in one of the local villages, Mr Thorne was walking home, stumbled off the road and got lost in the woods. He fell into an old well that no one used any more and was badly hurt. I guess he was stuck down there for two days. He can't even remember who found him and helped him out of the well. But when he finally recovered from his injuries he realised that he'd hit rock bottom in his life and would soon die if he didn't change his ways. So he decided to make a better man of himself.'

'What does that mean?' she asked, thinking the whole story sounded like two buckets of hogwash, and that Mr Bendel had been pulling Braeden's leg.

'Mr Thorne got a job working in a factory in the city. He learned about the machines and got promoted to manager.'

'The machines?' Serafina asked in surprise. 'What kind of machines?'

'I don't know, factory machines. But after that he became an attorney.'

'What's that?' she asked. She couldn't believe all the stuff she didn't know.

'A lawyer, sort of an expert on laws and crime.'

'How did he become an attorney when he was working in a factory?' The whole story was getting crookeder and crookeder.

'That's the thing,' Braeden continued. 'He worked and he applied himself and he made himself a better man. He travelled for a while, then he moved back here, bought a grand house in Asheville, and started buying land in the area.'

'Come on . . .' Serafina said incredulously. 'You're saying he went from a drunken, poverty-stricken wretch to a gentleman landowner?'

'I know the whole thing sounds impossible, but you've seen him. Mr Thorne is a very smart man, he's very rich and everyone loves him.'

She shook her head in frustration. There was no denying any of that. But, still, something wasn't right.

She looked out across the valley and the mist, just thinking. Nothing about Thorne's story made sense to her. It was like one of those tales that's filled with half-truths and deceptions, little twists in the telling. And she'd learned from hunting rats that where things were a-jumble that's where the rat had been.

'So where did your uncle meet him?' she asked.

'I think they were both being fitted for shoes at the custom shop downtown.'

'Which explains why Mr Vanderbilt's shoes sounded like his . . .'

'What?'

'Nothing. Why does Mr Thorne always wear gloves?' she asked, seeing if she could pick up the scent on a different trail.

'I never noticed that he did.'

'Is there something wrong with his hands? He plays the piano with his gloves on. Doesn't that seem very strange? And he was wearing leather gloves the morning the men found you in the carriage on the forest road, even though it wasn't that cold. And you said he was an expert at machines . . . Do you think he could break a dynamo so that not even the smartest mechanic in the world could fix it?'

'What kind of question is that?' Braeden asked in confusion. 'Why do you –'

'And how did a Southern plantation owner learn Russian?'

'I don't know,' Braeden muttered, becoming increasingly defensive.

'And what did he say to Mr Rostonov?'

Braeden shook his head, refusing to believe any of it. 'I don't know! Nobody's perfect.'

'You said he was extremely smart, could even beat your uncle at chess.'

'Well, maybe I was wrong. Maybe he just made an honest mistake with Mr Rostonov.'

'Then why did poor old Mr Rostonov get so upset? He was

as nettled as a badger in a porcupine fight. But he wasn't just upset. He seemed scared.'

'Scared? Of what?'

'Of Thorne!'

'Why?'

Serafina shook her head. She didn't know. Her thoughts were all discombobulated, but it felt like the clues to the mystery were swirling all around her. All she had to do was put them together. Where exactly was the rat hiding? That was the question.

'You told me that when your aunt met Clara Brahms she wanted you to be friends with her,' Serafina said, trying yet another path.

'Yes.'

'How did your aunt and uncle first meet the Brahms family?'

Braeden shrugged. 'I don't know. My uncle knew them somehow.'

'Your uncle . . .' Serafina said, sensing another connection there.

'Why do you say it like that?' Braeden asked defensively. 'My uncle doesn't have anything to do with any of this, Serafina. So just take it back!'

'Who told him about Clara being good at piano? How did he hear about her?'

'I don't know, but my uncle isn't responsible for any of this I can tell you that much.'

'Try to remember, Braeden,' she said. 'Who first told him about Clara Brahms?'

'Mr Bendel and Mr Thorne. They're always going to symphony concerts and things like that.'

'And Clara was an exceptionally talented piano player . . .' she said, remembering the maid's words to the footman. She kept trying to think it through. She was getting the same tingling feeling she felt when she was closing in on one of her four-legged enemies.

'Yes, I heard her play the first night she came to the house,' Braeden said, nodding. 'She was extremely good.'

'And you've heard Thorne play . . .'

'Yes, you heard him. He's an excellent player.'

And then Braeden paused. He frowned and looked at her in surprise. 'You don't think . . .'

She just stared at him, seeing if he would come to the same conclusion she had.

'Many people know how to play the piano, Serafina,' he said firmly.

'Not me,' she countered.

'Well, no, me neither, not like that, but I mean a lot of people *do* know how to play the piano really well.'

'And speak Russian and play the violin too?'

'Well, sure. There's Tchaikovsky and –'

'I don't know who that is, Mr Know-it-all, but is he also a chess expert?'

'Well, probably not, but –'

'And can he turn a team of horses and a full-size carriage around on a narrow mountain road?'

'You've gone crazy!' Braeden exclaimed, looking at her in bewilderment. 'What are you talking about now?'

'I'm not sure exactly,' she admitted, 'but think about it . . .'

'I *am* thinking about it.'

'And what do you see?'

'It's just a big mishmash as far as I can tell. Nothing means anything!'

'No. Everything means something. Think about the Black Cloak . . . You've seen it . . . It seems to allow the wearer to wrap people up and murder them, or at least capture them in some way . . .'

'It's horrible!' He shuddered.

'Maybe it doesn't just murder them . . .'

'I don't understand.'

'Maybe it *absorbs* them.'

'That's disgusting. What do you mean?'

'Maybe that's why Thorne accidentally addressed Mr Rostonov as "Father" and "Papa." Because Thorne had absorbed his knowledge of the Russian language from Anastasia.'

'Are you saying that he consumed Anastasia's soul?'

She grabbed Braeden's arm so fast that it startled him and he jumped. 'Think about it,' she said. 'The owner of the cloak absorbs his victims – their knowledge, their talents, their skills. Think about what that would mean, what that would be like . . . If he absorbed enough people, he'd gain many skills and talents. He'd become the most accomplished man in society. He'd be smart. He'd be rich. And everyone would love him. Just like you said.'

'I refuse to believe Mr Thorne would do that,' Braeden said. 'It's just not possible.' His whole body seemed to be tightening against her.

'It makes sense, Braeden. The whole thing. He's stealing souls. And he's coming for you next.'

'No, Serafina,' Braeden said, shaking his head. 'It can't be. That's crazy. He's a good man.'

At that moment, she heard a door from the main house creak open and the sound of someone approaching.

18

Serafina whirled round, ready to fight.

'Braeden, darling, what are you doing out here? It's time to come in now,' Mrs Vanderbilt called as she walked towards him.

Serafina breathed a sigh of relief, then darted into the bushes, leaving Braeden standing there alone.

'Who were you talking to just now?' Mrs Vanderbilt asked.

'No one,' he said, moving towards his aunt to block her view. 'Just talking to myself.'

'It's not safe for you out here,' Mrs Vanderbilt said. 'You need to come in now and go to bed.'

Serafina had never heard Mrs Vanderbilt sound so tired and

upset. The lady of the house clutched a long black coat round her waist to ward against the night's cold. It was clear that the disappearance of the children was taking a heavy toll on her.

Hesitating, Braeden glanced back into the bushes in Serafina's direction.

'Please come inside,' Mrs Vanderbilt said softly but firmly.

'All right,' he said finally.

Serafina could tell that he didn't want to go, but he didn't want to upset his aunt any more than she already was.

Mrs Vanderbilt put her arm around him and they began walking back toward the house.

'Lock your door!' Serafina half coughed, half whispered to Braeden, covering her mouth with her hand to garble her words.

'Did you hear something?' Mrs Vanderbilt said, stopping and looking out into the darkness.

'I think it was just a fox-call out in the woods,' Braeden said casually, but Serafina could see him smile and was relieved he wasn't still cross with her for suspecting Mr Thorne.

Stay safe tonight, Serafina thought as Braeden and his aunt continued towards the house.

'Listen, your uncle and I have been talking,' Mrs Vanderbilt said. 'We're worried about you.'

'I'm all right,' Braeden said.

'Your uncle and I need to stay here with the guests, but we've decided that it would be best if you went away from Biltmore for a little while. We tried it before, but we think it's more important than ever now.'

'I don't want to go away,' Braeden said, and Serafina knew he was thinking of her.

'Just until things settle down and the detectives figure out what's going on,' Mrs Vanderbilt said, her voice getting progressively harder to hear as they went back into the house. 'It'll be safer.'

'All right,' he said. 'I understand.'

'We've asked Mr Thorne to take you with him in his carriage first thing tomorrow morning,' she said. 'Won't that be nice? You like Mr Thorne, don't you? You'll get to see his house in Asheville.'

As the door closed behind them, Serafina's heart filled with dread. Braeden trusted Mr Thorne and would have no choice but to agree with his aunt and uncle's wishes.

The Man in the Black Cloak would finally get what he wanted.

I need a plan, Serafina thought as she went down the stairs into the basement. *And it has to be tonight.*

As she ate a late-night dinner with her pa in the workshop, she wanted to tell him everything and beg for his help to save Braeden, but there were no bodies, no weapons, no evidence of any kind to support what her pa would call her 'imaginings' about the Vanderbilts' most trusted guest. Even her best friend didn't believe her! Her pa never would. But, more than that, her pa looked so worn out. His hands were blackened and raw with the day's work on the Edison machine. He was under fierce pressure to get the lights back on. And rightly so. The darkness made the whole house the demon's domain.

But then she stopped in mid-thought and realised something. The darkness made it *her* domain as well.

'Are you all right?' her father asked as he scraped up the last of his potatoes with his spoon. 'You haven't eaten anything.'

She pulled herself out of her thoughts, looked at her pa and nodded. 'I'm all right.'

'Listen, Sera,' her pa said, 'I want you to hunker down tonight. Keep to yourself, you hear?'

'I hear, Pa,' she said obediently, but of course she wouldn't. She *couldn't*.

When they went to bed and her pa began to snore, she slipped out of the workshop and climbed the stairs that led outside to the estate grounds. Her mind was a-whirl with thoughts and images and fears. She knew her pa wanted her to stay close to him, but for the first time in her life she didn't feel safe in the basement. Staying in the basement tonight was death. It was doom. It would lead to a loneliness she could not bear. Over the last few days, she had felt increasingly constrained there. She didn't want to be inside any more. She wanted the freedom of open space and true darkness.

As she walked outside, it was a beautiful moonlit night with a light snow gently falling on the grass and trees. She tried to think it all through. She knew what she had to do; she just didn't know how to do it. What stratagem could she devise to defeat the Man in the Black Cloak? If he were a rat, how would she catch him?

She walked to the edge of the forest and paused at the point her pa had told her she should never go beyond. Her first foray into the shadows of the forest two nights before had been difficult, terrifying.

But she kept going.

She pushed through the thick brush and walked into the trees. She delved into the forest using the moonlight and the starlight to illuminate her way. Despite all that had happened, she was still drawn here. This was where she wanted to be.

A glint of light caught her eye. She looked up and saw a falling star. Then another. Then ten dashing through the blackness. Then a hundred at once. A shower of falling stars streaked across the sky, filling the crystalline black heavens with blazing light. And then the shower was gone, leaving nothing but the stillness of the glistening stars and the glowing planets in the infinite space above her.

She heard tiny footsteps behind her, a small country mouse out foraging and now making his way back home to his family, warm beneath a hollowed log.

The forest was alive at night, filled with motion, sound, creatures and light.

She felt comfortable here. *Connected.*

She walked a little further, studying the lichen-covered rocks, the trees with their outstretched limbs and the little rills of glistening water that ran beneath the ferns. Was this the forest her mother had come from?

Was this where she belonged?

She thought about why *she* could see that Mr Thorne was the Man in the Black Cloak but no one else could. Not even Braeden. Why could *she* believe it but they could not? Because they were normal, mortal human beings, and she was not. She was closer to the Man in the Black Cloak than she wished to admit. Closer to being a demon.

She knew she couldn't fight the Man in the Black Cloak directly. He was far too strong. In their first encounters, she had barely escaped him with her life. A shiver ran down her spine just thinking about it. But she couldn't just keep running away and hiding from him, either. Somehow, she had to *stop* him. But he possessed an otherworldly power – if her theory about him was correct, then he had within him all the strength and capability of every person he'd ever absorbed into his cloak. And, if she gave him another chance, he would surely absorb her as well.

No, she couldn't fight the Man in the Black Cloak head-on. Not alone.

She looked around her, and a dark idea formed in her mind. She asked herself the question again: if he were a rat, how would she catch him?

Suddenly, she knew the answer.

She'd bait him.

Fear rose up in her like bile from a half-digested meal. She wanted to turn away from the idea, to avoid it, but her mind kept going back to it as the only solution.

She thought of her pa's words once more: *Never go into the deep parts of the forest for there are many dangers there, both dark and bright . . .*

You're right, Pa, she thought. *There are. And I'm one of them.*

Standing in the woods, she came to a conclusion about herself, something that she'd known deep down for a long time but that she had never wanted to come to grips with: she was not like her pa. She was not like Braeden. She was not human.

At least not entirely.

The thought of it brought a lump to her throat. She felt a terrible loneliness. She didn't know what it meant she wasn't even sure she *wanted* to know what it meant but she knew it was true. She was not like the people she loved. She'd been born in the forest, a forest as black as the Black Cloak and as haunted as the graveyard. She was one of them, a creature of the night.

She'd overheard Mr Pratt say that the creatures of the night came straight from hell, that they were evil. She wondered about it again, her mind pushing through thorny brambles of conflict and confusion. Did evil creatures think of themselves as evil? Or did they think they were doing what was right? Was evil something that was in your heart or was it how people viewed you? She felt like she was good, but was she actually bad and just didn't know it? She lived underground. She slunk through the darkness without being seen or heard. She secretly listened to people's conversations. She pawed through their belongings when they weren't in their rooms. She killed animals.

She battled. She lied. She stole. She hid. She watched children lose their souls. And yet she was still living – thriving, even – drawing energy and knowledge and awareness from each and every night that she prowled through the darkness and another child was taken.

She stood for a long time, thinking about why she was alive and the others weren't, and she asked herself again: was she good or was she evil? She had been born in and lived in the world of darkness, but which side was she on? Darkness or light?

She looked up at the stars. She didn't know what she was or how she got that way, but she knew what she wanted to be. She wanted to be *good*. She wanted to save Braeden and the other children who were still alive. She wanted to protect Biltmore. She thought about the inscription on the base of the stone angel's pedestal: *Our character isn't defined by the battles we win or lose, but by the battles we dare to fight.* Standing in the forest at that moment, that's what she chose to believe. It was true that she was a creature of the night. But *she* would decide for herself what that meant.

She had two choices before her: to slink away and hide, or to dare to fight.

At that moment, she saw a plan in her mind and knew what she must do.

A part of her didn't want to do it. It would mean she could well die this very night. And her death would come at the moment in her life when she had finally crawled out of the basement and found a friend and begun to understand and connect to the world around her. She wanted to go home and sleep in front of Braeden's fireplace, and eat chicken and grits with her pa, and pretend that none of this was happening. She wanted to curl up in the basement behind the boiler and hide like she'd done all her life. But she couldn't. Thorne was going to keep coming. He was going to take Braeden's life. She had to stop him. She might die, but it meant that Braeden might live. He'd go on with Mr and Mrs Vanderbilt, and his horses, and with Gidean at his side. And that, she decided, more than anything, was what she wanted. She wanted Braeden to live.

She'd seen with her own eyes that the Man in the Black Cloak absorbed any child he encountered, but she knew that he wanted Braeden Vanderbilt next. She'd seen this when the Man in the Black Cloak attacked them in the forest. He hadn't come for Nolan, he had gone straight for Braeden. There was a talent in Braeden that Thorne craved: Braeden's expertise in horse-manship, but, more than that, his almost telepathic connection with animals. She imagined what it would be like to be able to befriend all the animals around her, even to control them.

But she sensed there was something more as well, something that obsessed Mr Thorne, that drove him even beyond Braeden. More and more, he had to take a child every night. Any child. And she'd use that need against him. She would meet him face to face on the most deadly battlefield she could think of. She would defeat him once and for all. Or she'd die trying.

She turned around and headed back towards the estate. As midnight approached, she went down the stairs towards the workshop.

It did not surprise her that her pa was asleep in his cot, snoring gently, exhausted from a long and difficult day. But then she saw something lying on her makeshift bed behind the boiler. As she stepped towards it, she realised it was the dress that Braeden had given her. Braeden must have come down and laid it there while she was gone. There was a note attached:

S,

A and U are determined. I'm leaving early in the morning with T. I'll see you in a few days. Please stay safe until I return.

– B.

Serafina stared at the note. She didn't want to believe it. He was really going to do what his aunt and uncle wanted.

But then she looked at the dress.

She was sure it wasn't Braeden's intention, but it was a perfect addition to her plan. Now she would look the part.

The time for sneaking and hiding was over.

She was going to make sure one man in particular saw her.

And tonight was the night.

The Chief Rat Catcher had a job to do.

20

Serafina put on the beautiful, dark maroon winter gown that Braeden had given her the night before.

The intricate black brocade corset felt tight round her chest and back, and she worried that when it came time to fight it would restrict her. She twisted and turned to test her freedom of movement. The long skirt hung heavily around her legs, but even as unfamiliar as the girls' clothing felt she couldn't help but be taken by it. It felt almost magical to be putting on a dress for the first time in her life. The material was fine and feminine and soft, like nothing she'd ever worn before. She felt like one of the girls in the books she read – like a *real* girl, with a real family, with brothers and sisters, and a mother and father, and friends.

She quickly scrubbed her face and brushed her hair and made herself as pretty as she could. It felt silly, but she needed to look the part. She tried to imagine that she was going to an extravagant dance, in a ballroom crowded with glittering ladies and gentlemen, and boys who would ask her to dance.

But she wasn't, and she knew it.

When she thought about the place she was going and the dark forces she'd meet there, it felt like she was jumping a chasm and she wasn't going to make it to the other side.

She tried to block it out of her mind and just kept lacing her dress up her back with shaky fingers, but she was having a terrible go of it. *Normal girls must have extremely long and bendy arms to do this every night*, she thought.

When she was finally done, she looked around at the workshop one last time. She couldn't tamp down the feeling that she wouldn't be coming back. She looked over to where her pa lay sleeping. She had seen how tired and overwhelmed he was. His struggles with the dynamo and searching for her these last few days had taken a toll on him. She wanted to curl up in the crook of his arm like she used to, but she knew she couldn't.

Sleep well, Pa, she thought.

Finally, she gathered her courage and turned. She made her way through the basement, and then climbed the stairs to the first floor.

At the top, she paused. She took a deep breath, and then walked down the darkened corridor of the house.

She walked slowly, deliberately, not darting and hiding like she normally did, but walking down the centre of the wide hallway like a proper young lady. She walked like the girls she had watched from the shadows so many times over the years. She did everything she could to take on the appearance of the helpless young daughter of one of the guests. She was no longer a predator; she was a vulnerable child.

The air was very still. Moonlight shone in through the windows, falling onto the marble floor. The grandfather clock in the Entrance Hall chimed off the twelve bells of midnight. The corridors of the house were mostly empty because it was so late, just a candle here and there to light the way for guests. But she sensed that there were a few people still awake.

As she made a slow promenade in her long, wide dress through the broad corridors of the house, it felt deeply strange not to be hunting, not to be the eyes of the predator but the prey that is seen. Her stomach churned. Her muscles flinched and twitched, begging her to dash away. She hated walking straight. And she hated walking slowly.

You're a normal girl, she told herself. *Just keep breathing, keep pulling air into your lungs. You're a normal girl.* It took every ounce of courage she had to just keep walking a straight line in the open.

She'd come up against the Man in the Black Cloak before,

but she was determined to make this time different. Tonight, she was going to fight – fight on her own terms and in her own way, with tooth and claw.

She lingered near the Winter Garden, with its high glass ceiling, just outside the door into the Billiard Room, where she knew from what she'd learned at Mrs Vanderbilt's gathering earlier that evening she had the best chance of setting her trap.

Suddenly, the door to the Billiard Room opened. Mr Vanderbilt, Mr Bendel, Mr Thorne, and several other gentlemen were sitting together in the leather chairs and drinking out of odd-shaped glasses. The smell of cigar smoke wafted into the corridor. Mr Pratt came out of the room with a large silver tray balanced on his hand and hurried down the hall.

Serafina stepped into a shadow behind a column to avoid being seen, and there she waited, lingering on the edge of darkness. She was a china doll, and she was a wraith, in and out of the shadows, a girl in between.

Finally, the fireside chat began to break up. Mr Vanderbilt stood and said goodnight to each of his guests. Mr Bendel shook everyone's hand, and then retired as well. In the end, only Mr Thorne remained.

Serafina watched him through the open door, her heart pounding slow and heavy. He sat in the candlelit Billiard Room alone, sipping from his glass and smoking his cigar.

Come on out, she thought. *We have business to attend to.* But he seemed to be enjoying a moment of personal triumph. She couldn't read his mind, but she tried to piece together what she knew about him and imagine what he was thinking at that moment.

After losing his plantation in the war and falling to the depths of ruin, here he was now, finally back in his rightful place again, a distinguished gentleman of the highest order, a personal friend of one of the richest men in America. All he had to do to get here was steal the souls and talents of a hundred lousy children, with their small, frail bodies and their pliable spirits.

But, she wondered, why didn't he absorb adults as well? Were they more difficult? And now that he had achieved his position in society, why did he continue with the attacks and risk discovery? If he'd been doing this for a long time, then why the sudden greed for young souls? What was driving him to absorb a child night after night? It had to be more than just the pursuit of talents. It had to be a need greater than anything that had come before.

She watched Mr Thorne as he sat on the sofa, puffing on his cigar and sipping his cognac. There was something different about him tonight. His face looked grey. The skin under his eyes was wrinkled and flaking. His hair seemed less shiny and perfect than it did the morning in the Tapestry Gallery when she saw him for the first time, or when he arrived with the rescue party to take Braeden back to Biltmore.

Mr Thorne set his empty glass on the end table and stood.

Serafina's muscles tensed. The time had come.

Like the other gentlemen, he wore a formal black jacket and tie, and she could hear the movement of his patent-leather shoes on the Billiard Room's hardwood floor. But when she saw what he was carrying draped over his arm her breath caught in her throat. It was the Black Cloak. Satin and shimmering and clean – the cloak was as much in disguise as she was. To anyone else, it was but a fashionable covering. To anyone else, it might have appeared that the handsomely attired gentleman intended to take a quiet stroll in the grounds before he retired for the evening, but she knew the truth: it wasn't just a cloak, it was the Black Cloak, which meant he was bent on malevolent purpose. Here was her enemy. Here was the fight she'd come for. But she could feel her whole body quaking in her gown. She was scared to death.

At least I'm going to die in a pretty dress, she thought.

He walked out of the room and into the corridor where Serafina was hidden in the shadows. She stayed perfectly still, but then he stopped just outside the Billiard Room door. He could not see her, but he could sense her there. He stood just a few feet away from her. Her heartbeat pounded. She had trouble controlling her breathing. He was right in front of her. All her well-laid plans seemed foolish now. She wanted to cower away, to flee, to slink, to hide, to scream.

But she steadied herself. She forced herself quiet. And she did what for her was the most terrifying thing to do in the world: she stepped out into the open.

21

Serafina stood in her dress in the candlelight of the corridor, where Mr Thorne could see her.

His hair wasn't as dark as she recalled, but far more silvery now, and his eyes were a striking ice-blue. He looked much older than she remembered, but he was a startlingly handsome man, a gentleman of distinguished character, and for a moment she was taken aback by it.

Her plan had been to pass herself off as a helpless little rich girl, a child guest of the Vanderbilts for him to prey on. Appearing to be easy prey was going to be part of her trick, the rat bait.

It was a perfect plan. But she realised now that it wasn't going to work.

As they looked at each other face to face, she could tell by his expression that, despite the beautiful gown she wore and her unusually well-combed hair, he knew exactly who she was. And it filled her with a wave of terrible dread.

She was the girl who had escaped his clutches the night he absorbed Clara Brahms. She was the girl who attacked him in the forest the night he took the stable boy. She was the girl who skulked through the darkness without need of a lantern, the one who could run and hide and jump and seemed to have impossibly fast reflexes. She was a girl with many talents . . .

And now here she was, standing right in front of him. A prize for the taking.

It was too late to run.

When Mr Thorne smiled, she flinched. But she stood her ground.

She was so scared that it hurt to breathe. Her corset felt like Satan's bony hand gripping her round her chest and squeezing her tight. Her limbs were hot with the burning drive to flee.

But she didn't. She mustn't. She had to stay.

She took in a long, slow, deep breath. Then she turned her back to him and slowly walked away.

She walked at what felt like a snail's pace down the corridor, pretending as though she had no idea who he was or that her life was in danger.

Her back was to him now, so she could not see him anymore, but she could hear Mr Thorne's footsteps following her, getting closer and closer behind her, so close that the hairs on the back of her neck stood on end. Unable to control her fear, her arms and hands began to tremble. His footsteps behind her pounded in her temples.

There was no doubt in her mind that they were not the footsteps of a mortal man, but of the Man in the Black Cloak. This was the Soul Stealer. This was the fiend who had taken Anastasia Rostonova, Clara Brahms, Nolan, the pastor's son and countless others.

And he was right behind her.

She looked down the corridor at the small side door ahead of her.

Just a few more steps, she thought, and she kept walking.

Three more steps . . .

Slowly walking.

Two more steps . . .

Finally, she slipped out through the door in one quick movement and into the cold darkness of the night.

Mr Thorne followed her outside, pulling his billowing black cloak and hood up around his head and shoulders as he entered the night.

As the snow fell gently down from the moonlit sky, she ran across the grass and ducked into the Rambles. The maze of twisting paths was a bewildering convolution of bushes and hedges with dark shadows, blind corners and dead ends – a place where the Man in the Black Cloak had killed before. But she knew this place too. She knew it better than anyone.

She moved swiftly through the maze. She imagined she'd

see the ghost of Anastasia Rostonova searching the paths for her little white dog.

The Man in the Black Cloak followed her down one pathway after another.

'Why are you running away from me, child?' he asked in a hideous, raspy voice.

Too frightened to answer, she just kept moving. When she looked over her shoulder to see how much of a lead she'd gained, she saw him coming up behind her. In the long, flowing black cloak, he flew a foot off the ground, standing erect, his arms stretched out like a wraith, his huge bloodstained hands reaching to grab her.

Her breath caught in her throat so severely that she couldn't even scream. Terrified, she sprinted forward with a burst of speed.

To stop was to die, and it was far too early to die.

Seeing a hole in the bushes, she dived through it. She left the manicured paths of the Rambles behind her and ran into the wild forest.

Tearing through the underbrush, she made quick time. She ducked behind trees. She scurried into and through thickets. She delved into the deepest shadows of the forest. She ran, and ran, and ran, deep into the darkest night, her nemesis close on her tail.

The thickness of the forest made it difficult for her pursuer. The trees grew so close together that an adult could barely squeeze between them. The spiny thickets were so bristling with thorns that they were nearly impenetrable. But with her smaller size and her agility, she could move easily, darting betwixt and between, scrambling below and leaping above. She moved as swiftly as a weasel through the brush. The forest was her ally.

She was terrified that he'd catch her and kill her, but she didn't want to lose him completely, either. When he fell behind or lost her trail in the snow, she slowed down to let him catch up. Deep into the woods she led him. She had studied the way and formed a map in her mind. But even with the shortcut she planned to take, they still had miles to go.

As she ran, she kept thinking about Braeden, her pa and the Vanderbilts. She kept thinking about what had happened to Clara, Anastasia and Nolan. She had to defeat Mr Thorne. She had to *kill* him. Her only chance lay ahead of her.

She was out of breath and desperately tired. Her legs ached, and her lungs felt like she was breathing through steel wool. She wasn't sure how much further she could run. But then she finally saw what she'd been running for.

Gravestones.

There were hundreds of them standing in the silver light of the moon beneath the bare branches of the gnarled old winter trees.

This was the place that terrified her, but she knew she must come.

She ran through the old cemetery. An eerie fog was rising among the twisted branches of the ancient trees and the decaying monuments of the dead.

She looked behind her. The Man in the Black Cloak flew towards her out of the mist, his bloody hands reaching for her.

Serafina ran with all her heart.

She dashed past Cloven Smith, the murdered man.

She leapt over the two sisters lying side by side.

She raced through the sixty-six Confederate soldiers.

She arrived, finally, panting and exhausted, at the small glade with the statue of the winged angel.

Serafina could hear the Man in the Black Cloak crashing through the brush behind her. She had only seconds before he arrived.

Fear flooded through her veins. She became sickeningly aware that she was bringing two great forces together and she was between them. From one direction or another, there was a good chance that death would soon be upon her.

She ran to the edge of the moonlit glade where the old willow lay with its upturned roots. The thick trunk and heavy branches of the fallen master of the forest swirled with ghostly mist. Its delicate leaves, somehow still growing bright green in the winter, glistened with the starlight.

Praying that the great yellow-eyed prowler of the night was out hunting, Serafina found the hole in the ground beneath the roots. She dropped down onto her hands and knees and crawled into the mountain lion's den.

She came face to face with the two spotted cubs, who stared at her with large, frightened eyes as she moved towards them.

'Where's your momma?' she asked them.

When the cubs saw that it was her, they jumped up in relief. They moved towards her, smelling her and rubbing themselves on her body.

She crawled past the two cubs and curled into a little ball in the earthen den.

Now the trap was laid.

Just as she had done when she crawled inside the machine in Biltmore's basement, she made herself very still and very quiet.

She steadied her lungs and her heart. She shut her eyes and concentrated, extending her senses outward into the forest.

I know you're out there someplace, hunting in your domain. Where are you? Your cubs are in danger . . .

Serafina could feel it. Out there in the darkness of the woods beyond the graveyard, the mother lion paused in her hunting. She tilted her head at the sound of two intruders in the forest. *Her* forest. Her cubs were in danger. She turned and charged back towards her den with all her speed.

The Man in the Black Cloak came into the angel's glade and looked around him. 'Where have you led me, dear child?' he said, trying to figure out in which direction Serafina had gone. He circled the stone pedestal of the moss-covered angel. 'Do you think you can hide from me, little rabbit?' he asked.

I'm not a rabbit, Serafina thought fiercely. For a brief moment, she felt a sensation of triumph because it seemed like her plan was going to work. The Man in the Black Cloak would be left standing haplessly in the angel's glade. He would have no idea where she'd gone. She had disappeared. She had escaped him.

But then she remembered the snow. She had not accounted for the snow. Her tracks led straight to her hiding place. The tracks would betray her.

'Ah . . .' the Man in the Black Cloak said when he saw the tracks. 'There you are . . .'

He walked over to the den, got down on his hands and knees, and looked inside. 'I know you're in there. Come on out, my dear child, before I become angry with you.'

Serafina tried not to breathe. The Man in the Black Cloak reached deep inside the den, his bloody hand searching in the darkness. She could smell his horrible, rotting stench. The folds of his slithering cloak twisted and turned as it snaked its way through the opening, rattling in anticipation of the coming meal.

Holding the cubs against her chest in terror, Serafina pulled back as far as she could go. She knew that if that man's hand or the folds of his cloak grabbed her, he'd drag her out of the den and her life would end in the most hideous way.

'I'm not going to hurt you, child . . .' he rasped as he reached for her.

At that moment, all the power and ferocity of clawed motherhood came ripping out of the woods. Enraged by the intruder at the mouth of her den, the lioness pounced upon his back. The terrific momentum of her attack rolled him to the ground. She struck her front claws into his back and chest even as she sank her teeth into his neck and head.

The Man in the Black Cloak shouted out in a shock of pain. He fought hard to defend himself from the powerful cat. He drew his dagger, but the lioness slashed his hand. Hissing and growling in fury, the lioness bit and clawed him repeatedly, mercilessly.

The Man in the Black Cloak punched and kicked and tried to get to his feet, but the furious lioness was too fast and too strong. He didn't have time to find the fallen dagger. He tried to slam her with a large branch, but she swatted him so hard with her razor-clawed paw that it ripped open his flesh and knocked him to the ground. Then she lunged at him and bit down on his neck, forcing him to the ground with her weight the way she would kill a deer. She held her powerful jaws clenched on his throat until he slowly stopped struggling and finally became still.

The Man in the Black Cloak went limp.

The lioness dropped him into a bloody black heap like the carcass of a dead animal.

The trap had sprung. A rush of joy and relief poured through Serafina. Her plan had worked! She'd finally defeated the Man in the Black Cloak. *She'd done it!* She'd saved Braeden. She'd saved Biltmore. *She'd really done it!* Her skin tingled with excitement. She wished she could somehow magically communicate with Braeden from a distance and tell him what had happened. It almost felt like she could turn herself into a bird and fly away. She'd fly up into the sky like a whip-poor-will and do loop-the-loops in the clouds until she was too dizzy to fly any more.

Ecstatic, she began to crawl towards the entrance of the den so that she could run home, but it was too late.

Death was upon her.

The lioness, still fiercely angry, entered the den to kill the second intruder.

Her.

22

There was only one way in and out of the den, and the lioness was going to tear Serafina to shreds. The lioness would kill her the same way she had killed the first intruder. To the lioness, there was no difference between them.

With a surge of panic, Serafina scrambled to the back of the den, trying desperately to get out of the lioness's reach. She sucked air in and out of her lungs. Her legs were kicking and thrashing like the hooves of a panicked horse, but she had no place to go.

The lioness came straight in. Her muscles bulged and rolled beneath her tan coat. Her eyes blazed. She held her mouth partly open. Her massive, sharp teeth gleamed. Her breaths froze in the frosty air as her sides heaved in and out. Steam rose off her body. As she pushed her way in towards Serafina, the lioness growled a low and menacing growl, fiercely determined to kill the creature that had invaded her den.

Serafina cowered behind the cubs with her back against the earthen wall. She tried to brace herself, to stay strong, but she shook uncontrollably. Unable to escape, she pulled her legs up against her chest, ready to defend herself, ready to kick. She tightened her hands to scratch and claw. She snapped her teeth and snarled.

Just as the lioness was about to lunge towards her and snap her neck, Serafina looked straight into her face and screamed as loudly and violently as she could, her teeth bared and threatening, like a cornered bobcat. She wanted to let this lioness know that she might be small, but she wasn't going to die easy.

Undeterred by Serafina's defence, the mountain lion stared her down with her huge, penetrating yellow eyes. Serafina gasped. The cat's eyes were the exact same colour as her own.

She looked into the cat's face. And then, in the next second, she saw what appeared to be a flicker of recognition in the lioness's eyes.

The lioness hesitated, stopping just a few inches in front of her.

She could see in the animal's expression that the lioness was thinking the same thing she was: their eyes were the same.

They weren't predator and prey.

They weren't protector and intruder.

They were connected.

She looked into the lioness's eyes, and the lioness looked into hers. There were no words between them. There could not be. But, in that moment, there was *understanding*. There was a bond between them. They were the same. They were hunters. They were prowlers of the night.

But, even more than all that, they were *kin*.

23

With her back crammed up against the rear wall of the den and her knees pulled up to her chest, Serafina stared at the mountain lion in amazement. Her heart pounded. Her body was folded up so tightly that she could only take short, shallow breaths.

The lioness gazed at her with the most mesmerising amber-gold eyes she had ever seen. How was it possible that they looked just like hers? Images and ideas flashed through her mind in a swirling confusion, but none of it made sense.

The lioness leaned closer to her.

Serafina remained perfectly still, trying to breathe as steady as she could. She made no sudden movements.

She saw an intelligence and awareness in the lioness's eyes. They were filled with a gentleness and understanding far beyond that of a wild animal. She knew she could not speak to the lioness in words, but she yearned to.

The lioness pushed her nose against Serafina's shoulder and smelled her. The lioness's breath was loud in her ears, her lungs sounding like a bellows, the air rushing in and out. The moisture around the lioness's partially open mouth glistened, and her teeth shone. Her deep scent was both foreign and familiar to Serafina. She'd never smelled a lion in her life, but it smelled exactly the way she expected it would.

As she looked at the lioness, she wished more than anything in the world that she could somehow communicate with her. She felt a deep longing to know what she was thinking and feeling in that moment.

Serafina exhaled gently and then took in a breath and held it as she slowly raised her trembling hand and touched the side of the lioness's head. She caressed the lioness's fur.

The lioness stared at her, her eyes locked on her, but the big cat did not move, she did not growl or bite, and Serafina began to breathe again.

She stroked the side of the lioness's head and then down her neck. The lioness rubbed her shoulder against Serafina's body, and Serafina felt the power and weight of the animal against her, so much weight that it prevented her from breathing for several seconds and she almost panicked, but then the lioness moved again and she could breathe once more. When Serafina relaxed her folded knees, the lioness put her head against Serafina's chest. Serafina touched the back of her neck and her ears. Then the lioness slowly leaned down and lay beside her, with her cubs around her, and swished her long tail.

Serafina held the fuzzy little mewing cubs in her arms and hugged them. She felt her chest swelling and her limbs tingling. She was filled with pride and happiness. The little lions were welcoming her – *they loved her* – and for a moment she was swept up with the feeling that she had finally come home.

She thought about how she was different from other people, the seeing in the dark, the moving quietly, the hunting at night. She looked at the palm of her hand and opened her fingers, and then examined her fingertips one by one. Were they fingernails or were they claws? What was her connection to the lioness? Why did she feel like she belonged here?

But the more she thought about it, the more ludicrous it became in her mind. She was a person. She was wearing clothes. She lived in a house full of human beings. And that's where she wanted to be. She had to get back to Braeden and her pa and the world she knew, the world she loved.

Clenching her teeth and shaking her head, she crawled out of the lioness's den. She stumbled into the open glade and stood beneath the stars in utter confusion.

She looked over at where the battle had taken place. The Black Cloak lay in a heap on the ground. Thorne's bloody body lay beside it. His other clothing had been shredded by the lioness's claws. Blood stained his white shirt. A large open wound bled at his side. His head and face were badly bitten and clawed. She could see his blood glistening, and she knew from watching rats die that glistening blood meant he wasn't completely dead yet. But he soon would be. Sometimes you killed a dying rat, but other times you just let it die.

Standing in the angel's glade, she looked up at the sky and the trees, and all around her. She had won! She had defeated the Man in the Black Cloak! It felt like every muscle in her body was alive and moving. There was a part of her that felt elated, almost euphoric, like she was floating on air. But another part of her was deeply confused. She had solved one mystery only to be confronted with another. Why did she feel this way inside? And why hadn't the lioness attacked her?

'What does it all mean?' she asked aloud in frustration. She took a few steps, kicking her feet roughly through the snow. She was so sick of not knowing anything, not having the answers. 'Tell me what it all means!' she shouted to the heavens.

Put me on . . . came a raspy voice.

24

Serafina looked around her.

Put me on . . .

She felt the words in their ancient, raspy voice more than she heard them, and she knew exactly where they were coming from. She looked at the Black Cloak, lying there on the ground beside Thorne's body. The cloak lay crumpled in the snow by itself, torn from him by the force of the attack.

Imagine knowing all things . . .

'Shut up,' she told the cloak, her words spitting out of her like she was reprimanding an uppity rat she'd captured.

Imagine being able to do anything you wanted to do . . .

She gritted her teeth and snarled at it. 'You're dead! Now hush up!'

There's nothing to fear . . .

Serafina felt the trembling agitation of pure fear growing deep within her. Every muscle in her body was telling her to flee, but she was too angry to go. She clenched her teeth. She wanted to fight. She wanted to win.

Put me on . . . the raspy voice came again.

She looked at the cloak. It was the cloak of power, the cloak of *knowing*. She felt an overwhelming desire to touch it. She wanted to hold it in her hands. She could feel it using its power to draw her in, and she didn't care. She wanted the power.

Imagine understanding and controlling everything around you . . .

She took a step towards the cloak.

Put me on . . .

She reached down and picked up the Black Cloak. The satin material reflected the sheen of the moonlight as she turned it over in her hands. Despite the running through the thickets, the flying through the forest and the battle with the mountain lion, the cloak wasn't torn or dirtied in any way.

She examined the cloak carefully, looking for any sign or symbol of the power that it contained. As she moved the material through her hands, it didn't feel like a normal piece of clothing, but like a living, pulsing thing, like holding a giant snake.

Put me on . . . the cloak said again in its low, raspy voice.

She looked at the cloak's silver clasp, which was engraved with an intricate design: a tight bundle of twisting vines and thorns. When she held the clasp in the moonlight in just the right way, she could see the image of tiny faces behind the thorns.

She didn't know what it meant. It felt like she didn't know what anything meant any more. A black and terrible loneliness welled up inside her, an anguish stronger than anything she had ever felt before. But what did the cloak do? How did it work? Did it really give its master the blessing of profound knowledge? Could it answer the questions that stormed through her mind?

You will become all-knowing, all-powerful . . . the cloak whispered.

Her head spun in confusion. Cloudiness closed in on her mind. She was unable to control herself. Her fingers grasped, her arms moved and she began pulling the cloak around her. Drawn in by its powerful spell, she draped the Black Cloak over her back and shoulders just for a brief moment to see what would happen. She only wanted to wear it for a few seconds, just long enough to see how it felt.

As she pulled on the cloak, it spoke to her once more.

Welcome, Serafina. I'm not going to hurt you, child . . .

25

As soon as Serafina put the cloak on, her world changed. The weight of the cloak on her shoulders felt strangely satisfying. The cloak gave off no stench or foul smell. There was no blood or fear while she was wearing the cloak. It made no rattling sound. Everything about it felt fine and good.

She used her fingers to clasp the cloak at her throat. Although it had been a full-length cloak on the much taller Mr Thorne, it fitted her body perfectly. She held out her arms and pivoted and looked at the cloak on her body. She thought she looked very sophisticated and aristocratic wearing it. Then she walked a few paces back and forth, testing how it draped and flowed. It felt like she was dancing with every movement she made.

'I look good in this,' she said. Her voice sounded strong and confident.

She didn't feel nearly as confused, tired and discouraged as she had just a moment before. No, she wasn't tired at all any more. She felt rested, capable. Optimistic. She felt *powerful*. Wearing the cloak, she felt as if she could do almost anything, solve any puzzle, accomplish any task, play any instrument, speak another language and, if she tried, maybe even *fly*. It was a wonderful, glorious feeling, and she spun around the angel's glade kicking up the snow.

The power is within us . . . the cloak whispered.

She tried to imagine it. She'd be famous and popular, and everyone would love her. She'd have many friends and a huge family of people who adored her. She'd travel all over the world. She'd know more than everyone else. No one could defeat her.

We will work together . . .

She'd be the most powerful girl in the entire world.

We will be a great force . . .

With the fabric of the cloak wrapped around her, she began to understand things about it that she could not before. She could see its history, like a dark dream in her mind. The cloak had been conjured by a sorcerer who had lived in a nearby village. He'd intended to use it to gain talents and understanding, to learn languages and skills, and to become a great, unifying leader in society, but his creation went terribly awry. He hadn't just created a concentrator of knowledge: he'd created an enslaver of souls. When he realised what he had done, he tried to hurl the cloak into the village's deepest well. He fought with the cloak, tearing and pulling and throwing, but the cloak grasped at him and twisted around him and would not let go until, finally, the sorcerer threw himself and the cloak together down the well, thinking that he would destroy them both. As the years passed, the sorcerer's body rotted in the well, putrefied, but the cloak remained, perfect and unharmed, until years later when it was found by the drunken and desperate Mr Thorne. The cloak had the power to acquire knowledge and capability, to concentrate the talents of a hundred people into a single person. She had seen what Mr Thorne did with that capability. She imagined what she could do with it. She'd be able to do anything she wanted. She could go anywhere. She'd know *everything*. She'd finally find all the answers.

She ran her fingers down the fabric of the cloak and felt its potency coursing through her. It contained such tremendous capability, she thought. She tried to imagine what great things she could do with it, what good and beneficial deeds she could accomplish in the world. It seemed like it would be such a shame to waste that power. Someone had to use the cloak; it might as well be her.

Lift the hood of the cloak . . .

She felt good and hopeful and buoyant.

Put on the hood . . .

She reached up and gathered the cloak's hood in her fingers and pulled it onto her head.

Then she screamed in horror at the shock of what she saw.

The edges of her sight blurred into a dark and vibrating tunnel. She could still see the physical world directly in front of her, but the hood pressed in on her peripheral vision with a crush of dead children and adults pushing their faces up against hers. The faces of the dead children surrounded her.

A little blonde girl cried as she pressed her cold dead face against Serafina's, touching her pleadingly with her grasping fingers. 'I can't find my mother! Can you help me?'

'*Pozhaluysta, skazhite gde moi otets?*' a girl with long, curly black hair said, pressing her face against Serafina's.

'Please help me!' wailed a woman, only to be pushed out of the way by two more faces. The visages of terrified children and adults were crowded inside the cloak.

'The horses are trapped!' a boy shouted, pressing his face in among the others. 'Watch out!'

Serafina screamed and ripped the hood from her head. She gazed around the empty glade, shaking and gasping for breath.

The souls of the dead people were imprisoned in the black folds of the cloak. This was the cloak's power: to enslave people's talents and hold their souls prisoner in a ghastly cage.

Come, little creature . . . We shall be together . . .

She shook her head, trying desperately to resist the cloak's powerful spell.

We shall control the world . . .

'No,' she said, gritting her teeth.

Everyone shall love us . . .

'No!' she shouted. 'I won't do it!'

She unclasped the cloak from her neck and tore it away. The act of ripping it from her body struck her such a blow that she fell onto her hands and knees, suddenly debilitated by extreme fatigue and despair. But, filled with determination, she got back up onto her feet. She tried to hurl the cloak to the ground, but the slithering creature tangled itself in her arms and wouldn't let go. She couldn't free herself from it.

Alone you are a weak little creature, but together we are strong . . .

'No!' she shouted.

She knew that she had to get rid of the cloak. She had to *destroy* it. As the cloak roiled and twisted like black snakes in her hands, she tried to tear the material in her fingers, but they weren't strong enough to rend it. The cloak, seething and hissing, wrapped around her arms and her legs, clinging to her.

A bloody hand reached up from the ground and gripped her ankle.

26

Serafina screamed.

'Don't hurt the cloak, you stupid child!' Thorne snarled. Wounded and crazed, he yanked her to the ground, knocked the wind out of her, and held her down. 'If you destroy it, then we'll lose everything!'

She struggled to escape him, but he clenched her by the arms and she couldn't get free.

'We'll work together,' he rasped. 'You with your abilities and me with mine. Don't you see? We're the same. We're on the same side.'

Something was happening to him. Thorne's face was grey and deteriorating, his skin flaking off around his cheeks and eyes. His hair had turned grey and wiry. His mouth dripped with blood.

A wave of revulsion poured through her. She tried to kick him and bite his hands and pull herself free, but she couldn't wrest herself from his grip.

He held her to the ground with all his weight, pushing the air painfully from her lungs. She could feel her ribs bending, starting to crack. Despite his wounds and his decomposing condition, Thorne seemed to be getting stronger and stronger, driven by his greed for the cloak.

'I'll never give in to you!' she snarled into his face. 'Never!'

'Then you're going to die, little mouser . . .'

Pressing her down, he crushed into her. She couldn't breathe. Without air flowing through her lungs, she couldn't move, couldn't think. Even as she fought to get away, she felt her life draining from her, her arms and legs falling limp, her mind clouding with the white light of death.

She thought there was supposed to be a sense of peace when death finally came. But she didn't feel it. There was still too much to do in her life, still too many questions to answer, too many mysteries to solve, and it was the mysteries, the unfinished business, the *want*, that kept her going. She didn't want to die, especially not this way. But she could feel herself drifting now, the life ebbing out of her, her soul slipping away.

But she kept seeing a vision of her pa in her mind. She could hear his voice. *Eat your grits, girl*, he demanded.

I'm not gonna eat my grits! she shouted back at him.

Her pa gazed at her dying on the ground beneath her enemy's weight and he shook his head. *The rat don't kill the cat, girl*, he said. *That just ain't right.*

The rat don't kill the cat, she thought as she pulled her wayward soul back into her body with fierce determination. *The rat don't kill the cat*, she thought again as she felt a burst of new strength. She began to fight anew, pulling her arm free from her captor.

At that moment, a large black shape lunged out of the mist with a ferocious snarl and a flash of white teeth. At first she thought it must be some kind of black wolf. But it wasn't a wolf. It was a dog. A Dobermann.

It was Gidean!

Gidean bit into Thorne's side and pulled him to the ground, then plunged in for another attack, biting and snapping. Thorne grabbed his fallen dagger from the ground and slashed Gidean in the side. Gidean yelped in pain and pulled back. Then the mountain lion charged out of her den and dived into the battle. She attacked Thorne with rapid swats of her clawed paws, her teeth snarling and her ears pressed back against her head, as if she was mightily perturbed that he hadn't stayed dead. Plunging back into the fight, the wounded Gidean chomped Thorne's arm, forcing him to drop the dagger, then tore into his shoulder and dragged him viciously across the ground, shaking him.

Serafina spotted the Black Cloak lying on the ground. She darted into the battle and snatched up the dagger that had fallen from Thorne's hand. Then she attacked the cloak with the blade. She was sure this was the answer. She cut and stabbed, trying to slice through the material, but the cloak fought against her, twisting and turning and rattling. Becoming a black seething coil in her hands, the cloak clutched at her and wrapped itself round her arms and then her body, and began to crush her. No matter how hard she tried, she could not cut the snaking cloth.

As the folds of the Black Cloak slithered round her neck and began to tighten, she tried to scream for help, but the cloak choked her breath short. Nothing but horrible gagging noises escaped from her clasped throat. Gasping for breath and clutching at her neck, she struggled to get up onto her feet. She stumbled towards the statue of the angel in the middle of the glade. *It had sliced my finger with the slightest touch.* In one swift motion, she hurled herself onto the point of the angel's gleaming sword. The sword slashed the side of her neck with searing pain as its tip pierced into the folds of the Black Cloak. The cloak screamed and hissed as the razor-sharp edges cut into it. Serafina grabbed at her neck and tore the cloak away, then clenched the material in her fists and slammed the cloak onto the sword point. She pierced it again and again. The cloak slithered and screeched, coiling like a tortured serpent. It writhed in her hands as she tore the cloth, but she did not relent. When she was finally done, there was nothing left of the Black Cloak but shreds lying at the angel's feet.

Serafina fell away, panting and exhausted, pressing her hand to the wound at her neck to staunch the bleeding. She looked over and saw Thorne pinned to the ground beneath her allies. Thorne was strong, but without the Black Cloak he was no match for the speed, power and jaws of both Gidean and the lioness.

Serafina felt a wave of triumph pass through her. They'd done it. It was all over. It had to be.

But as Gidean and the lioness struck the final, killing bites into Thorne, his body emitted a frightening sizzling sound, like meat burning on a fire. His carcass vibrated as his skin burned and peeled down into blood and bones. A thick cloud of smoke emanated from his body as it rapidly disintegrated, as if enkindled by the air itself.

Gidean stepped back and tilted his head in confusion. The lioness retreated into the den to protect her cubs.

The stinking black effluence poured forth until the roiling smoke filled the entire glade. The whole area became a great, choking cloud. Serafina coughed, waved her arms and tried to escape from the smoke.

'Come on, Gidean,' she called, and pulled him back as she gagged on the horrible taste of the smoke in her throat.

Overwhelmed by the fumes and unable to see, she tripped over something and fell face-first to the ground. Whatever she tripped over was hard, like a branch. But when she looked she realised it wasn't a branch. It was a human leg. She whimpered in horror and scrambled away from it. The body of a little girl lay on the ground, her arms and legs tangled and bent at crooked angles.

27

Serafina crawled several yards across the angel's glade, then got up onto her feet, her whole body shaking with fear. She looked again at the body of the girl lying on the ground. It had blonde hair and wore a yellow dress. A yellow dress! How was that possible?

The body was face down. Serafina couldn't see the face, just the hair, the sickly pale legs and the crumpled fingers of the hands.

Just as she took a small, tentative step towards the body to get a closer look, one of the fingers twitched.

Serafina leapt back, grabbing Gidean for protection. Gidean barked and snarled at the body, his teeth white and gleaming.

The hand bent. Then the body's arm moved, then a leg. It was like a carcass crawling its way out of a grave.

Serafina's instinct was to run, but she forced herself to stay.

The body slowly got up onto its hands and knees, the hair falling around the face and covering it.

Serafina was horrified to think what the face was going to look like, imagining it to be the face of a carcass, bloody and rotted.

The thing stood erect on two feet.

Serafina watched in a paralysed state of horror. Gidean lunged and snapped repeatedly, warding off the zombie's attack.

But then the head slowly turned and the hair parted and Serafina looked into the face. It wasn't a rotting monster, but the perfect features and lucid, pale blue eyes of Clara Brahms. Clara opened her mouth and spoke in a desperately sweet voice, 'Please, can you help me?'

Serafina froze, astounded. Clara was alive! She stood before her in her yellow dress as bright and bold as a Sunday morning. Her body and her soul had been freed.

'I remember you,' Clara said to Serafina. She reached out and clutched Serafina's hand. Serafina flinched back reflexively, but the hand that grasped her was warm and full of life. 'I saw you,' Clara said. 'I called out to you. I *knew* you'd help me. I just knew it!'

Too shocked to speak or respond to Clara in any way, Serafina turned and looked across the glade. As the smoke cleared, it revealed the bodies of many children and adults lying on the ground.

The victims of the cloak woke up slowly, as if from a long, nightmarish sleep. Some of them sat on the ground in confusion for a long time. Others stood and looked around them.

A tall girl with long, curly black hair came up to Serafina and started speaking to her in Russian. She seemed very sweet, but scared and anxious to reunite with her father and her dog.

And there was a young man, as well, who didn't understand what was happening. 'Have you seen my violin?' he asked repeatedly. 'I seem to have lost it . . .'

A small boy with a mop of curly brown hair, wearing an oversize coachman's jacket, touched Serafina's arm. 'Pardon me, Miss Serafina, but have you seen the young master? I've got to get home. My father is going to be worried about me, and the horses need to be fed their grain. Do you know the way to Biltmore?'

'Nolan! It's you! You're alive!' Serafina grabbed the little boy and hugged him. 'I'm so glad to see you. Don't worry. I'll take you home.'

'You're bleeding, miss,' he said, gesturing towards her neck.

She touched the wound. It hurt a bit, but the bleeding had stopped. 'I'm all right,' she said. The truth was, she'd suffered multiple cuts and bruises, but she didn't care about that. She was just so happy to be alive.

She looked at all the children, took a long, deep breath, and smiled. She felt a tremendous sense of relief, a sense of exultation. They were alive. They were safe. She had saved them.

Then Serafina saw among the cloak's victims a woman with long golden-brown hair, lying on the ground. She looked weak and confused, but she was alive.

Serafina went over to her. She got down on her knees and comforted the woman. As Serafina took her arm and helped her stand, she noticed how lean and muscular the woman was, but she seemed even more disoriented than the others.

'Where are my babies?' the woman muttered in slurred, hard-to-understand words.

When Nolan came over and covered the shivering woman with his jacket, she pawed it slowly and awkwardly around herself with her open hands, as if her fingers were stiff and didn't bend.

'You're safe now,' Serafina assured her. 'You're going to be all right.'

The woman just stared at the ground, her hair hanging loose around her head. When Serafina slowly brushed back the woman's hair from her face, what she saw startled her. The woman had the loveliest face Serafina had ever seen. She had a perfect, pale complexion; high, protruding cheekbones; and long, angled cheeks. But her most striking feature was her amber-yellow eyes.

Serafina frowned. She looked at the woman in confusion and disbelief. The woman looked so familiar to her, and yet Serafina was sure she had never seen her before.

It was at that moment that she realised that it felt like she was looking into a mirror.

Serafina opened her mouth to speak, but her voice was trembling so badly she could barely get the words out.

'Who are you?'

28

The woman did not answer the question. She rubbed her eyes and face with the backs of her hands, then she looked around, glassy-eyed, taking in the forest and the angel's glade as if she did not understand what she was seeing or how she came to be there. The woman stumbled toward the opening of the lion's den beneath the roots of the willow tree.

'Where are my babies?' she asked frantically.

Seemingly ignorant of the severe danger of entering a lion's den, the woman went to the mouth of the den and looked in. She appeared to think her babies were in there. Serafina felt so sorry for her. The poor creature must have lost her mind in the imprisonment of the cloak. Worried that the lioness would attack the woman, Serafina reached to pull her out of harm's way. But then the woman made a series of sharp, guttural hissing noises, and the lion cubs came trundling out of the den in response to her call. Laughing, the woman dropped down onto her knees and encircled the cubs in her arms as they rubbed their shoulders against her, purring.

Serafina cringed, expecting the mountain lion to come charging out of the den at any second. But when she checked the den, there was no sign of the mother lion. Serafina scanned the trees nervously.

The woman, still on her knees with the cubs, lifted her hands and looked at her palms, as if they were things of amazement, opening and closing her fingers repeatedly, and she smiled. She rubbed her arms and her head and brushed back her hair like a person who had woken up from a terrible nightmare and had to reassure herself that she was still in one piece. She stood and looked up at the night sky and took a long, deep breath. Then she turned rapidly around, holding Nolan's jacket to her body. She laughed. She tilted her head back and shouted up at the stars. 'I'm free!'

Still smiling, the woman looked around at her surroundings with a new brightness in her eyes. She looked at the graveyard, the stone angel, and the other victims. Then she looked at Serafina. The woman froze. She stopped smiling. She stopped moving. She just stared at Serafina.

Serafina's heart began pounding in her chest, a slow, steady rhythm. 'Why are you looking at me like that?'

Suddenly, the woman lunged at her with a startling burst of speed. Serafina leapt back to defend herself, but the woman caught her with ease and held her by the shoulders, looking into her face.

'You're her!' the woman said in astonishment. 'You're really her! I can't believe it! Look at you!'

'I – I . . . I don't understand . . .' Serafina stammered, trying to pull away.

'What's your name, child?' the woman asked. 'Tell me your name!'

'Serafina,' she mumbled, staring wide-eyed at the woman.

'Let me look at you!' the woman said, turning her first one way and then another, as if to take her measure in every way. 'Just look at you! You're so big! How wonderful you are. You're amazing!'

Serafina reeled with dizziness as a new wave of confusion swept through her. What in heaven's name was this woman doing?

'Who are you?' Serafina asked again.

The woman paused and looked at her with compassion. 'I'm sorry,' she said gently. 'I forgot that you don't know me. My name is Leandra.'

The name meant nothing to Serafina, but the woman's eyes, her voice, her face – everything about her mesmerised her.

Serafina felt like sparks of a crackling fire were popping in her mind.

'But who *are* you?' Serafina asked again, clenching her fists in frustration.

'You know who I am,' Leandra said, studying her.

'No, I don't!' Serafina shouted, stomping her foot.

'I'm your mother, Serafina,' the woman said softly, reaching out and touching Serafina's face for the first time.

Serafina went quiet and still. She frowned in confusion. How could this be possible? She studied the woman's face, trying to make sense of its configuration, trying to understand if she should believe what she was seeing in front of her. Her mouth felt terribly dry. She licked her lips and then clenched them together, breathing through her nose. She tried to steady her breathing as she looked at the woman's hair, her hands, her sinewy body. But it was her eyes more than anything, her yellow eyes, that told her that it was true. This was her mother.

Serafina felt her face flash with heat. Suddenly, the image of her mother blurred as the tears welled in her eyes and brimmed over. She released a sigh that turned into a sob, then heaving sobs that she couldn't control, and her mother reached for her and pulled her into her arms.

'Oh, kitten, it's all right,' her mother said, as her own sobs rolled against Serafina.

When Serafina finally spoke, her voice was so weak with emotion that she could only manage one frail and breathless word.

'How?' she asked.

29

The children and adults who had been freed from the cloak began to wander through the graveyard. Some of them spoke to each other, trying to understand where they were and what had happened to them, but their minds were beset by confusion. Many were too bewildered to speak at all. Nolan and Clara, along with the other children, stayed nearby; for they recognised Serafina, and they huddled together; but many of the adults wandered off, trying to remember their lives and their families. One man stood staring at a gravestone.

'That's me,' he said, in shock. 'That's my name. My wife and children must have thought I died . . .'

Serafina understood now why some of the graves in the

graveyard had no bodies, but she still didn't understand how the woman standing before her could be her mother.

'What happened to you?' she asked.

The stars glistened in her mother's mesmerising eyes. 'I am a catamount, Serafina,' she said, her breath filling the icy air as she spoke. 'My soul has two halves.'

Serafina breathed slowly in and out, trying to comprehend what her mother was saying, but it made no sense.

'Come,' Leandra said gently, touching her arm. 'Sit here with me for a moment.' They sat on the ground beside the pedestal of the stone angel, facing each other. 'I once lived in a village near here. I was a normal human woman, but I could also change shape into a mountain lion whenever I wished to.'

As Serafina listened to her mother's story, everything else fell away. The cold air, the gravestones, the other victims of the cloak . . . Everything disappeared except the quiet, soothing tone of her mother's voice.

'I was married to a man who I loved dearly, and we were going to start a family. I was pregnant. He, too, was a catamount, and we spent much of our time together out here in the forest, running and hunting.'

As her mother spoke, she gently wiped away the snow that was falling onto Serafina's hair. 'But those were difficult times for all of us. The forest in this area was dying, twisted and withered by an evil force . . .'

Serafina looked over at the remnants of the Black Cloak and the scorch marks on the ground.

'One day,' Leandra continued, 'I was walking down a path in human form, and I was attacked by an unimaginable darkness . . .'

'The Man in the Black Cloak,' Serafina whispered.

'During the battle, he wrapped his cloak around me. I fought for my life, but he was far too strong. My husband heard me screaming and came running. He, too, began to fight, but we were losing. I saw the Man in the Black Cloak strike your father down. In a matter of seconds, I was going to be overcome in the cloak's black folds. I was terrified. I feared for the lives of the babies inside me. I tried to change into a mountain lion to fight him with tooth and claw, but in that instant, the cloak sucked in the human part of my soul. I kept fighting, as fierce as any mother lion has ever fought, and I finally escaped and fled, but the cloak had torn me asunder.'

'I don't understand,' Serafina cried. 'What do you mean? What is *asunder*?'

'The Black Cloak tore me apart, Serafina. It absorbed the human part of my soul, for that was its purpose, but it had never encountered a catamount before.'

'So you were stuck in your lion form . . .' Serafina said in amazement.

'Yes,' Leandra said, her voice ragged. 'I became sick with grief. I couldn't find your father and feared that he was dead. My soul, my body, my love – they had all been torn apart, shredded to pieces. I did not want to live.'

Her mother's voice faltered from a whisper to nothing at all, but Serafina moved closer to her. 'But you were pregnant . . .' she said, urging her to continue.

'That's right,' her mother said, lifting her head. 'I was pregnant. It was the only thing that kept me going. I gave birth a few months later, but it was not as it should have been. You were the only one of my four children to survive, and I did not know if you would make it through the night. And what was I to do from there? You were human, and I was not! How could I care for a human baby?'

'What happened next?' Serafina pleaded.

'That same night, I heard the steps of a man walking through the forest,' her mother said. 'Thinking him an enemy, I almost killed him. I circled the stranger in the darkness and watched him for a long time, trying to look into his heart. Was he a good man? Was there strength in him or weakness? Would he defend his den with tooth and claw? This was not your true father, but he was a human being, and he was the only choice I had. I made the decision to let him take my baby. I prayed that he would carry you into the human world and make sure that someone took care of you, for, though it broke my heart, I knew that I could not.'

'That was my pa!' Serafina cried out.

Leandra smiled and nodded. 'That was your pa. You were curled into a ball and so covered in blood that I barely got a good look at you that night. I honestly didn't know whether you would even survive, Serafina, and, if you did, I worried that you would be terribly deformed. I had no idea whether you would come out normal.'

Serafina went very quiet, and then she lifted her eyes and looked at her mother. In the frailest of voices, she asked, 'Did I?'

Her mother's face burst with joy, and she threw her arms round her and laughed. 'Of course you did, Serafina! You're beautiful. You're perfect. Look at you! My God, I've never seen a girl so lovely and perfect in all my life! That night when you were born, I thought that man might take one look at you and drown you in a bucket like an unwanted goat. I had so many crazy, dreadful worries. But here you are. You're alive! And you're perfect in every way.'

When Serafina looked up at the sky, the stars were all glimmering and splotchy as she wiped her tears from her eyes. It felt like her heart was overflowing. She reached out her arms and hugged her mother. She wrapped her arms tightly round her, feeling her warmth and her strength and her joy and her happiness. And her mother held her close, almost purring, and tears fell from their cheeks, and the little cubs, Serafina's half brother and half sister, tumbled around their feet, joining in the family reunion.

'I can see that your pa raised you well, Serafina,' her mother said, separating them a little bit and looking into her face. 'When I saw you the first time here in the cemetery, I thought you were an intruder, and I attacked out of pure instinct. After twelve years, I was far more animal than I was anything else. It wasn't until tonight when I saw your eyes up close that I slowly began to realise who you were. And now here you are! And you freed me, Serafina. After twelve years, you have healed my soul. Do you realise that? I am whole again because of you. I have arms, I have hands, I can laugh, and I can kiss you! You saved me. And just look at you! You are the most perfect kitten I could have ever hoped for: you're fierce of heart, and sharp of claw, and fast and beautiful.'

Serafina's cheeks burned with heat, and her heart filled with pride, but then she looked at the children waiting for her.

'It was the Black Cloak that did all this,' she said.

'Yes.' Her mother looked around at their confused and frightened faces as they huddled together among the graves. 'They don't seem to know what happened to them.'

'But you do . . .' Serafina said, looking at her mother.

She nodded. 'Only half of my soul was in the Black Cloak.'

'That must have been awful,' Serafina said, trying to imagine it. 'But why were all of his most recent victims children?'

'Mr Thorne lived in this area for many years, avoiding detection by only capturing a soul every so often when he spotted a particular talent he wanted,' her mother said. 'But then something happened. The cloak began to take its toll on him. His body was ageing severely every day. He was dying.'

'The skin in the glove . . .' Serafina gasped.

'He started stealing the souls of children, not just because they had the talents he wanted, but because they had the one thing he most desperately needed.'

'They were young . . .' Serafina said. 'But how did you learn all this?'

Her mother stood, and brought Serafina to her feet with her. 'There is much for us to talk about, Serafina,' she said. 'But we need to get these children home to their parents.'

'But . . .' Serafina said. She wanted to keep talking, wanted to know more, and she was terribly scared that something would take her mother away from her again.

'Don't worry,' her mother said, touching Serafina's face gently with her hand. 'This isn't a fleeting run. I'm here now, and I'm whole again. In the days ahead, I will begin to teach you all that I can, just as a mother should. And you will tell me all about your life too, to help me come back into the human world that I've been absent from for so long. We are together now, Serafina. We are family and kin, and nothing shall ever break that bond between us again.' Tears streamed down her mother's cheeks. 'More than anything right now, I just want you to know how much I love you. I love you, Serafina. I have always loved you.'

'I love you too, Momma,' she said, her voice cracking as she wrapped her arms round her and wept in her mother's arms.

Serafina stood in the cover of the trees at the edge of the forest and looked towards Biltmore Estate. The sun was just rising in a clear blue sky, casting a golden light on the front walls of the mansion.

A large group of men and women on foot and on horseback were gathering together. There were ladies and gentlemen, servants and workmen, and there was an urgency in their movements.

They're organising a search, Serafina thought.

Mr and Mrs Vanderbilt stood among them, their faces troubled with the news of yet another missing child. Mrs Brahms stood with her husband, who was dressed in rugged clothing and ready to trek into the forest. Mr Rostonov was there as well, holding his daughter's dog in his arms. Even the young maid and the footman, Miss Whitney and Mr Pratt, had come out to help, along with the chief cook, the butler and his assistant boy, and many of the other household servants and men from the stables.

'If we're going to find her, we have to move quickly,' Braeden shouted as he mounted his horse in one swift, confident movement.

Serafina's heart swelled when she saw him. That's when she realised what she was seeing. *Braeden* had organised the search. They were going out into the forest to search for *her*.

'Everyone, please gather around,' Braeden called from atop his horse. She had never seen him so bold, so filled with leadership and determination. Rich or poor, guest or servant, he had brought them all together. It sent a wave of warmth through her cold, tired body.

Then she saw her pa. He must have woken up in the morning and discovered she was gone. Overcoming his fear of discovery, he went to the Vanderbilts for help, even though he knew it would expose her existence and betray the fact that they were living in the basement.

Braeden turned and gestured to the dog handlers. 'Give them this,' he said as he tossed a piece of clothing to the lead handler. It was her old shirt-dress. The four brindled Plott hounds bayed like it was a coon hunt.

'I looked for Mr Thorne so that he could join us in the

search,' Mr Bendel said from atop his thoroughbred. 'But I couldn't find him anywhere.'

And you're not going to, Serafina thought with satisfaction as she watched the search party gather. *Ever.*

'Mr Bendel, if you would, please take that group there and go east,' Braeden said. 'Uncle, perhaps you could take your footmen and go west.' Braeden turned to the dog handlers. 'When I put Gidean on Serafina's scent, he ran straight north, so that's where we'll try to pick up her trail . . .' Braeden turned in his saddle and pointed in that direction.

And there he stopped.

At that moment, when Serafina knew Braeden would see her, she stepped out of the woods.

Unsure of what he was seeing at first, Braeden lifted his reins, pivoted his horse and looked out across the lawn towards the trees. His eyes found her, and a smile spread across his face. She could see his relief and happiness.

'Who is that?' Mr Vanderbilt asked in confusion.

'Is that the girl we're looking for?' Mrs Vanderbilt asked.

Everyone turned towards Serafina and looked at her as she stood at the edge of the forest in her torn gown. Today, she wasn't hiding. For the first time in her life, she was being truly seen, seen by *everyone*. She stood there and just waited for them to understand the sight before them. There was amazement in their expressions, not just from the presence of a lone girl standing at the edge of the woods, but also because of what stood beside her – a large, full-grown mountain lion. Serafina's bare hand lay on the lioness's neck, touching the animal, holding her. The mountain lion wasn't just there, but *with* her, strong and silent at her side.

On her other side stood a black Dobermann. Gidean. The dog's shoulder was gashed and red with blood, but he stood strong and proud with the knowledge that he had fought his battle and won.

Braeden smiled. 'I knew you'd find her, boy,' he said under his breath.

When a young lad in a coachman's jacket stepped out of the woods and stood beside Serafina, expressions of surprise and disbelief and happiness spread across the faces of the search party. Then a young blonde girl came out. Then several more children. Soon, a whole group of children stood with her and her two animal companions at the edge of the forest.

For a long moment, no one moved or said a word. No one could believe what they were seeing.

Then the little white dog leapt out of Mr Rostonov's arms and ran as fast as its legs would take it. Everyone watched in stunned silence as the dog ran barking across the lawn and leapt joyfully into the arms of a raven-haired girl who laughed and hugged and kissed the little dog with abandon.

'Anastasia!' Mr Rostonov cried out.

Anastasia Rostonova ran to her papa. They kissed each other on both cheeks, then she threw her arms round him and cried in desperate happiness. The sight of Mr Rostonov finally reuniting with his long-lost daughter made Serafina want to cheer.

'There's my boy!' Nolan's father shouted and pointed. 'Come on,' he told the others. 'It's the children! They're safe! They're all safe!'

Nolan ran across the lawn and embraced his father as the other stablemen patted the boy on his back, congratulating him on his safe return, and Serafina could see how pleased Braeden was that Nolan was all right.

Clara Brahms ran to her mother and father and swept her arms round them.

'Oh dear, oh dear, you're finally here,' Mrs Brahms cried as she held her little girl. 'We've been looking for you everywhere.'

As the lost children and their parents came together in joyful embrace, Serafina remained standing at the edge of the forest with the lioness. Her mother had been living in the forest for many years, and she was not yet ready to rejoin the world of humans, especially with a den of new young cubs to care for.

My brothers and sisters, Serafina thought, with a smile. She saw her mother staring at the great house, studying the crowd of people and dogs and horses gathered in front of it. Then her mother turned and looked at her. Serafina looked back at her, and she understood what she was thinking. As the lioness nuzzled her, Serafina hugged her, and kissed her, and ran her hands across her powerful shoulders.

'I'll see you soon, Momma,' she said. 'I'll come to the den.'

Then the lioness turned to the trees and disappeared into the underbrush.

When Serafina looked towards the estate again, Braeden

was riding to her, and she couldn't help but take a breath when she saw him coming. He dismounted and dropped the reins. He stood in front of her and looked at her, and for what seemed like a long time he did not say a word. She knew that her long hair was full of leaves and twigs, and that her face and neck were scratched and bleeding. The lovely dress he'd given her was stained with dirt and blood, and torn in many places. But she could tell by the beaming expression on Braeden's face in the warm light of the rising sun that he didn't care about any of that; he was just immensely glad to see her.

'I like what you've done with the dress,' he said.

'I think this is going to be the new style this year,' she said.

Then they laughed and stepped towards each other and hugged.

'Welcome home,' he said.

'I'm so glad I'm back,' she said. Braeden felt so warm and strong and loyal in her arms. This is what she'd dreamed of, to have a friend, to have someone to talk to, someone who knew her secrets. She didn't know what the future would bring, but she was just glad that she'd have Braeden with her when it came.

After a few seconds, her thoughts turned to what had happened during the night. The next time they were alone she'd tell him everything, but she didn't bother with that now.

'It's over,' she said.

'Was it really Thorne?' he asked.

She nodded. 'The cloak's destroyed, and the rat's dead.'

Braeden looked at her. 'You're amazing, Serafina. I'm sorry I didn't believe you.'

Feeling left out of the homecoming, Gidean barked. Braeden knelt down and hugged his happy, wiggling dog.

'You did good, boy,' he said, rubbing his head.

'Thank you for sending him,' Serafina said, kneeling down with him.

'I knew he'd find you.'

'He found me, all right, just in time, and he fought like a champion,' she said, remembering Gidean's heroic leap. Then she looked at Braeden again. '*We did it*, Braeden,' she said. 'You and Gidean and I, we found the Man in the Black Cloak and we defeated him.'

'We make a pretty good team,' Braeden agreed.

As she was speaking to Braeden, she saw her pa standing on his own at a distance. He was looking at her in amazement, relief and uncertainty all at once. It was obvious from his shocked expression that he couldn't believe his eyes. Serafina could only imagine what he was thinking as he looked at her. His daughter, the girl he'd been hiding and protecting her entire life, was standing in broad daylight for all to see. She'd gone into the forest, deep into the wild. She'd stood with a lion. And now she'd come back home to him. She had led the lost children out from the forest, and now she was talking with the young master Vanderbilt like they were best friends.

She looked at her pa and thought about everything he'd

done for her, all the risks he'd taken, all the things he'd taught her, and she loved him more than she ever had.

'It's just like you told me, Pa,' she said as she approached him. 'There are many mysteries in the world, both dark and bright.'

As she put her arms round him, he pulled her into his huge chest and embraced her. Then he swung her round in a great circle while she laughed and cheered and cried.

When he finally put her down again, he looked at her and held her hands. 'You're a sight for sore eyes, girl. I've been worried sick about ya, but ya done good, real good.'

'I love you, Pa.'

'I love you too, Sera,' he said, looking into her eyes. He turned and gazed around at all the people and commotion and then turned back to her. 'Not that it matters none, but I finally got the dynamo workin' again,' he said happily. 'And I put a good strong lock on the electrical room's door.'

'It *does* matter, Pa. It matters a lot,' she said, smiling, thinking about how Mr Thorne had sabotaged the dynamo to plunge Biltmore into darkness each night.

'I'm sorry, sir, I need to borrow your daughter,' Braeden said to her pa as he grabbed her hand and yanked her away.

'Where are you taking me?' she asked nervously as he pulled her through the crowd of people gathered in front of the estate.

'Aunt, Uncle, this is the girl I told you about,' he said, dragging her in front of Mr and Mrs Vanderbilt. 'This is Serafina. She's been living secretly in our basement.'

Serafina couldn't believe it. He had just blurted it all out, her name, where she lived, everything!

She slowly lifted her eyes and looked at Mr Vanderbilt, expecting the worst.

'I'm very pleased to meet you, Serafina,' Mr Vanderbilt said, smiling and cheerful, and he shook her hand. 'I must say, young lady, that you are my great hero today for what you've done. You are my Diana, goddess of the Wood, goddess of the Hunt. In fact, I shall erect a statue in your honour on top of the tallest hill in sight of the house. You have done what I could not. The police couldn't do it, and the private detectives couldn't do it. You brought all the children home. It's simply wonderful, Serafina! Bravo!'

'Thank you, sir,' she said, blushing. She'd never seen him so full of praise. She couldn't help but laugh at herself for thinking that fancy shoes were the root of all evil. It seemed ridiculous now that she had been so suspicious of him.

'So, tell me what happened, Serafina,' Mr Vanderbilt said. 'How did you find the children?'

She wanted to tell him, tell him everything, like a proud, four-legged mouser that lays her nightly kill on her master's doorstep. But then she remembered everything that had happened: the cloak, the cemetery. They were adults, and they were human. The last thing they wanted to hear were the grisly details of the rats she'd killed.

'The children were in the forest, sir,' she said. 'We just had to find them.'

'But where?' he asked. 'I thought we looked everywhere.'

'They were in the old cemetery,' she said.

Mr Vanderbilt's brows furrowed. 'But how did they get there? Why didn't they come back?'

'The old graveyard is heavily overgrown, like a maze now. Once you wander in, even by accident, it's a very dark and difficult place to escape.'

'But *you* did, Serafina,' he said, tilting his head.

'I'm good in the dark.'

'But you were injured,' he said, gesturing toward her neck and her other wounds. 'You look like you battled the devil himself.'

'No, no, nothing like that, sir,' she said, covering her crusty neck wound self-consciously. 'I just had a run-in with a nasty thorn. It'll mend. But the children were hungry and scared when I found them, sir, very confused, filled with nightmarish stories of ghosts and ghouls. They were terrified.'

'It sounds like you all went through an extremely harrowing experience . . .' Mr Vanderbilt said, his voice filled with both sympathy and respect.

'Yes, sir. I think we should try to make sure that none of our future guests go in that direction again,' she said, thinking of her momma's den with her brother and sister. 'I think the old cemetery is best left alone.'

'Yes, that's sensible,' he agreed. 'We'll be sure to tell visitors to avoid that area. Far too dangerous.'

'Yes, sir.'

'Well,' he said finally, sighing in relief and looking at Serafina. 'I can't say I understand everything that happened, but I do know a hero when I see one.'

'You mean a *heroine*,' Mrs Vanderbilt said. She put her hand out to Serafina in the fashion of fancy ladies. Serafina quickly tried to remember what she'd seen young ladies do in these situations, and did her best to approximate the motion of shaking her hand. Mrs Vanderbilt's hand felt so soft and pillowy and clean compared to her own, and so different from the sinewy tautness of her mother's hands.

'It is very good to finally meet you, young lady,' Mrs Vanderbilt said, smiling. 'I knew there must be someone new in Braeden's life. I just couldn't decipher who in the world it was.'

'I am pleased to meet you as well, Mrs Vanderbilt,' Serafina said, trying to sound as dignified and grown up as she could.

'Braeden said that you live in our basement. Is that really true?' Mrs Vanderbilt asked kindly.

Serafina nodded, terrified at what she was going to say next.

'Do you have a job in the basement, Serafina?' Mrs Vanderbilt asked.

'Yes,' Serafina replied, feeling a smidgen of pride shining through her. 'I'm the C.R.C.'

'I'm so sorry, darling. I'm afraid I don't know what that means.'

'I'm Biltmore Estate's Chief Rat Catcher.'

'Oh my,' Mrs Vanderbilt said in surprise, looking over at her husband and then back at Serafina. 'I must admit, I didn't even know we had one of those!'

'Yes, you've had one for a long time,' she said. 'Pretty much since I was six or seven.'

'It seems to me that it must be an extremely important job,' Mr Vanderbilt said.

'Well, yes, I take it quite seriously,' Serafina said.

'You can say that again,' said Braeden.

Serafina poked him in the side with her elbow and tried to keep from smiling.

'Well, in any case, thank you, Miss Serafina,' Mrs Vanderbilt said warmly. 'We all appreciate what you've done. And you're such a little thing. I really don't understand how you did all this, but you brought the children home, that's the important thing. Thanks to you, we'll hear laughter again at Biltmore. It brings great happiness to my heart.'

'Amen,' Mr Vanderbilt said, nodding. Then he turned and stepped toward her pa. 'And you, sir. Where have you been hiding this daughter of yours all these years?'

'She's a good girl, sir,' her pa said, both proudly and protectively as he came forward. Serafina could see the worry in his eyes about how Mr Vanderbilt was going to react.

'I'm sure she is,' Mr Vanderbilt said, laughing. 'And it's to her father's credit, I say.'

'Thank you, sir,' her pa said, taken aback by Mr Vanderbilt's generous words as Mr Vanderbilt shook her pa's hand. She could see the relief in her father's expression as he looked over at her.

Then Mr Vanderbilt looked at his nephew. 'And you, sir, where have *you* been hiding this new friend of yours?'

'Here and there,' Braeden said with a grin. 'Believe me, sir, she's easy to hide.'

'Well, I can say this much, Braeden,' he said as he put his arm warmly round him. 'You know how to pick good friends, and there are few skills more important in the world than that. Well done, I say, well done.'

She loved the smile that flooded across Braeden's face when his uncle congratulated him.

Mrs Vanderbilt reached out and led Serafina by the hand. 'Come with me into the house, little darling.'

As she walked towards the house with Braeden and her pa, and several others, Serafina thought about what a wondrous thing it was. She had lived in the basement of Biltmore all her life, but this was the first time that she had ever walked in through the front door, and it made her feel like she was walking on a cloud. She felt like a real person.

'Now, let's us girls talk, shall we?' Mrs Vanderbilt said as she put her arm round her. 'Tell me, do you and your pa like it down in the basement?'

'Yes, ma'am, we do, but don't you mind that we're living there?'

'Well, I can't say it's the norm, and I can't imagine it being very comfortable down there for you. Do you even have proper linens?'

'No, ma'am,' she said sheepishly. 'I sleep behind the boiler.'

'Ah, I see,' Mrs Vanderbilt said, horrified. 'I think we can do better than that. I'll send down a couple of proper beds with nice, soft, down-filled mattresses; a full set of sheets and blankets; and, of course, some pillows. How does that sound?'

'It sounds wonderful, ma'am,' Serafina said, glowing with anticipation. She just hoped she'd do it soon, because after all that had happened she wanted to get under those covers and sleep for a week.

'Good, it's settled, then,' Mrs Vanderbilt said, pleased, as she looked at her husband.

'Sounds like a perfect plan,' Mr Vanderbilt agreed. 'It's important that we take good care of the estate's C.R.C., especially with the kind of rats that we have around here.'

Serafina smiled. Mr V. didn't know the half of it.

As they went into the house, she turned and looked out across the forested mountains.

She knew now that there were darker forces in the world than she had ever imagined, and brighter ones too. She didn't know exactly where she fitted into it all, or what role she would play, but she knew now that she was part of it, part of the world, not just watching it. And she knew that her fate wasn't set by how or where she was born, but the decisions she made and the battles she fought. It didn't matter if she had eight toes or ten, amber eyes or blue. What mattered was what she set out to do.

She wondered with excitement what her mother would teach her in the days ahead, what new skills she'd learn and what new things she'd see, walking through the day and prowling through the night.

She looked at the statues of the stone lions just outside the mansion's front doors. She wasn't just the Chief Rat Catcher any more, but the defender against intruders and evil spirits. She was the protector of Biltmore Estate.

She was the hunter, the *Guardian*.

And her name was Serafina.

Acknowledgements

I would like to thank the staff and management of Biltmore Estate for their support of *Serafina and the Black Cloak* and their commitment to preserving an important part of America's history for the public to enjoy. Biltmore Estate is a wonderful place to visit and see where Serafina prowled, including the basement, the Banquet Hall, the Winter Garden, Mr Vanderbilt's library, the hidden door in the Billiard Room and so much more.

I would like to thank my wonderful editors at Disney•Hyperion, Emily Meehan and Laura Schreiber, and my excellent agent, Bill Contardi, for their belief in Serafina, their insightfulness in improving the manuscript and their dedication to bringing her story to the world in the best possible way.

I would also like to acknowledge my wife, Jennifer, and my daughters, Camille and Genevieve, who played an important role in the creation and refinement of the Serafina story. My name may be on the cover, but this has been a grand labour of love for our whole family. I would also like to thank my two brothers, Paul and Chris, who have been with me from the beginning.

Finally, I would like to acknowledge the people who helped me to become a better writer over the years, including Tom Jenks and Carol Edgarian at *Narrative* magazine for their friendship and writing mentorship, Alan Rinzler for his editing and guidance, Allison Itterly for her work on the early version of *Serafina*, and all the other editors and readers who provided feedback on my writing over the years. If I have any ability to write at all, it's because I've been listening carefully to all of you.